GREY MAGIC

JT LAWRENCE

FIRE FINCH

ABOUT THE AUTHOR

JT Lawrence is an Amazon bestselling author, playwright & bookdealer. She lives in Parkview, Johannesburg, in a house with a red front door.

* * *

www.jt-lawrence.com

ALSO BY JT LAWRENCE

* * *

FICTION

WHEN TOMORROW CALLS

• SERIES •

The Stepford Florist: A Novelette (Oct 2017)

The Sigma Surrogate (2018)

1. Why You Were Taken (2015)
2. How We Found You (May 2017)
3. What Have We Done (October 2017)

* * *

STANDALONE NOVELS

The Memory of Water (2011)

Grey Magic (2016)

* * *

SHORT STORY COLLECTIONS

Sticky Fingers (2016)

Sticky Fingers 2 (2018)

Sticky Fingers 3 (2018)

* * *

NON-FICTION

The Underachieving Ovary (2016)

* * *

To my daughter, Alexandra.
May you find, and celebrate, your inherent power.

A sense of humour helps, too,
but I see that in you already.

GREY MAGIC

Spells are like knives,
capable of good or evil.

* * *

PART I

WATER

1 / A GOOD TRICK

No one appreciates the irony of her situation more than Raven Kane. She would have laughed, except that it doesn't seem so funny at three in the morning when she is lying, skin-on-fire, in a strange hotel bathtub.

Raven Kane. Burnt-out witch. Hot skin, blue lips.

The burning always starts with a fever. Not a regular high temperature caused by a velcro-legged virus, but a fever of the skin. The first time it happened — 27 years ago — Raven had just lain there, in her nursery nightgown, while the fire spread from her feet upwards, as if she were burning at the stake in some parallel life — paralysed by the fear of her destiny. Sometimes she had wished to burn up altogether, to blaze away the worried looks of her parents, to incinerate the innate knowledge that she was so very different to the other kids. Sometimes, as a child, she wished to relinquish her strange power altogether; to be nothing more than a sad glint of ashes in the creeping morning light.

Now she lies in the cold water listening to her heart slow. Watching, as the red burn leaks out of her skin. The opposite of a sun lizard. Raven likes to think of herself as a hip, multi-tasking, hexing-and-texting witch. That has always been her highlights reel. But the dark and sticky truth is —

There's a tentative knock on the hotel room door. It's the waiter from the downstairs bar.

"Hello?" he calls. "Miss Kane?"

"Bring it in here," Raven says. "Quickly."

She hears his footsteps stutter into the empty room, allows him to see a flash of flesh through the slightly ajar bathroom door: a long, blushing arm resting on the lip of the tub. Raven senses his hesitation; hears him clear his throat. Imagines him adjusting his bowtie.

"I'll just leave it here," he says. "Just call down if you need more."

"I need it in here!" yells Raven. Is the man deaf? How can you be a decent bartender if you're hard of hearing?

The barman teeters into the tiled room. When he sees Raven he jumps and tries unsuccessfully to cover his eyes. "Oh my God, I'm so sorry."

"You're sorry?"

"You're naked!" he says, as red wings bloom along his cheeks like Rorschach ink blots.

"Of course I'm naked," Raven says, "I'm in the bath."

The waiter quickly averts his gaze; searches for something else to focus on. Raven sees him look at the spider-shaped pile of lingerie on the counter — black satin, charcoal lace — and sees his eyes skitter away from that, too. Finally, with some relief, he finds a safe zone: her worn-out toothbrush, reposing happily in a scuffed glass mug. Beyond the mug and its identical twin, Raven is still there, inside the mirror.

"The ice," her reflection says. Of course he has forgotten. He lifts the metal buckets as if to prove he hasn't.

"Pour it into the bath," she says.

He still seems uncertain but does as he's told. The ice crashes in. Raven closes her eyes and sinks down into the arctic water with a sigh. She feels his gaze sweep over her body as her heat melts the ice. Despite so much of her skin being on show, she feels his eyes inspecting her face, looking at the silver amulet — a wolf's head — on a chain around her neck. Her Fenrir. She knows that her dark make-up is smudged. He will be wondering why she has been crying.

"Stop looking at me," she says, startling him.

"More ice?" he asks.

"More ice," she says.

You shouldn't do that to them, you know, says a voice that sounds like a masculine version of her own.

Do what? asks Raven.

You know full well what, says the voice.

You're no fun.

Fun is not my mandate.

I wasn't doing anything. I needed the ice.

Did you have to embarrass the boy?

Are you kidding? This is probably the most interesting thing that's ever happened to him.

You give yourself a lot of credit.

Yes, well… Someone has to.

She hears sounds deep in the walls. Moaning. Whispering. Who else is awake at this hour? Certainly no one from the conference. It must be the staff getting ready for the day. Hotels never sleep.

Is it normal, do you think, says Raven, to have conversations with yourself?

What do you mean 'normal'?

Well, do other people do it?

Would that make it 'normal'? Anyway, what does it matter?

She sinks down, trying to immerse her whole body, but she's too tall and her knees stick out of the water like hot, pink islands.

Joan of Arc heard a voice, says Raven.

So did Jesus.

That doesn't bode well.

What do you mean?

Well - look what happened to them.

She runs an ice cube over her thigh. It glides over her flickering skin and vanishes. It is its own magic trick.

It's getting worse, says the voice. *You have to do something about it.*

The waiter reappears. Without hesitating, as if he had planned his actions while walking up the stairs, he marches in and dumps the contents of his pails at Raven's feet.

"More?" he asks, his cheek-flush faded.

Raven opens her legs a fragment. "Please," she says.

The silver buckets clatter out of the room.

Sometimes the skin-fever brings with it auditory hallucinations: chanting, shouting, the sound of an angry mob. The crackling of a spiteful fire. Raven has always dreamt of pitchforks and pyres, but her current predicament is far less dramatic. It's a slow burn — a burning out — an unhurried ember losing its glow. Descending, devolving, degenerating into those familiar grey cinders. A well-known curse in Chinese witchcraft is: 'May you get what you wish for'. That and 'May you live in interesting times'. Raven has been hexed with both.

She often wonders if she experiences these episodes because her energy has an intense empathy for her foremothers in Essex or Salem; if the attacks are, in fact, echoes of her previous or future lives. Whatever the reason, she thanks the Universe daily for the Age of Enlightenment.

She slips her body further down, puts her face under the water, holds her breath for as long as she can. Her knuckles hum with the cold.

Of course, she uses the term 'enlightenment' loosely. There are still plenty of Pitchforks around.

2 / OLD CLAW

The hotel porter swings open the main door and Raven thinks she has made a lucky escape. The 6 a.m. air streaming into the stale lobby is cool and fresh. She can smell toast and car exhaust fumes and jasmine blossoms. In short: she can smell freedom. She quickens her pace but, as she's about to step over the threshold and into the sky-coloured world outside, there is an old claw on her shoulder. Rum and maple cigarette smoke.

Damn it! thinks Raven. Caught out! I knew it was too good to be true.

"Raven Kane," says the crone, who seems to have appeared out of nowhere.

Raven recognises the scented voice. Spins around. Lavinia Barkridge, resplendent with her coiffed blue-grey hair, hipster pin-striped suit, roll-up glowing from in between her immaculately varnished fingernails. Eighty years in the shade and more fashion-forward than Raven could ever hope to be.

"High Priestess," Raven says, forcing a smile.

"You're not staying for breakfast? I heard that their Eggs Benedict is outstanding."

"I have to be somewhere."

"You're going to hospital," says Lavinia. She frowns.

There's no use asking her how she knows. Raven herself didn't even know up until twenty minutes ago.

"You're ill?"

"Oh, I'm not going for myself. I have a… client there."

"I hope it wasn't your doing."

It was indeed Raven's doing. She opens her mouth to answer but the High Priestess squeezes her shoulder, then lets go. Her eyes are twinkling. "I'm only joking."

Raven attempts to laugh. It doesn't work.

"Are you quite sure you're not ill? I had a vision of you. Pale. In a hospital bed."

The idea is inviting. She wouldn't mind a couple of days off, lying in a white room with no responsibilities, with people to bring her tea and badly-made cheese sandwiches.

"Will you come back here afterwards?" asks Lavinia. "The Coven was hoping to have a proper catch-up with you."

"Sorry Lavinia but I have to get back to the menagerie. Eternally hungry maws. You know how it is. The Grimm Brothers have probably eaten Lily Lightfoot on toast. And I have so much work to catch up on…"

Lavinia looks into her face. Her eyes may as well be titanium-tipped electric drills.

"That's a shame. We were worried about you last night when you left the forum discussion so abruptly."

"Yes. Well, er… I had to —"

There was no point in telling Lavinia about the attack. Raven pulls her sleeves down to hide her mottled skin.

"To be honest, we were worried about you before your hasty exit. You haven't quite… been yourself."

What she actually means, says the voice, *is that you HAVE been yourself. They would rather you be more polite and pro-social. Tactful. In other words, NOT be yourself.*

"You weren't at the Gibbous ritual last month or the Michaelmas Feaste."

"I've been extremely busy."

Don't lie to the High Priestess! cautions the voice. *She sees through anything. I'm convinced that she can see through a bulletproof car.*

I *have* been busy!

Busy lying on the couch, says the voice. *Busy binge-watching television series. Busy staring at your house crumble around you. Busy procrastinating. Busy Not Writing Your Book.*

"I've been having… some problems," says Raven, taking a sideways step in the direction of her emancipation.

"Problems? What problems?"

"I don't want to bother you with them," says Raven. "You have enough to deal with."

"I do," says Lavinia. "And I need you to do your job with regard to the Wicked Witches."

"The Witchcore Wenches?"

"They've changed the name of their coven again."

Raven had read a Tumblr post of a fan of theirs that said they were 'too cutting-edge' for a name to stick. The press has settled on calling them 'The Wicked Witches' so that their audience will at least know who they are reporting on.

Lavinia shakes her head in disapproval. Her hair stays perfectly in place. "They are causing untold mischief."

"They are, I know." Despite being especially good at ignoring her phone, Raven hasn't missed the Google alerts or the mayhem on her Twitter newsfeed. "But there is no malice in their magic."

They just like shaking up the *status quo*. Challenging the beliefs of the 'brainwashed sheeple'. They're too young and too energetic for their own good.

"No malice, perhaps, but their reckless behaviour will have consequences."

Last week they hexed the stock exchange. The week before that they'd released a colony of white rats into shopping centres to 'mirror the culture of consumerism'. They were always up to some kind of roguery. Just thinking about their capers exhausts Raven.

"They give us a bad name, you know," Lavinia says. "I have *not* worked this hard for this long for some Dabblers to sully our good reputation."

"Yes, High Priestess."

Raven's phone starts to ring. She silences it and chucks it back into her bag.

"They are your responsibility, Raven."

"Yes. I'll sort them out."

Raven crabs her way out. The High Priestess narrows her eyes. "Let's do coffee," she says. "Soon. We need to catch up."

"Great idea!" yells Raven from the parking-lot.

"Email me!" shouts Lavinia, but Raven pretends not to hear as she jumps into her faded Morris Minor. The High Priestess is still watching her as she almost reverses into a jogger, stalls, then screeches off.

Why do you even attend these damn things? asks the voice.

You can make fun of it, but it IS important. Witchcraft is all about community. And being a practising witch in this city can be... solitary.

You LIKE solitary.

True. But one has to make an effort to...

To what?

To... network.

My God, woman! Who are you and what have you done with Raven? I never thought I'd hear you say that word. I should wash your mouth out with soap.

Ja well... Scoff all you like. Times are tough. You know, the economy.

What do you know about the economy?

Raven's phone, now on silent, buzzes impotently from inside her bag.

It might be important, says the voice.

Then they can leave a message.

What if someone wants to actually, you know, speak to you?

Texting is far more efficient.

Raven decides to take the scenic route to help reduce the anxiety bubbling in her chest. The trees are in full leaf and the air is clear.

You should answer your phone, says the voice.

I'm driving! says Raven.

I don't mean that you should answer it this minute. Just that you should answer it sometimes. That you should not avoid it altogether.

I hate answering my phone.

What does it feel like?

What? says Raven.

To have so many issues. I mean who hates answering their phone?

I do.

Yes, I think we've established that.

There, it's stopped ringing. Now we can stop talking about it.

Why didn't you stay for Eggs Benedict? asks the voice.

I think I bonded more than enough. And I had to escape the crowds. You know me.

I do know you.

I don't like crowds.

You're agoraphobic.

No, I'm not. Agoraphobic is a fear of open places. I love open places. I hate crowds. They make me nervous. Bad things can happen in crowds.

Raven brakes for a red light. She looks around for hijackers. A beggar is rooting through a pavement dustbin. He spots her and starts making his way to her car. He holds a sawn-off plastic coke bottle bottom which he shakes at her. She tries to wind the window up but the mechanism jams and it sticks halfway. She waits for green but it doesn't come. Raven checks for cars and then runs the light.

Demophobia, says the voice.

Hey?

Fear of crowds.

Yes, that's it. Not to be confused with demonophobia.

There's really a condition called demonophobia?

I'm not sure. I could have made it up. But if there's not, then there should be. I haven't had much sleep.

You haven't had such a bad attack in ages. Since you were a little girl.

How do you know?

Because I was there.

My skin is still tingling, says Raven, looking down at her arms.

That's what she said.

What?

That's what she said. It's a joke.

You're telling jokes now?

I wouldn't go that far. One joke does not a joker make.

That's better.

Is it?

More philosophising. Less joking.

Okay.

You're supposed to be my Voice of Reason, says Raven.

Am I?

God knows I need one. Besides, shouldn't it be 'That's what HE said'?

Wait...

What?

You didn't?

Oh yes I did!

The bartender? That pupa of a human? How could you?

Very easily, if you must know.

You're terrible!

What? You're the one who said I should give him a tip. He was an eager learner and very... grateful.

You're terrible. You're a terrible human being.

That's not what he said.

3 / RAVEN CHICKS

The grumpy nurse behind the reception counter at Saints hospital motions for Raven to take a seat.

"It's full in there," she says, frowning, as if it is Raven's fault that Celeste has friends visiting her to meet her newborn baby. As if Raven is the reason that gentle laughter and helium balloons are spilling out of the private ward where her client is recovering.

"I'll only be two minutes," says Raven, gesturing at the uninspired pharmacy-bought flowers in her hand. "I just came to drop these off."

The nurse purses her lips, crosses her meaty forearms. She doesn't believe a word. She knows how these things work out.

"I'm in a hurry," says Raven. "Shall I come back another time?"

She doesn't like holding newborns anyway. They are too fragile. She imagines their skulls like bird eggs: ready to crack and spill open at the smallest trauma. And their skin! That pink, fragrant, never-been-touched-before skin. Their pink peril is almost too much for her to bear. She had read before that, in the Middle

Ages, Europeans wouldn't name a baby in the first year because of the high rate of infant mortality. It was a different world entirely, one in which naming a child was seen as brazen: a way of tempting fate.

"Sit," says the nurse. "I'll chase the others out in five minutes."

Raven sees then that this staunchly-built nurse is absolutely perfect for her job. This is the position of Gatekeeper, not friendly push-over. She's here to protect the new mothers from the barrage that comes with bringing a new life into the world. She will keep the well-meaning crowd from overwhelming the over-vulnerable. Raven sits down.

She pulls out her phone, swears at the number of missed calls and notifications that her iCloud storage is full. She ignores them and checks her Twitter account. May as well do some work while she's waiting.

Dear Raven @turningtricks, reads the first tweet.

I need a spell to help me lose weight. Can you help? #havetriedeverything.

Dear @Jozifoodie, types Raven. **There's nothing wrong with a little junk in your trunk. What's the real problem?**

@Turningtricks, reads the next one, **I need a spell to keep my husband faithful.**

A newborn starts wailing in the room next door. It's a brutal sound.

@frankieJ, if you need a spell to keep your husband faithful, you're doing it wrong.

After clicking TWEET she wonders if that was a bit blunt. Oh, well, she doesn't have the energy to sugarcoat it. What else could she say anyway? Maybe he's just not built for monogamy? Not many animals are. Maybe he's just a lying bastard you shouldn't be with? Or maybe he's a wonderful man with a weakness. We all have our flaws. Maybe she should have told her that cheating is a symptom not a sickness and that she needs to find the root cause.

What her followers need most is not magic, but common sense. Sometimes, they just need help to identify the problem correctly. Sometimes, they just need a strategy. A more business-savvy witch would just comply with the requests (at R500 a spell) instead of dispensing practical advice. Today's 58 tweets would certainly come in handy for her giant echoing cave of a bank account.

@Turningtricks I've lost my lucky socks and I have an important game coming up. Can you find them for me?

Dear Ms Kane @turningtricks, my #lavender plants are wilting — any advice?? #Organic #HerbHippie #Notsogreenfingers.

My toddler loves my husband more than me. What can I do? @Turningtricks.

@Turningtricks Do you have a spell to make my mother-in-law vanish? LOL.

@Turningtricks I need your help. It concerns a rash. Picture in PM. #askingforafriend.

Do you believe in a Higher Power? @TurningTricks.

Raven replies: **@LightSeeker — I believe in a Deeper Power.**

Dearest Raven @turningtricks, please help me. I need some fertility magic. #DesperatelyTTC.

Now fertility, she can help with. The reason Raven is sitting here, in the maternity ward, with wilting flowers by her side, is because of a similar plea for help that she received ten months ago. Raven knows she'll never have children of her own, but she's single-handedly responsible for a large number of conceptions. Sometimes she pictures all the little grubs — they never grow up in her imagination — chubby-cheeked and gurgling. Bonny. Sturdy. Her own little baby army. Her raven chicks.

Celeste had been trying to conceive for six years. Raven could sense, in the first consultation, that the woman was perfectly fertile (her energy was the colour of a ripe mandarin) but despite this, her womb remained stubbornly barren. Celeste was Afrikaans and used some colourful phrases to describe her infertility, including calling her own uterus "an empty *papsak*" (which, in English, is the silver bladder that contains the wine in boxed wine). She would make them both laugh, and then she cried. The constant dashing of her hopes was exhausting her. She was falling into depression. Raven promised she'd have her pregnant within three new moons. All it would take was some skilful spell-crafting, an eggshell sail and a little resourcefulness on her side. In Medieval England witches were called 'the cunning folk' for good reason.

It was clear to Raven that the husband's sperm was the problem, although Celeste wouldn't entertain this idea, wouldn't even 'insult him' by having him tested, as if he were some kind of paleo caveman with the emotional intelligence of a Sumatran Orangutan. The matter of their infertility was not even discussed in their household, apart from their monthly ritual of him shooting reproachful looks at her tear-stained face, raw and bruised by her steady disappointment.

Raven asked her if they would consider fertility treatment but Celeste dismissed the idea as 'unnatural'. Raven had to check her impulse to argue that there was nothing unnatural about science — that in fact, science was the very study of nature — but it wasn't her place to challenge Celeste's beliefs. Besides, she knew she could solve their problem 'naturally'.

They had been trying for six years, which was good news for Raven. Six is an incredibly fertile number as one can possibly guess from the shape. It also told Raven that, if it hadn't happened spontaneously by now, it probably wasn't going to happen unless she took some drastic action.

When Celeste was mid-cycle and the moon was full, it was time to cast the spell. Celeste had invited her sister, Danielle, for moral support, as she was keeping Raven's services a secret from her Orangutan.

"I just want you to know that I don't approve of what you do," were the first words Danielle uttered.

Raven continued to unpack her things.

"I just don't think it's right," she continued, insisting on a confrontation that Raven had no intention of participating in.

"Oh, Danielle," sighed Celeste.

"In fact, I think..."

Raven could tell that she was about to hit her stride.

"You are more than welcome," Raven said, "to wait outside."

"Out-Side?" As if it was the first time she'd ever heard the word. Raven found herself wishing that she would close her gaping fish-mouth. If they were characters in a comic book she could have waved her wand — abracadabra — and turned her into a puffer fish, bouncing and flapping on the kitchen floor!

"There is no place for negative energy here tonight," Raven said, slowly and clearly. "If you have a problem it's best to go and leave this sacred space." Raven hammed it up a bit, for effect.

"Sacred?" Danielle gasped. "Sacred?"

One is bound, Raven knows from bitter experience, to bump up against some people in this business who believe that witchery is inherently wicked. Little do they know that they cast spells themselves when they curse other drivers in traffic, touch wood, or make a wish when they blow out birthday candles.

"I need this to work," Celeste said.

"Listen to me," whispered her sister, frantic, bunching up her fists around the flea-market crucifix that dangled from her moist and unpleasantly chunky neck. "You don't need to do this. Come to our church! Our cell group has been praying for you —"

Raven had no choice now but to speak up. "And she is yet to conceive. You say you don't like spells but what do you think prayer is? You just haven't been saying the right ones."

Heathen! Danielle's aura had shouted. Evil woman! "And I suppose you know the right ones?"

She eyed Raven: seeing a wolf in wolf's clothing.

"Yes," Raven said. "It's my job."

With Danielle unhappily dispatched, Raven began the ceremony by smudging the room with the sweet smoke of lavender and white sage. With a piece of chalkstone she cast a circle on the pine floorboards around Celeste, on which she placed six green candles. She anointed the candles with vanilla oil, lit them, then began her fertility incantation. Celeste was instructed to close her eyes and sit as still as possible, as if meditating, and just allow the spell to wash through her. Her hands were placed over her abdomen, sending warmth and acceptance deep into her pelvic chakra. Afterwards, they sailed the eggshell by moonlight while Celeste recited a poem she had written, inviting the soul of her baby into her body.

Raven found her openness touching, and couldn't help thinking that she would make a tender mother. She gave her a silver bracelet with a charm of a carnelian-eyed hare —which she had charged with pentacle-cast spells — as well as a gift of bespoke tea: stinging nettle, red clove and raspberry leaf, which Celeste was to drink every day.

On her way out Raven gave Celeste a syringe she had been keeping warm in her bra, snug between her breasts. Raven told her it was a potion to open and soften her cervix and that she should keep it at blood temperature and use it as soon as possible before making love.

A fortuitous two weeks later Celeste was pregnant and the rest, as they say, is history. Her Orangutan will never know that the child is not biologically his.

The timing of Celeste's luna-cycle couldn't have been more perfect. Raven had been consulting that day with another client of hers who was having trouble sustaining his phallus. Feri, or sexual mysticism is her speciality and she was training him in the art of Tantra. This client wasn't dissimilar looking to the man in the framed wedding photo that Celeste had given her and he had inadvertently given Raven the means to help Celeste. The universe was particularly supportive that day, as it can be when you are following a beneficent course of action. Neither client was aware of the transaction and they were both extremely pleased with the results.

The nurse, true to her word, marches to Celeste's room and rounds up the visitors. She deftly shepherds them out of the door and in the direction of the elevator that will transport them from the east wing. On her way back to the reception counter she winks at Raven and Raven takes her cue and slips into the private ward.

"Raven," says Celeste, smiling, a host of sterile white pillows behind her. She is glowing like a Madonna on oxytocin. "I'm so glad you could come."

"I'll only stay a minute," says Raven. "I'm sure you'd like some alone-time with —"

"Bobby," she says, holding him out towards Raven. He is impossibly small and calm, with perfect blue eyes and a button nose. "My little Robbins."

"Bobby," says Raven. "What a beautiful boy! Congratulations."

"Hold him," she says.

"I don't know," says Raven, holding the drooping roses to her chest. "I'm not very good with — "

"Nonsense," says Celeste. "He wants you to hold him. You're the reason he exists."

The room is full of flowers and crunchy silver balloons and teddy bears. There's not an empty vase in sight. She dumps the bouquet into the small porcelain basin and washes her hands over the shucked stems.

"Hello Robbins," she says, as he is placed in her arms, as light as a raven feather.

"What is *she* doing here?" says an angry voice at the door. Raven turns around to see a shocked Danielle holding two paper cups of coffee. "You're letting her HOLD your baby?"

"Of course!" says Celeste. "Why wouldn't I?"

"Because she's a —"

"Yes?"

"Because she's a *witch.*"

"Oh, Dani, please. Don't make a scene!"

Danielle's décolletage flushes with patches of ire. She's about to say something but then changes her mind and turns on her heel.

"Sorry about that. She's always been —"

"Don't worry. It's not your fault," says Raven, twinkling. "Besides, I don't take being called 'a witch' personally."

Raven doesn't tell Celeste that Dani has in fact been stalking her on social media ever since the conception spell worked. She had used different names, fake profiles, anonymous comments on her blog, but the message was always the same: that Raven was an agent of evil and that the Almighty would soon put a stop to her devil worshipping ways.

"I'm so glad you could come," Celeste says, as Raven hands the baby back to her along with some myrrh incense. "I feel like... like we've closed the circle."

Raven glances at the skulking Danielle on the way out. She has been talking to the Orangutan in the corridor and they both look up at her as she sees them. Raven's black-hilted *athamé* — her double-edged ritual knife — tingles against her thigh. She has a feeling that this particular circle is not yet closed.

When Raven pulls into her driveway at Colborn Manor she

quickly closes the gate behind her before the animals realise she's home. Max, the perennially bad-tempered ginger Maine Coon mudblood, jumps up onto Morris's bonnet and stretches out on the engine-warmed metal. Licks his paws in a bored kind of way, as if to say that he didn't even know she had been away for the night. She can hear Eli chatting inside. "Raven," he chirps, "Raven!"

The Grimm Brothers, Jake and Bill, bound around the side of the house and Raven steadies herself to accept the battering of their excitement.

"Hello my devil hounds!" she says, ruffling the midnight fur on their Rottweiler heads. "Miss me?"

They bark as if to say 'Yes, yes, we missed you. Where were you? Where were you? We thought you were never coming back'.

4 / DEAD & BURIED

Benjamin is wearing his usual workman's clothes: soft, faded checked shirt; dirty denims, stubby HB pencil that lives in the crook between his ear and his skull. He has a lumberjack air about him, thinks Raven, as all good carpenters do, and a dark, steady beard. They are standing on the porch of Colborn Manor and Benjamin is uneasy. He strokes one of Raven's cats, Cocoa, who is strutting on the table. She hasn't yet seen Lightfoot. The Grimm Brothers are chasing pigeons in the garden.

"It's bad, isn't it?" Raven already knows the answer. She is holding one of the new baby rabbits. It's mink-soft and the warmth is comforting.

"Yip," says Benjamin. "Bad."

He's never been one to mince the few words he deigns to mutter.

"How bad?"

"Hmm," Ben scratches his beard. "Hmm."

It is like trying to coax a bear from a cave. Even Cocoa eventually loses interest and jumps down. Raven checks her phone: 28 missed calls.

"How much is it going to cost me?"

The African Grey swoops down and perches on the back of one of the bentwood chairs. He does a foot shuffle and then shows Benjamin his beak.

"Hello Eli," says the carpenter.

"Hello Eli," chirps the bird.

Ben sighs and leans his hip against the table. "Look, it depends."

Raven puts the rabbit down and denies the urge to cross her arms. "It depends? What does that mean? Won't it cost what it costs?"

"There are a few possible scenarios."

"Okay."

"First, we can just fix what you've asked me to fix: The loose planks on this porch. The stair banister. The floorboards throughout."

"The bedroom ceiling. The office wall."

"Right. So… that's already a broad scope of work."

"Right."

"So we'll be looking at around R60K for that."

"Jesus Christ!" Eli shouts. That's his favourite phrase.

"Sixty THOUSAND rand?" says Raven.

"I would charge anyone else 100."

She knows he's not lying. Ben doesn't have a deceitful bone in his body, unlike her. She has become used to embroidering the truth to suit her own or her clients', needs.

"And the other scenarios?"

"Well," says Benjamin, "the second option would be to do all that, plus… a lot more."

She waits for him to continue, but he bites his lips and looks out at the oak tree. Good Goddess, she wishes that he would speak faster. Should she put a temporary spell on him to speed up his thought process?

"I'm listening."

How does his wife do it? Raven would've bludgeoned him to death with his own glow-in-the-dark hammer by now. He sighs again, runs a calloused hand through his hair, causing his bicep to flex. He has the body of a lumberjack, too.

Ah. Maybe that's why his wife hasn't done away with him.

Eyes, says the voice.

What?

Stop ogling him. He is not a piece of flesh. Look him in the eyes.

Oh. Yes.

"Look, Miss Kane. I'm not going to beat around the bush."

Well that is hardly surprising, she thinks. Also, you'd think that after working for her on and off for the last 12 years he would call her by her first name.

"This house…"

"My house."

"Your house. Colborn Manor. It's falling apart."

"You always say that," says Raven. "And you always fix it."

"This time I just feel that —"

"Yes?"

"That it's too late. Too far gone." He knocks on the wooden panelling behind her. It sounds worryingly hollow. "The house is just too... old. A timber house, in this climate — it's just asking for trouble."

Raven doesn't know what to say. Eli keeps quiet too.

"I would take it up with the architect but I'm sure he's dead and buried by now."

If he wasn't before this conversation then he certainly is now.

She leans against the crumbling wall, feels the sap drain out of her.

"It's not just a house," she says. "You know that."

"I know that. I'm sorry."

You should listen to him, says the voice. *He knows what he's talking about.*

"How much for the second option? You know, to fix everything?"

"Broad strokes? 500. 550. Let's say an extra 50 contingency. So you can budget on R600K."

"Holy shit," says Raven. "I don't have R600K."

"Holy shit!" chirps Eli.

"I don't have anything close to R600K."

"Not many people do these days."

"In fact," she says, "I have the opposite of R600K. I have a bond to pay off. I have minus R600K."

Ben shrugs. It's not his business.

"So, it'll be 60, or 600?"

"Or anywhere in between. Or less, or more. It's difficult to know how much it will deteriorate. If you like, you can give me a budget and I can do as much as I can for that amount."

"But you don't recommend it?" says Raven, leaning harder against the wood, wishing it would swallow her and all her earthly problems.

He shakes his head.

"What would you do?"

"Honestly? I'd sell. Get out while it's still standing. Buy myself a cheerful little lock-up-and-go in a secure complex in a safe neighbourhood."

The cheek of him! Next he'd be telling her to sell her soul to the Death-eaters.

"You know I'd never do that. I inherited this property through blood. It's sacred ground."

"Sacred ground," says Eli. "Blood."

"Well, in that case, I'd demolish."

It's like a wooden arrow in her heart.

"Start again," he says. "Build with bricks and mortar."

The Grimm Brothers start going mad. They must have caught a pigeon. Fred, the albino peacock, is screaming. Eli launches himself into the air to investigate.

"But you're a carpenter! You're supposed to love timber architecture."

"Bricks and mortar," he says. "Dry-walling. It's the sensible thing to do."

"Yes, well," sighs Raven. "I've never been very sensible."

There is a crack from the brittle slat she is leaning on, and with a crash, she falls through the wall.

5 / ADDER STONES

"What happened to you?" Jessica is, of course, as perfectly made up as ever, despite the baby clinging to her jacket like the little chimpanzee that he is.

"What do you mean?" says Raven, dusting the wood-chips from her hair. She tries to hide her irritation at her sister's unexpected visit.

"Ah, never mind. Here, take the baby, will you?"

"Er, okay."

Jess unclamps Matthew's chubby fingers and hands him over. The baby starts to wail. He wants his mother. Raven holds him stiffly as if he's a strange new animal which may or may not bite. Two babies in her arms in one day: it's a record she is quite sure will never be broken. Heartsore, he continues to cry directly into Raven's ear canal. Jess pays him no mind and just speaks louder to be heard over the sobbing.

"His bottle is in the bag. Hot water to warm it up. Don't put it in the microwave."

"I don't own a microwave."

"Really? What? Oh my God. Let me guess – now you don't believe in microwaves?"

"Nope, it's not that."

There was no way she was going to tell Jess that she couldn't afford to replace the original nuker that now sat, sulking, in her storeroom, with its broken carbon-coloured innards.

"What then? You can't run a microwave on your kooky solar system?"

"It's not 'kooky' to live off the grid, Jess. It's clever. It's progressive."

"It's a bit kooky."

"Well, I'll keep that in mind. You know, the next time you come over to charge your phone during load-shedding."

"Whatever." Jess smoothes her hair. "I don't have time."

"Time for what?"

"To stand here and debate your… your eccentricity."

What's to debate? asks the voice.

"What's to debate?" asks Raven, jiggling the baby on her hip.

Jessica blows her hair out of her face. A strand stays glued to her lipgloss, irritating her.

Raven doesn't understand women who wear a) lipgloss or b) high heels. It's like purposefully handicapping yourself. As if women don't have enough handicaps.

Handicaps? says the voice. *What rubbish!*

Easy for you to say, says Raven.

Give me an example of a woman's 'handicap'.

A uterus, for one.

Jessica teeters over the stones to fetch an unwilling Rebecca from the car.

I hate it when people pop in unannounced, says the voice. *Chuck some tea down her throat and boot her out. We have work to do.*

Raven stands in the doorway holding Matthew, who is now whimpering into her shirt, glazing it with snail-trails of snot. She hears Jessica having a shouting match with her daughter who clearly wants to stay in the air-conditioned Land Cruiser. Eventually Rebecca is hauled out of the 4x4 and pushed up Raven's footpath.

"Here," says an out-of-breath Jessica. "Say hello to your aunt."

Rebecca glares at Raven from under a perfectly blunt-cut fringe; her outfit just as immaculate as her mother's.

"Hi Becks!" says Raven, feigning enthusiasm. Rebecca narrows her eyes. She has never been a good actress. "Come for a visit, have you?"

The girl pouts. Is she wearing lipgloss, too?

"How about some yummy juice?" says Raven.

Rebecca crosses her arms. "I'm not a CHILD."

Jess barks her fake laugh. "She's going through a phase."

Rebecca has been 'going through a phase' for the full six years she has been alive.

"I'm not going inside," says Rebecca.

"Suit yourself." Raven turns and walks towards the kitchen. "Tea, Jess? Coffee? I've just made a jug of —"

"I'm not staying," says Jessica.

Raven whirls around. "What do you mean you're not staying?"

"I have an important appointment. I can't cancel. I'm late! That's why I asked you to baby-sit."

Shit, thinks Raven. Had she forgotten? Was her memory fading now, too, as well as her magic?

"When did you ask me to baby-sit?"

"Half an hour ago!"

"What?"

"Jesus, Raven. I tweeted you!"

"You do realise that Twitter is not a personal messenger service?"

"If you ever answered your phone, you know, like a normal person, then I wouldn't have to resort to tweeting you!"

They stand facing each other with twin frowns. Matthew breaks the spell by farting into Raven's hand. She laughs and the baby joins in.

"Whatever," says Jessica. "I'm late. I need to go."

"Where's Thabisa?"

"Busy. You know what nannies are like. Totally unreliable! When did the help become so damn entitled? Really, the sooner I get rid of her, the better."

She wouldn't last a day without a nanny, says the voice.

"Well," says Raven, as she tries to hand Matthew back. "You can't leave them here."

Jess takes a step back. "What? Why?"

"You can't just leave your kids here, Jessica. I'm being serious. I don't have time to look after them today. My work — I was at the PaganCon the whole day yesterday —"

"Do you know how hard it is to have two children?" says Jess, tears in her eyes. "Tim is always working. He's never around on weekends. I'm practically a widow. I'm a corporate widow! And on weekends, I'm a golf widow. Do you know how hard that is?"

Oh, boo hoo, says the voice. *Poor Jessica. Everything's always a fucking national disaster.*

"Jess."

Don't fall for her crocodile tears, says the voice. *Don't let her take advantage of you.*

I'm her sister, thinks Raven.

That doesn't mean you have to be her doormat, says the voice.

"I never have time to myself."

She's the one who decided to HAVE children, says the voice.

"You're the one who... oh, never mind," says Raven, taking the nappy-bag from her sister and slinging it over her shoulder. "Go."

Doormat, says the voice.

I am *not.*

Why is it that you can say no to absolutely anyone in the universe apart from the person who treats you the worst?

She's my sister. She needs help.

That's an understatement.

"You're the best!" says Jess, tears instantly evaporating. She air-kisses Raven's cheek and pats Matthew's moon-bald head. "Just the best."

Typical. Where's she off to, anyway? Movies? Lunch? Cocktails with her band of bored housewives?

No, she said it was an appointment. An important appointment.

"You'd better be back in an hour," says Raven.

"I need three hours!"

"No," says Raven, firmly. "One. Two at the most. I need to work."

"Thanks again!" shouts Jess as she runs down to her monster of a car. The engine is still running.

Raven yells after her, "If you take one minute more than two hours I will dump these kids at social services!"

Jessica barks her fake laugh again, checks her reflection in the rearview mirror, and sprays gravel at them as she accelerates up the drive.

Matthew has gone from Wailing Chimp to Nestled Monkey; his breathing even, his warm ear pressed against her chest. Raven relaxes a little; strokes his back. Poor sausage. She warms the milk for him and pours out two glasses of cold lavender lemonade. Decorates the glasses with a sprig of blossoming lavender from her potion garden. Takes the drinks back to the angry niece in the doorway.

Rebecca stands her ground, her arms in the shape of a cross, like a wrong answer. Raven's arm feels like it is about to drop off, but she doesn't want to put the baby down. Instead she sighs and sits outside, on the ground, her back resting cautiously against the disloyal timber slats, the baby snug in the make-shift cradle of her vaulted legs. The girl glares at her: she has storm-clouds for eyes.

“I’m not going to drink that witch’s potion!” Rebecca says.

“Good,” says Raven, taking a long sip. It’s aromatic. Crisp and delicious.

“Good?”

“More for me!”

Rebecca rolls her eyes.

“Besides. I put a spell on it.”

“What do you mean?” she says, paying attention.

“I hexed it. If you were to drink it, it would make you turn into a frog!”

“No it wouldn’t!”

“Yes it would.”

“No it wouldn’t.”

“You’re right. It wouldn’t.”

“I was right. You were lying.”

“No. I was playing. Remember that? Playing? What you used to do before iPads and smart TV?”

“Playing is for children,” Rebecca smoothes her hair in exactly the same way her mother does. Her nails are painted pink.

Raven sighs, gives baby Matthew his bottle which he sucks at with furrowed brows.

"What happened, Becks? How did you grow up so quickly?"

What she really meant was: how can such a small soul like you be filled with so much venom? Where does it come from? What are you going to do with it?

Matthew chugs.

"It can't be easy with your dad working all the time. And your mom, well —"

"And Mom always trying to get rid of us!"

"She's not trying to get rid of you. She just needs some time to herself. It's difficult."

"So she keeps saying."

Matthew finishes his bottle and shows Raven his big shark-like grin.

"Your mom loves you, Becks. She does. Even if it doesn't always feel like it."

"Whatever."

The baby pulls a face; he squirms.

"He needs to burp," Rebecca says. She uncrosses her arms and moves to lever Matthew upright, who promptly belches obediently. He relaxes again into his leggy cradle. He smiles at his sister. She doesn't smile back. Raven picks up an Adder stone, polishes it with her thumb.

"What are these?" asks Rebecca. "These strange stones?"

"They're Adder stones."

"Adder?"

"Adder, as in snake."

"Snake stones?"

"Also known as Hag stones. Witch stones. Serpent's eggs."

"Gross."

"They're rare. And very valuable. I collect them. I used to keep them in a bowl inside, but they grew out of it. So now I have them in the garden. They are all around the house, in a circle. Not many people notice them. Or, if they do, they think they are ordinary garden pebbles."

Rebecca holds it up to her face to examine it. Looks through the hole.

"You know,' says Raven, "I'm not surprised you noticed them."

"What do you mean?"

"From the day you were born I had a feeling about you, that you were special. I've never told you this before but I think you're old enough now. I think you're like me. I think you have a gift."

Rebecca looks at her. "I don't want to be like you," she says. "I don't want to be a witch."

"I'm not talking about becoming a witch. I'm talking about magic, Becks. I think you have some."

"Can I keep it?" Rebecca asks.

"The Adder stone? Of course."

The girl puts it into her pocket.

"The reason they are sought after is because they have power," says Raven. "Adder stones offer protection and they draw out poison. Take care of it and it will take care of you."

Matthew is getting restless. He wants to explore.

"Shall we go through to the back garden? Let Matthew crawl around? See the animals? I'm sure that Applejack will be very happy to see you."

"Okay." Rebecca's energy is lighter now. The pale cool-blue of a shallow ocean. They stand up and dust themselves off. Raven heads in first and Rebecca follows. Out of the corner of her eye she sees the girl take a tentative sip of her lemonade.

Raven has long since forgotten about her mounting work schedule and is throwing a naked Matthew into the air. He gurgles in delight. Much to the Grimm Brothers' delight, Rebecca is riding the pony around the giant oak tree. They lope alongside her, barking and nudging Applejack with their warm snouts. Toby, the ancient tortoise, has been decorated with a garland of wild flowers and the snowy peacock is watching the humans with a look of resigned disdain. With the exception of the peacock, they are all spattered with mud.

"Rebecca!" shouts Jessica. "Your dress!"

They stop playing and look up at her standing stiffly on the stilted verandah. Raven hadn't heard the doorbell. Jessica must have let herself in.

"Hi Mom!" shouts Rebecca. "Look at me! I'm riding Applejack!"

Hearing his name, the pony speeds up a little, to show off.

"Mama!" says Matthew. "Mama!"

"Hi Jess. Nice of you to join us."

She has been away for over four hours.

"My appointment ran over," sniffs Jess. "How did you all get so grubby?"

"We made a mud castle!" says the girl. "Look!"

There is a mud castle: a clay version of Raven's house, dirty, and just as dilapidated.

"Matthew was King Kong!" shouts Rebecca. "He King-Konged it!"

"Do you know how much that dress cost?"

Rebecca blinks at her mother.

"Does it matter?" asks Raven.

"Of course it bloody well matters!"

"*Ag*, leave her. She's having fun. It's just a dress."

"Just a dress? It's BratCouture! It cost over seven hundred rand!"

"Oh well. Soap?"

"SOAP? You think soap will get that mess out? It's ruined! Rebecca, get off that smelly animal immediately!"

"But, Mom, I wanted to show you how I —"

"OFF, Rebecca! OFF!"

Applejack, confused by the shouting, stops in his tracks.

"Why are you so upset?" asks Raven.

Rebecca climbs off the pony, puts her arm around his neck.

"Why am I so upset? Because you have no respect, Raven, you never have had."

Raven's mouth hangs open. "Respect? For a designer dress for a six-year-old?"

"Don't be facetious! I mean respect for things. Respect for hard-earned money."

Raven doesn't call her out on her blatant hypocrisy. Doesn't remind her that she has dropped out of every study course and job she has ever had; that she hasn't been in the workplace since she fell pregnant with Rebecca; that she has a housekeeper, a full-time nanny and a night nurse and she still complains about how hard it is to be 'a full-time mother'.

Raven stares up at her sister. It has always been a complicated relationship. Jess likes to say it was because, as a child, Raven fed her pet hamster to a toad, but the truth is more complicated than that. For one, Jessica is an A-type personality who likes things a certain way, and it drove her crazy when her younger sister came along and coloured outside the lines. It still makes her furious that Raven is immune to her bossiness.

"Mama!" says Matthew, reaching out for her. Jessica remains on the porch.

"Have you at least fed them?" she asks.

"Yes." Rebecca twirls, stroking her thyme-blossom tiara. "We picked grapes and kumquats and gooseberries."

"And figs," says Raven. "And mint from the potion garden."

The mention of the potion garden makes Jess blanch.

"And granadillas!" says Rebecca.

"Your kids are very good at foraging," says Raven. "They're right on trend. I think their chances of survival on a desert island would be average to good."

"Rebecca, Matthew, come. We're going."

Rebecca gives Applejack an affectionate pat. He snorts in reply, lifts a foreleg. She hugs his neck and makes her way up the grassy slope, dusting sand off her dress as she climbs the wooden steps. Raven follows, holding Matthew close.

Jessica's face has that post-facial just-scrubbed look and her anger glows in a halo around her. Raven notices that she's had her hair done. Can smell sweet aromatherapy massage oil. Bergamot.

Matthew starts to whimper.

"Why is he naked? Where are his clothes? His nappy?"

"They're inside."

Jessica stomps into the house.

"Listen," says Raven, trying to make peace for the sake of the kids, "why don't you pour yourself a glass of wine, put your feet up. I'll chuck the kids in the bath and they'll be as good as new."

Matthew roars in his new King Kong voice.

"Well, almost as good as new."

Doormat, says the voice.

"No." Jessica turns and takes Matthew, who leans into her, happy and exhausted. "Their nanny is back. She'll sort them out."

"I don't want Thabisa, I want you," says Rebecca. "I want you to get us ready for bed."

Raven throws things haphazardly into the nappy-bag and hands it to her sister. Gives the baby a cheek-squish and a kiss, tries to high-five her niece but is left hanging.

"Get in the car." Jessica unlocks the doors with her remote. "There's a present in there for you."

The girl trudges down the footpath. The storm-clouds are back.

6 / FISH-GUT WHISKERS

Raven checks her email. The machine pings with 256 unread emails. Scanning the titles she sees there are more than 50 work leads that she must urgently follow up on and a message from the High Priestess. She knows she and her empty pockets should feel grateful for the potential work, but sometimes being so needed feels like she is being attacked. It's as if too many people want a piece of her and soon she'll be taken apart, broken into pieces and carried away like a peeled carcass in a desert, until there is nothing left of her but powder-dry bones the colour of clouds.

Hello Raven Dear

We must meet for coffee. The Wicked Witches are out of control. We don't want them igniting the ignorami.

We need a plan.

Also: I'm worried about you. You haven't been to any of the coven gatherings. The Moon Chapel ceremony last night was particularly dull without you.

I know something is wrong. I can help.

Let's get together and sort this out.

Blessed Be

Lavinia

Ping, ping, ping, goes her laptop. So many people looking for magic. What they don't know about earth magic is that it can go either way. We are all under the influence of so many factors at any one time that it's not an exaggeration to say that anything can happen. Without even knowing it, our destinies are pushed and pulled by the sparkling cosmos, kneaded and knocked back like baker's dough. You can try your best to stake out your life's path — or others' lives, as Raven does — but our human influence is limited. There are people — women and men — who become taken with a neo-pagan lifestyle, study Wicca, indulgently call themselves White Witches, but if they truly knew the Craft they would know that there is no such thing. These Dabblers are the moths of the sorcery world, not unpleasant to have around unless they become confused and start battering themselves against a light-source that is not the moon. Some are elegant and pretty to look at, others leave moth-dust and holes in your winter underwear.

Raven knows there is no such thing as white magic. Real magic covers a wide spectrum encompassing good and evil and there are very many shades of grey in-between. The reason a spell can never be pure white is because of the cosmic baker's influence. A sorceress may start out with a clear, benevolent purpose, unalloyed ingredients and a pure heart and may perform the incantation as close to perfectly as she can manage, but after that she has little influence. Once it is out of her mouth the spell is out of her hands and cannot be kept un-grubby. Just as a person cannot be 100 per cent good, a witch, as pure-thinking as she may be, cannot achieve Perfect Snow. She may be milk, ivory or limestone, or one of the hundreds of shades between them, but never fresh snow. You have this trembling human spectrum overlapping and interweaving the sure orbit of magic and it becomes evident — despite the illusions of the giggling wiccans — that a white witch is nothing but a fairytale.

Raven doesn't buy into any of these pagan pretences. She practises Grey Magic; more dove-grey than charcoal. Or, more accurately: the colour of a raincloud, as it swells and shrinks and flickers between shades of pearl and slate. She has to be careful of slipping towards the sooty part of the spectrum. The darker the magic, the quicker the flame takes, the more powerful you feel. You have to be on your guard and think things through: sometimes you set out to do good and the result is murky, or worse. Raven once killed someone with a simple love spell. The spell had been one of her best: refined over and over again to be as straightforward and striking as possible. But setting out she hadn't been told the whole story and had thus made the mistake of not binding the spell. A woman had left a man and the spell had been intended to reunite them. What she hadn't been told was that the woman had left the man for 'someone else'; that someone else happened to meet with a freak accident the day Raven triple-cast the reunion conjuration: he was an innocent bystander, shot in a cash-in-transit heist. Raven's client, his grief-stricken lover returned, was delighted and paid her double. Of course the fatal shooting had not been Raven's intention.

Apparently the reunited couple are happily married now. He still sends Raven fruit baskets.

Raven types 'WICKED WITCHES' into the search bar of Vimeo and watches through her fingers as she sees them protesting outside the Xosmetix building in the CBD, demanding that they stop testing on animals. There is a flash of a T-shirt with 'Twisted

Sisters' on it. They have red-spattered placards with slogans and toy animals in cages: rabbits, monkeys, rats. It's like a plush parade of the Chinese zodiac. Hope; intelligence; vitality. Plastic pastel colours and fish-gut whiskers.

That's not too bad, she thinks.

She spots a pentagram on a poster.

But this is not good.

The pentagram is a sacred symbol which is most maligned, and for PR reasons it is a mark best employed in relative privacy. The Wicked Witches don't seem to agree.

She understands their fire, their rebellion. She admires their revolutionary thinking, but young spirits don't always know what's good for them. What they don't understand is the danger of mob mentality. Getting people with closed minds riled up is never a good idea.

The next clip is of the coven breaking into the building. It's shot at night with a shaking hand and some kind of night-vision lens. Her root chakra twinges. It feels like a horror film. It's scary until she realises what they are doing: you see the green eyes of the animals twitch with nerves. The witches open the cages and let the test animals free.

Well, thinks Raven, you can hardly blame them for that.

Another video, from a few days ago, shows the Wicked Witches mid-ritual.

Uh-oh.

Thirteen sky-clad women stand in a circle, faces shining in the dusk light. They are chanting. The flames of a hundred candles illuminate the space and flicker on their naked bodies.

Where are they? A forest? The trees are black in the background.

The chanting gets louder and deeper as they move into their collective trance. Some of them tremble, some of their heads are flung so far back that they look decapitated. Others start gibbering as if there are speaking in tongues.

“Holy Shit,” says Raven. What the fuck are they doing? She’s about to close the browser when the video jump-cuts to a blank screen. Then a close-up of Luella flickers on and off. Her signature candy-cane hair flashes red and white, and she’s wearing more dark eye make-up than a model sporting heroine-chic. Her skin is luminous.

Slowly and deliberately, she says: “You want to know who we are?”

The question echoes in the black box.

Are they finally going to settle on a name?

“We are the daughters of the witches you couldn’t burn.”

The video flickers again to a blank screen and the clip ends.

“Holy Hecate,” says Raven. Lavinia is right. They have to do something.

7 / TURNING TRICKS

Raven takes a wineglass out of the kitchen cupboard and puts it on the counter. It's her favourite glass, so thin that it is almost invisible. A ghost glass. She's about to pour a generous and well-deserved drink when she recalls how much of her work remains undone. She'd love to just sit out on the porch with her bare feet up, watching the sun set in silence. Or climb up into her oak tree. Polish an acorn. Rest her scratchy eyes. But she has a long night ahead of her, so she re-corks the Pinotage and boils the kettle instead. Makes herself a double-strength french press with cream and hunts for a rusk. Coffee is one of her daily reminders that magic does exist.

Holding her MacBook aloft, she tries to find space on her chaotic writing-desk to put it down. It's crowded with toppling towers of reference books and sheafs of papers. A mosaic of rippling Post-It notes.

You really need to sort this lot out, says the voice.

It's organised chaos, says Raven. I know where everything is.

No you don't.

Okay, you're right. I don't. But I don't have time to tidy it now, I need to work.

The machine pings. More emails.

You see?

A cluttered desk is a sign of a cluttered mind, says the voice.

Rubbish. Have you seen pictures of Einstein's desk?

No.

Well, then, I think you should keep your opinions on housekeeping to yourself.

I just —

Yes?

I just worry that you're turning into one of THOSE witches, says the voice.

Which?

You know what I'm talking about.

I don't.

You know the type. The ones that give the Craft a bad name. They let everything... slip.

Slip? You think I'm slipping?

They're like those caricatures of witches you see in fairy tales with the grey hair and the warts on their noses.

It was one grey hair! One! And I pulled it out!

But you haven't had your hair done in months.

That's because I have better things to do! More constructive things. Trying to finish this book, for one!

Raven smacks the pile of notes in front of her. It's not going to write itself, you know.

I know. But —

But, what?

What are you wearing?

These? These are my *schlumperdincker* pants. They're the most comfortable pants ever. They are ideal for *schlumperdincking* in. It's not like I go out in public in a dressing gown and dirty slippers.

Except for that one time.

That was an emergency.

Raven. Double-chocolate ice-cream swirl at 11 p.m. is not an emergency.

...You think I'm slipping?

It's not about the hair. Let's be honest, you'd look good with a crew-cut.

I don't know about that.

You would.

Ah well! I can't take any credit for that. Good genes are hardly an accomplishment.

It's not about the hair. It's about the out-of-control desk, the bursting inbox, the unfinished manuscript, the unwashed dogs, the crumbling house. The pigeon infestation.

What pigeon infestation?

The insomnia. Most worrying of all, your attack last night, at the conference. I don't want to use the phrase 'downward spiral' but –

But?

Well it seems to me that you're in a downward spiral.

You can be such an asshole, says Raven.

You do realise that you've just called YOURSELF an asshole?

Will you please leave me alone for a few hours? I need an empty head to deal with this. Raven gestures at the mess. This downward spiral on my desk.

I think you need an intervention. Like those hoarders on ReelTV.

I do not!

Just because you don't keep old newspapers and dirty take-away polystyrene clamshells from 1984 doesn't mean you don't need help.

Will you please be quiet?

What would it be called? A witcher-vention, says the voice.

Quiet.

A wicca-vention?

Go away.

This conversation is not over.

"God Almighty!" chirps the African Grey, making Raven jump.

"Thank you, Eli," says Raven. "My thoughts exactly."

She blinks, takes a sip of coffee, prepares to concentrate, looks at the piles of pages demanding her attention and feels like giving up before she starts. Maybe she'll just go onto Facebook first, just to ease herself into it. She scrolls through pictures of her acquaintances' children, political rants and some vaguely funny memes. She knows that she should update her status but can't think of anything interesting enough to say. She just types "Carry two seeds for luck" and clicks 'post'.

She knows she should check Twitter, with her 108 notifications of tweets addressed to her *@turningtricks* handle, but she's not in the mood for giving advice. Twitter is part of her witch's social media platform — to 'get her name out there' as her business coach had said. To remain up-to-date, clued-in, relevant. Engaged and engaging. Okay, she doesn't have a business coach — perhaps she should — but she's sure it's what she would have said. *@turningtricks* is her contemporary equivalent of an 80s *YOU* magazine agony aunt column, except the aunt in this case isn't a moustached middle-aged lady with false nails and a rotary telephone on her desk, but a smart, savvy sorceress.

That's what she's supposed to be, anyway. That's the idea you'd get if you looked at her website, her Instagram account. But at the moment she feels more hip-replacement than hip, and the only multi-tasking she's done lately is feeding the animals while she's scrolling Tumblr.

As if reading her thoughts the Grimms saunter in.

"Is it dinner-time already?" says Raven. The Rottweilers look up at her with their dog-smiles.

"Okay, then," she says, and stands up, leaving her Pilates ball to roll into the corner.

In an ordinary household it would take, perhaps, two minutes in total to feed the pets. At Colborn Manor it could take anything from twenty minutes to an hour, depending on how amusing the animals were being. The Grimm Brothers, Jake and Bill, are the easiest to satisfy, with just a firm jiggling of their pelts and a scoopful of kibble each. If she has time she throws in a few sentences in a really deep voice, which they love. She does it now. "You are a bit smelly," she says, channelling Ramtha, "but still very handsome" and they show her their happy teeth and scalloped gums. So predictable. That's one of the reasons she loves dogs.

Next up are the cats, who require filtered water after tasting it a few years ago and refusing to drink regular tap water ever since, and a scoopful of their own special kibble mix: *Gourmiaow High KittyJoule* for Cocoa, who, despite being three years old, still looks like a kitten and has to be coaxed to eat, like a fussy child; *High Protein Anabolic* mixed with *Kat deLight* for snowy Lily Lightfoot, who is rudely accused of being fat at every vet check-up, and boring old *Feline Senior+* for Max, the cantankerous ginger who Raven found in a storm-drain fifteen years ago. Sometimes she tops the bowls up with tuna as a treat, garnishing it with fresh catnip, but when she checks the larder cupboard she sees that she's out of tuna. Goddess, how she hates shopping.

Next on the list is Eli, the African Grey, who eats parrot pellets. When he feels like a fresh, non-pelleted snack, he helps himself from the garden. He loves grapes and strawberries, in particular. The chickens get chicken feed mixed with some crushed seashells for calcium to harden their eggs. Raven doesn't name the chickens, for obvious reasons. Fred, the albino peacock, gets the same, although he never seems very impressed with it.

Toby, the 200-year-old tortoise, gets cherry tomatoes, carrot sticks and red lettuce — homegrown, organic — and the food has to be placed a metre or so in front of him, to encourage him to exercise, otherwise he just stays put for days and Raven has to knock on his shell and wake him up to see if he's still alive. Then, of course, there is Applejack, the dearest grey pony, whose name says it all. He also loves lavender lemonade and walking in circles around the massive oak tree as if he is hypnotised by it, or wants to hypnotise it.

In return, Raven gets three eggs from the chickens, which she thanks them for. Thinking of having an omelette for dinner, she makes her way around the house to the potion garden outside her kitchen door to pick some thyme and oregano. Maybe she'll Instagram a shot of what's blooming in the Smudge section.

An unpleasant surprise awaits her in the form of bird waste splattered all over her herbaceous border. For a moment, she's confused. How did this get here? Was it Fred, throwing one of his tantrums? Was it —

"Mother of God!" shouts Eli.

"Eli! Was this you?" Raven says, but she knows it wasn't. Eli has impeccable manners, apart from his habit of blaspheming. Then she hears the cooing of the feral pigeons, who have clearly built a nest in the eves above.

"Damn it," she says. "Look at this mess." Looking up, she counts 13 birds.

"Damn it!" says Eli. "Mother of God."

Raven picks up her straw broom and chases the birds away. They flap and flutter in dumb indignation and perch on the boundary wall, waiting for Raven to go inside so that they can swoop back to their new home.

"Shoo! Shoo!" she shouts, waving the broom at them like a mad woman. They wobble their heads at her.

Her crop of Italian herbs is ruined, as well as her camomile and St John's Wort. There is acidic guano all over her Devil's Shoestring, her Kava Kava, her Mugwort. She knows that she should love all the universe's animals equally, but she has to draw a line somewhere. Orwell certainly had a point with his tongue-in-cheek observation in Animal Farm. She blinks into the setting sun, then gives them a good glare.

Be gone! she thinks. She scatters some Graveyard Dust around.

Away, away. You're not welcome. Do not stay.

They coo at her. Eli coos back.

"Don't make friends with those pigeons, Eli," warns Raven. "They're a bad crowd. They carry diseases, you know. Lice. They're vermin. That's what they are."

Eli nods, then bows in for a stroke of the head. Raven complies.

"Rats with wings," she says, and shudders.

"Rats with wings," Eli agrees.

8 / STOP EATING WEEDS

Raven is dreaming that she is falling. Her soul is tumbling from some astral plane and then - BANG! It's back in her body as she hits the ground. She opens her eyes and sees the Pilates ball roll into the corner. She stays still for a moment, trying to make sense of why she is lying on the floor. Then she remembers that she was working on her book, finishing an important chapter. She loves this feeling, of having completed good work, even if her back is aching, even if her cheek is glued to the grain of the pine boards. How long has she been sleeping?

Good morning, Sunshine, says the voice.

Morning? Is it? Damn!

She sees the beginning of dawn floating into the room. Light swirls in like smoke.

You shouldn't fall asleep at your desk. It's not good for you.

It wasn't intentional.

You have some... I think you have some drool on your chin.

I like it there.

You did well last night. The book is coming along. I can feel it.

Yes. It was a good session.

It's exciting. I think you may be close to finishing, now, says the voice.

It's only taken 15 years.

How much longer do you need to finish it?

Another lifetime.

You don't have another lifetime.

Well, technically…

What?

Technically I have till the end of time, if I want it.

How convenient.

What?

To bring up reincarnation when you're trying to procrastinate.

Yes, well. Sometimes these things work in your favour.

No. You need to finish it in THIS lifetime.

I know.

You can't not finish it. You have to get it out there, into other peoples' hands.

That is the idea.

You can do it!

It doesn't feel like it, says Raven.

You can. You're so close.

I don't have the energy.

You must.

Argh.

Remember what your dad used to say?

Stand up straight? Mind your manners? Stop eating weeds? Stop locking your sister in a cage?

He used to say: How do you eat an elephant?

I don't remember him saying that.

Well, how do you eat an elephant?

I don't know. Roasted? With rosa tomatoes and thyme? Are we banting? Is it a free range elephant?

That's a dark thing to say for someone who loves animals.

Raven laughs.

You're calling me dark?

Can we focus here please?

Okay.

How do you eat an elephant? The answer is: one bite at a time.

Okay.

You can do anything if you just do it a little bit at a time.

I get it.

That's what he used to say.

Don't say it like that. You make it sound like he's dead.

Sorry.

… He's not dead, is he?

Not as far as I know.

Still travelling the Pacific Islands?

I think so. Are you going to get up off the floor now?

Yes. Just give me a couple more minutes.

Good view?

Not especially.

Comfortable?

No.

Then what are you waiting for?

I don't know. That's the problem, you see. I need a reason.

Since when does anyone need a reason to get up off a filthy floor?

It's not filthy.

What can I say? We have different standards.

Lily Lightfoot sidles up to Raven and deposits an empty chip packet in front of her face. It's a brand she's never seen before, most likely garnered from the street where the white cat cleans up most frequently. Raven calls Lightfoot her reformed cat burglar. Despite being feline, Lily has always preferred gathering over hunting. In the early days she used to steal things from neighbours, small packets of nails and screws; to-do lists scribbled on the back of envelopes; keyrings; freshly-washed socks and bring them to Raven with a guttural miaowing to announce the sacrificial offering. Then, gradually, and with a little encouragement from Raven, she had mended her criminal ways. She still brought her daily gifts but now they were empty cigarette packets, biscuits wrappers and other such litter. Now she cleans up the streets.

A baby rabbit hops across Raven's line of vision. Is it the same bunny as yesterday? Lightfoot pounces on it, but it wriggles free and jumps away.

They're multiplying, says Raven.

She waits for an answer but the voice is gone. Where does he go?

It's a good example of magic, says Raven.

No reply.

It's like a magic trick. New rabbits just popping up everywhere.

The Grimm Brothers are chasing each other through the house. There is a crash as a side table falls down and a glass smashes against the hard wood.

"Holy Bible!" shouts Eli.

Lightfoot angles her cat's bum directly in front of Raven's face.

"Okay," sighs Raven. "Okay. I'm getting up."

She stands to survey the damage; grabs a broom, sweeps up the broken glass, wraps it in newspaper, double-bags it, mops up the spilled water and stray shards. The dogs seem contrite.

"It's okay," she tells them. "I never really liked that glass anyway."

9 / MAGIC TICKET

The doorbell rings. Someone is outside, at the pedestrian gate. Raven is in no state to open the door. She hasn't showered or changed in over 36 hours. She hasn't even brushed her teeth since yesterday morning. Her clothes are smudged with sawdust and animal hair. She's sporting double-bagged raccoon eyes: insufficient sleep; old mascara. She peers through a slit in the curtains trying to get a glimpse of who is attempting to invade her space. The perimeter fence is in bad repair which sometimes allows her to see who is there but at the moment she can't make anybody out. Maybe it's a child playing *tok-tokkie.* It wouldn't be the first time a kid had rung the bell and run away. What is it with kids and witches' houses? The last one she caught screamed as if Raven had skewered her, ready for the fire. A sweet and sour kebab.

They goad each other, the children. They take chocolate bets. They double-dog dare. Raven feels it's her duty to play the evil witch who likes to eat children, otherwise where's the fun in their games? If she's in the house she grabs a prop: a broom, a wand, a rubber frog left over from last Halloween and chases them with it. It's better if she's in her front garden when they call then she can pop her head through a hole in the fence and shout "BOO!" and see the pint-sized offender jump a metre into the air. It never gets old.

The doorbell rings again and then again. Raven grabs her spell-stick and marches down the front path. The hag stones are smooth and cool on her bare feet. The Rottweilers bound alongside her, whining, excited at the prospect of a visitor. When she gets to the gate she whacks the latch and wrenches the metal gate open, startling the man on the other side. The Grimm Brothers bark in happy greeting. He straightens his priest's collar in alarm; brings his scuffed leather Bible to his chest like a shield to protect his old heart.

Ugh. Her anger is replaced by foreboding. Father Stephen Bishop is her least favourite neighbour. What's he doing up so early, anyway? Aren't old people supposed to sleep in? She dislikes him so much that just seeing his neat, boring little face-brick house across the road makes her bristle.

"Yes, Bishop?"

"Good morning to you, young lady." The skin on his face is white, apart from the angry spider veins on his nose. Grog-blossom.

I am not young, nor am I a lady and it is certainly not a 'good' morning, Raven wants to say, but holds her tongue. Next he'll be telling her to smile or wear a pretty dress, or will call her a 'girl' in his clueless infuriating patriarchal misogynist way.

The dogs don't share her opinion. They love the priest and, if she doesn't hold them back, they'll knock him over with their boisterous regard. Sometimes she wishes they would. Sometimes she thinks she'll just accidentally let one of them go. A broken pelvis at his advanced age would surely discourage him from pestering her.

What is it about Bishop that infuriates her so? So he's ancient — not entirely his fault — with the old fashioned views to go with his old-person smell. Surely he can be forgiven for that? But it's his infinitely unwelcome presence in her life that irritates her so intensely. He's a complainer; an energy vampire and Raven resents having him standing, endlessly, at her gate.

"What is it this time, Bishop?"

He looks her up and down, taking in her wild appearance.

"Is everything quite all right?" Bishop nudges his spectacles up the bridge of his nose.

"I had a rough night and I'd very much like to get back inside. What can I help you with?"

"Well…" he presses a hand to his back, as if to settle in for a chat, "I wanted to talk to you about your animals."

The dogs bark happily, showing him their salmon tongues.

"Again? We spoke about them last week and the week before that. In fact, I think we've spoken about the animals every week since I moved in here 15 years ago."

"Well…"

"Well?" What can he possibly want to add to the conversation?

In the last month alone he had complained about Fred screaming, the cats fighting (almost certainly at Max's instigation) and the dogs howling at the moon. Raven knows they can get a little loud but can't he just turn down his hearing aid?

"It's the rabbits."

"The rabbits?" How can he not like the rabbits? How can *anyone* not like rabbits? They are such a sweet colony.

"They've been eating my iceberg."

Raven's thought processes are a little slower than usual. She needs more sleep.

"They've been eating your —"

"My lettuce. And my cucumbers! They are the most voracious little… things." Bishop shows Raven his long, tea-stained teeth.

"You mean they've been crossing this road and visiting your property?"

"Visiting," says the priest, "is not quite the word for what they do. More precisely: they plunder."

"Plunder?" Raven wonders if he's joking, but then remembers that he doesn't have a slip of a sense of humour.

"Pillage, rob, loot, raid," he says, like a talking thesaurus. "Ransack, strip, fleece, ravage." He's clearly completed his fair share of crossword puzzles in his time. Raven imagines what a thesaurus would look like if it was an animal. Old, with a thick, spiny back, ground-down teeth, a big skull to house a big brain.

"Miss Kane!" the priest ejaculates, "Are you listening to me? Your rabbits have devastated my vegetable garden! I have photos!"

He always takes photos. Of everything. Raven believes that he is, at heart, a frustrated photographer.

"I'm sorry. Really, I am." Hecate knows how much she despises the pigeons for spoiling part of her potion garden, so she is empathetic. But at least the rabbits are cute, not like those —

"Well?" demands Bishop. "What are you going to do about it?"

"My carpenter is coming in today to work on the house."

"Thank Heaven for that!" he says. (Another frequent complaint is that Colborn Manor is 'falling down before his very eyes' as if it's any of his business. "Of course it's my business! I have to look at it!" he had said. "No, you don't," Raven countered. "God gave you free will, didn't he?")

"I'll ask him to look at the fence."

"He'll have to do more than 'look' at the fence. He'll have to rip it all down and build a new one!"

Raven ignores the anger bubbling in her stomach. The Grimm Brothers are distracted by a sound in the garden and bolt away. Her phone starts to ring. She takes the opportunity to excuse herself.

"I'll ask him to look at the fence," she closes the gate on Bishop, "and I'll have a word with the rabbits, too."

"Wait," Bishop says, fumbling in his Bible. "I have something for you."

Before he lets her go, Bishop thrusts a flyer into her hand. Raven doesn't even look at it before tossing it into her compost bin. She's seen the advert a thousand times. It's like a magic ticket that keeps showing up. No matter how many times she tears it into strips to line the animals' beds, how many times she uses it as kindling for a fire, for food for the earthworms, how many times she scrunches it up into a ball for the cats to play with, it reappears: freshly printed and uncreased, in her letterbox or under the windshield wiper of her car, pushed under her door or stuck on her fridge, masquerading as the back of a scribbled shopping list. Raven is sure that one day it will arrive as a neatly folded paper aeroplane flying over her fence before swooping elegantly through an open window and onto her lap. The thing annoys her so much that she's stopped going through her mail. She now leaves the letterbox to get full to bursting and then takes the whole thing and shakes the crowded contents straight into the papery innards of the recycling bin. Who writes letters anymore, anyway?

The flyer is some kind of Christian propaganda. The logo is the Christian fish symbol with the name "7 LOAVES" inside it. The number 7 hides in the fish's tail and the 'S' is in the lips. There are bank details listed on it, as if God is asking for your money. If they knew what she knows, they'd know that the Universe needs a lot of things but that cold cash is not one of them. She's never bothered to actually read the advert, doesn't want to put that kind of nonsense in her head. Goddess, she hates religion. Her theory is that religious fundamentalism is a psychological disorder that is yet to be officially classified.

Father Stephen is NOT a religious fundamentalist, says the voice.

He is!

He's not.

Well then, he's an evangelist.

He's Catholic!

So?

So, Catholics are not evangelists. If you're going to cast aspersions on an entire faith I suggest you get your facts straight.

Fundamentalist, evangelist. ToMAYto, to*ma*to.

Let's not get into it. You have things to do.

I still think that he's an evangelist.

He's not!

Then why the magic ticket? Why the constant barrage of cheap flyers in my letterbox?

It's probably for some kind of good cause, you know, like Christian Crowdfunding. Maybe they're building houses for homeless people.

If only they'd learn the truth, says Raven. It would make my life and those of many others a lot easier.

The truth? And what's that?

That God is just a rumour which got out of hand.

Sometimes Raven fantasises that Bishop is an actual Bible-basher: that he literally goes around bashing people with that scuffed brick of a Bible he carries with him. She sees the victims as nails and his Bible as a hammer. Bang! Bang! Bang! And there is a trail of dead people. Or maybe he's really a secret wizard and his harassment of Raven is nothing but a clever and relentless façade.

It isn't just Bishop who spouts his dogma at Raven. She's often the victim of impromptu sermons delivered to her in the most inopportune places, like public restrooms, while she's searching for paper towels to dry her hands, or while standing in line for a double-shot *latté*. As if the pentagram tattoo on the back of her neck is an invitation to engage only the most mentally unstable person in the queue.

Raven's always amazed at how many religious fanatics there are in her midst, walking around like ordinary people dressed in slacks and crumpled Ts or polka-dotted summer dresses and cheap glass beads, doing things that ordinary people do: eating processed cheese and junk-bread sandwiches and listening to ballads on their phones. Using greasy hand cream that smells of artificial roses. They seem so normal from the outside. It's only when they start babbling about necromantic prophets and being 'saved' that you realise they have demons in their heads. When you look closely — although this should be avoided — you can see black scribbles on their auras.

You know what I don't understand?

What? says the voice.

The Grimm Brothers. Why do they like Bishop so much?

I don't know.

I thought Rottweilers were supposed to be excellent judges of character.

Maybe their Dog IQ is low, says the voice. *Maybe Dog IQ is the reverse of Dog Years.*

Or their Dog EQ, says Raven. Emotional intelligence.

I don't know. I think, canine or not, their EQ is higher than that of most of the humans I know.

That's true, says Raven.

Maybe he is really a nice person —

Ha.

— Or maybe they just like his collar.

10 / SNAKES & LADDERS

You're going to fall.

Give me some credit. I've climbed a bloody ladder before.

The board game doesn't count.

Ha.

What are you doing? asks the voice.

I'm looking for a message from Brenna.

I think the messages are finished.

How would you know?

You haven't found one in ages.

Yes, well, maybe I haven't been looking properly, hence: the ladder.

Do you know that more than half of domestic accidents involve a ladder?

I did not know that.

Well, technically, you did. Otherwise I wouldn't know —

Whoa! That was close.

Be more careful, will you?

I'm not TRYING to fall.

You think she'd put something there? Behind the kitchen cupboards?

Why not?

I don't know. It seems like a strange place to put a thing that you want to be found.

Maybe she wanted me to work hard for it.

Maybe. Still... seems a bit mean of her, don't you think?

My grandmother was a lot of things, but she was not mean.

I rest my case.

Ah! Look! I found something!

Please be careful - you're millimetres away from toppling off that thing.

I told you I had to look harder!

Please come down before you read it.

Okay, okay.

What does it say?

Oh.

Oh?

It's not from Brenna. It's just an old piece of newspaper.

An article?

No, just a random piece.

Sorry. Let's pack up that ladder and do something else.

No, I want to keep looking.

You need to be at your desk. People need you. Your book needs you.

I need a message from Brenna.

"Finally!" shouts Raven, and does an impromptu dance where she is, standing on the kitchen counter.

"Hello?" says Benjamin. He's holding his glow-in-the-dark toolbox. Every last one of his tools are spray-painted neon yellow. His wife does it for him to keep him from losing them.

"Oh, sorry," she says. "I didn't mean to startle you."

"I don't startle easily."

He's wearing his carpenter clothes and his ear-pencil. Raven wonders if he lifts weights or if his sculpted body is the result of his work alone. "I thought you were on the other side of the house."

"I was. I have a question."

"Okay," says Raven.

"The porch's hand-rail. The uprights are rotted through. Exposure."

"I like those uprights. They're elegant."

"They're matchsticks."

"Will you replace them?"

"Yes, but you need something more sturdy."

He's got really good skin for someone who works outdoors for a living, thinks Raven. And it's warm. You can tell it's warm without touching it.

"I'd go with maybe 20 by 20."

He measures 20mm with his fingers, holds the imaginary block of wood up for her to see.

"Okay. That's your recommendation?"

"It is."

"Okay, let's go with that."

"You know," the carpenter says. "You're almost the ideal customer."

"Almost?"

"Almost." He looks up at Raven who is still standing on the counter.

"Do you... often find yourself dancing on your kitchen counter?"

Raven laughs. He offers his hand to her, helps her down. She feels the strength in his grip, smells the wood on his shirt.

Careful, says the voice.

What? says Raven. I'm not doing anything wrong.

He's married.

So?

So... he's not available.

Everyone's 'available'.

I don't think his wife would feel the same way.

His wife is not my concern.

You don't feel some kind of responsibility towards her as a fellow woman?

Nope, not really.

You don't feel that their marriage vows should be respected?

They are both welcome to respect their vows. They're the ones who made them.

You're incorrigible. And I don't mean that in a good way.

Oh relax! I'm not planning on seducing him.

Thank God.

Unless ...

Unless?

Do you think he'd give me a discount? You know, on the work?

No!

He wouldn't give a discount? That seems stingy.

Raven, please. That would make you a...

Yes?

Well, you know what that would make you.

Clever? Business-savvy?

A prostitute! It would make you a prostitute.

And that is a problem... why?

Raven.

Every job is a form of prostitution.

Raven clutches Brenna's note which she has found in an old rusty tin at the back of the kitchen cupboard. The slip of paper is textured and is whiter than she expected it to be. She puts it to her cheek, then smells it. It carries the scent of old books and some kind of spice. Vanilla? Clove? She should be able to identify it immediately, given her experience with potions, but she is distracted by the anticipation that nips at her stomach. Then it comes to her: nutmeg. *Myristica fragrans.* Warm, sweet, aromatic, with sedative and anti-depressive effects. Not completely irrelevant to her situation. And, now more than ever, she needs insight from her grandmother. She had started to wonder if there were no more messages left, had thought that she might never hear from Brenna again, but, here she is, as always.

Of course the house is haunted. How could it not be when its previous owner had been one of the best witches Raven had ever known? Although she had never given herself that title, calling herself a housewife, keeping herself busy with a trio of babies and feeding everyone within a spoon's reach and creating the most wonderful, surprising, strange garden in the urban jungle that is Johannesburg. Some of Raven's favourite memories are here, tucked into this house, buried and blooming in the mysterious garden. She used to help her grandmother plant and tend and harvest. This was where her potion lore had begun, as well as her love of animals and mysticism and knowledge. It's where everything began.

There is just one word on the note: in an elegant script it reads *Temperance.*

How's that going to help me? says Raven.

What were you expecting? says the voice. *A map? A manual?*

Either of those would have been most helpful.

Raven empties out a third drawer of lingerie onto her bedroom floor.

You have a lot of lingerie, says the voice.

Mind your own business, says Raven.

In the bottom of the fourth drawer she finds the worn suede bag with her tarot deck in it. She sits on the bed and shuffles the cards. They feel good in her hands. Familiar.

She finds the Temperance card. It is a picture of a woman dressed in white, exactly as Brenna used to do. She is holding cups and there's a rainbow in the background. Raven knows the meaning of the card: it advises showing restraint; being more tactful than usual; embracing moderation. With this restraint, it promises personal alchemy and flow. The colours in the sky symbolise hope. She takes the deck into her office, pins the Temperance card to her wall.

Personal alchemy, she says. Flow.

Shall we get to work? asks the voice.

11 / PLUCKED & ROASTED

Raven is standing on the back verandah, her hands on the steady, new bannister. It feels good having something solid to hold on to. She's watching the green ripples of the oak tree leaves as they tremble in the bare breeze. Her eyes are half-moon apertures as she tries to un-focus her vision. She's trying to catch the unique energy of the tree instead of the fine details. Details are good and important for real-life consciousness, but magic requires a different view. Real-life consciousness is like a torch-light, a steady beam that reveals everything you need to know in that area which is illuminated. Magic, however, needs an entirely different perspective. It's starlight, as opposed to torch-light. It's wide and all-encompassing. It shows you the whole picture, so much so that sometimes you feel like it's too much to take in, and the edges shimmer as they are held back by the confines of your mind. The magic is always there. Your mind has to grow to meet it.

Raven's head is feeling especially confined lately. She can't seem to stretch her consciousness past any meaningful margin before it snaps back like a rubber-band. If she can't get to the starlight, she can't access her power. She tries again. She breathes deeply, using her diaphragm. She clears her mind. In and out she breathes until the light starts spilling into her head. Slowly, slowly… she knows not to rush it. She feels an opening, a broadening. The gossamer fringes are revealing themselves and then –

Her phone rings. The light disappears. The energy is gone. With a flash of anger Raven grabs the phone from the table and lobs it as far into the garden as she can. It lands somewhere between the arums and the Devil's Backbone. Before she has time to feel any kind of regret, the Grimm Brothers bound off, flying down the steps and into their large-leafed jungle. Jake finds the phone, Bill yelps in either envy or excitement and they bound back towards her and proudly drop the frothy phone at her feet. Again! Again! Again! they seem to say. New Game! Again!

Raven sighs; pats them both.

"Good boys," she says, wiping it on her jeans. It's still ringing. She taps the green icon. This had better be good.

"Hello?"

"I'm looking for Mrs Raven Kane," says an authoritative male voice. His energy is a bright blue. He plays with money for a living. He is single, but wishes he wasn't.

"Miss," says Raven.

"Excuse me?"

"It's *Miss* Kane… Never mind."

The man clears his throat right into the receiver and Raven holds the phone away from her ear. It smells like grass and dog breath.

"I'm calling to alert you to the notice of repossession of your property at 77 Elderberry Lane, Colborn Manor."

Raven loses the feeling in her limbs; her jaw muscles gape.

"Is this..." she says, "is this a joke?"

There is a pause. Static. He doesn't know what to say.

"I can assure you that it's not a joke."

"You can't do this," Raven says. "I've had no warning."

"Atlas Bank has sent you over twenty notices, ma'am. You are almost six months behind on your bond repayments. We have offered you adaptive payment plans and debt counselling, neither of which were accepted by you. We have tried to contact you on multiple occasions via telephone. Our messages were not returned."

Raven is struck mute. She can't lose this house.

"Look," he says, softening. "I'm sorry. These calls are never easy to make. And believe me, I've been making a lot of them lately."

If she loses the house she will lose her magic. Lose what is left of her magic.

"What can I do?" she asks the money man. She sits down on the ground. Lightfoot and Cocoa sense her distress and both pad over. Lily sits on her lap.

"It's too late for that," he says. "You have to vacate the property."

"There's no such thing."

"Excuse me?"

"There's no such thing as 'too late'."

"I have the notice in front of me. It says in black and white that —"

"Time is an illusion."

"...Hey?"

The Grimm Brothers are energetically digging holes in the garden; perhaps hoping to find more phones.

"Just tell me what I can do."

"I don't know what to say."

"Isn't there..." Raven says, grasping. "What if I made a lump sum payment now? That settles the overdue amount?"

"Do you have a lump sum?"

"No."

Eli flies in and lands on the hand rail, as if he has come to eavesdrop.

"Well, in theory, no, because the repossession notice has already been... well... noted."

"But?"

"But if you can get R100,000 together in the next couple of days I may be able to stall the proceedings."

"Okay. I can do that."

"That will be good."

Max stares up at Eli and licks her lips, perhaps imagining him plucked and roasted and served with sauce.

"What if I can't do that?" she asks.

"Then you need to pack your bags."

"What if I refuse to pack my bags?"

"That would be okay."

"What do you mean?"

"You don't need luggage for prison. Which is where you'd go for obstructing the law."

"I'll call my lawyer."

"That's a good idea."

You don't have a lawyer, says the voice.

Eli caws and swoops away.

12 / DETZEL DOLL

What are you doing? says the voice.

What does it look like I'm doing? says Raven.

Making a list?

Yes.

Does this mean what I think it means?

I don't know. What do you think it means?

That you... have a plan?

Yes. Well, I'm working on a plan, anyway.

You've taken the Temperance card down.

The time for temperance is over.

You're making me nervous.

Good.

What's the new card?

The Star.

Yip, I'm definitely nervous.

You can be nervous. I don't have time to be nervous. I have a rebellious coven to rein in and a manuscript to finish and a house to save.

Okay. What about the pigeons?

The pigeons?

Do you have a plan to get rid of the pigeons?

Not yet. I'll add it to the list.

They're ruining your potion garden.

I said I'll add it to the list. I'm about to lose my house. I need to prioritise.

You can't do magic without your potion garden.

Well, if it comes to it, I can order online. From that organic ingredient place - *Potions in Motion*.

Their produce will never be as good as yours. They don't have your —

I know. But desperate times, etc. etc.

But you need...

Yes?

I don't know how to say this without offending you.

Try.

I think you need to use your own herbs because... you need all the help you can get.

Raven, fuelled by coffee and an energy spell, whips around the house gathering material for the scarecrowess she's about to make. She finds a red dress in the back of her cupboard that she hasn't worn for years. It's practically a siren. You have to be in the right kind of mood to pull off that kind of dress. She can't remember the last time she felt up to it. At least now, she thinks, pulling it off its hanger, it can be useful. She also finds string and a spool of maroon thread, sack-cloth for skin, buttons for eyes and bells, broken broom-handles to be lashed together for the inner crucifix that will be her skeleton.

Having fun? asks the voice.

Raven tears through the sack cloth with her *athamé*.

Would that make me mad?

Not at all. Okay, maybe a little bit. It does bear a striking resemblance to the Detzel doll.

We don't know for sure that Katherina Detzel was insane.

She lived in a psychiatric hospital.

Yes.

That's not proof enough for you?

They used to lock women up for being different, for being eccentric, for having an opinion.

She ripped apart her only mattress to make a straw man.

It was her creative outlet. She was lonely. I would have done the same thing, in her position.

I rest my case.

Ha.

Raven?

What now?

It needs a little more stuffing.

Raven's needle slips and punctures her finger pad. She stops working for a moment to watch the bead of blood swell and then spill down her knuckle. A small dab of crimson lands on the scarecrowess's neck.

"Oops," she says. Does such a small amount matter? She knows that it does. Should she cut the stained piece out? She doesn't have time. So what if the scarecrow is now a poppet? A voodoo doll with Raven blood. No harm will come to the figure out in the garden, she's sure, so there should be no problem. Perhaps the blood will add to the doll's fright factor.

Before putting together the large scarecrowess she had made a mini version: a prototype. She had even taken some fabric from the hem of the red dress and made a make-shift wrap for it. Sewn a bobble of hair on top. Scrunched up some of Bishop's flyers and used them for stuffing. She'll give it to Matthew; she's sure he'll love to gum it.

She digs a narrow hole in the middle of her potion garden and plants the female scarecrow in it. She's surrounded by tender shoots and leaves and the earth feels good on her bare feet and in her hands. She should spend some time gardening, it makes her feel better: more in tune with the universe. The figure looks handsome and the pigeons are nowhere to be seen but Raven can hear them cooing somewhere in the distance. She takes out her wand and points it in the direction of the fowlish murmuring.

Now, vermin, with your louse-y feathers

Stay away and come back never.

Raven gives the doll's shoulders a tap each and scans the horizon for birds. The skirt of the red dress flutters in the breeze.

Still buzzing with caffeine and magic, she goes into her office and sweeps the entire contents of her desk onto the floor.

I guess that's one way to do it, says the voice.

Raven gives the oak surface a perfunctory dusting and a quick wood-polish spray, and positions her laptop in the middle, along with her Moleskine notebook. She places an antique pewter goblet next to it into which she deposits a clatter of pens. Without thinking too much, she opens her document and begins to write.

Six hours later she staggers out of the office in a stupor. The Grimm Brothers had hauled her upright by snacking on her slippers. When Eli sees her, he shrieks: "Good God!"

"Is it that bad?" she says to the bird. Not that she cares. She has written five thousand words and the ending, the glorious ending, is finally in sight. Something inside her has lifted; shifted.

"It's going to happen," she says. "It's actually going to happen. I'm going to finish this book."

13 / RAINBOW PONICORN

Raven's back is aching. Her stomach feels like it's eating itself; wrapping itself around her spine. She looks in the fridge, but it's empty, apart from an old piece of cheese and a crystallised jar of honeyed figs. She chooses the figs and a silver spoon.

Now it's time to do some spellwork and earn some money.

Do you know how many tricks you're going to need to turn, to earn R200K? says the voice.

R200K? The bank rep said R100K.

There's Ben's bill, remember? And the personal loans. Credit card. The interest is adding up. On that note, we need to think about consolidating your debt.

Holy Goddess. Why is adult-ing so hard?

Raven's phone rings. Fighting her natural instinct to allow it to go to voicemail, she answers it on the third ring.

Jessica is shocked. "Oh, I didn't expect you to answer."

"I can't have the kids. I've got, like 67 things to do on my To Do list and no time to do it in."

"I'm not phoning about that."

Raven stares at her list. How is she ever going to finish in time? She should highlight the absolute priorities. She circles MONEY (HOUSE); SHADOW BOOK; WICKED WITCHES. She ticks and crosses out SCARECROW. It feels good.

"You're phoning to apologise?" asks Raven.

"Why would I need to apologise?"

"Never mind. What's up?"

"I just wanted to remind you about Rebecca's birthday party."

"Oh," says Raven. "Yes." Raven searches the piece of paper for space to add another task, then scribbles it onto the side of the list. "That's, er, next week?"

"It's today, Raven," she says. "Now. In an hour. I sent you the invitation two months ago."

You don't have time, says the voice.

"Oh. Right. I don't think I'm going to make —"

"I knew you would forget."

"I'm sorry. I have a lot of stuff on at the moment."

Look, says the voice. *You seriously don't have time to go to a kid's party. You need to work.*

"I wouldn't have called except that Rebecca asked me to."

Raven stops. Glances out of the window.

"Really?"

"I know. I couldn't believe it either. I mean, she hates you."

"Thanks."

"Don't take it personally. She hates me too. It's a phase. She hates everyone. Except Justin Bieber."

"But she wants me at the party?"

"Yes. God knows why. I don't know what you said or did the last time we visited but it obviously made some kind of impression."

"I do have a gift for her."

"You don't need to bring a gift. Tim's bought her half of Hamley's."

"I hate kids' parties," says Raven. "They're full of... kids. No offence."

"Look, I understand if you can't come. I'm just phoning because Becks asked me to."

Raven kicks the couch, which hurts — an electric current zips up the outside of her ankle — and she moves the phone away from her mouth as she hops and swears. "No, I'll pop in. Just quickly."

"You don't have to."

"I'll see you in a bit."

"Well, if you're definitely coming could you pick up the balloons?"

"The balloons? Seriously? Can't Tim do it?"

"He's playing golf."

"Argh."

"You're the best. I'll text you the address."

Maybe... says the voice and then trails off.

Yes? says Raven. Spit it out.

Maybe you can ask Jessica for a loan?

No!

Just, you know, till you're back on your feet. They have so-o-o-o much money.

NO.

Look at it this way: you can ask your sister for a loan or you can lose the house.

I'll find another way.

You don't even have to ask Jessica, you could go directly to Tim.

Tim? Are you crazy? I'd rather take a long jump off a short cliff.

This house is being repossessed as we speak.

Re-possessed. Ha!

You think it's funny?

It is, a little. I live in a possessed house. The bank is threatening to re-possess it. I can picture the bloody little poltergeist in a pinstripe suit and tie, telling Brenna's ghost to leave.

We've run out of time. You NEED to make that lump sum payment.

I know. I know. I'll find a way.

The BoomBoom Party Room sales assistant looks uncertainly at Raven, then looks behind her, at her tiny Morris Minor.

"Is there a problem?" asks Raven. Does one have to drive a certain kind of car in order to be allowed to shop here, in this bright migraine space of candy stripes and polka dots? She assumes her appearance is a problem too - a midi-black dress and Wicked Witch stockings, unwashed hair swept up into a tousled bun revealing her pentagram tattoo. She couldn't look more different to the other customers browsing the party supplies in their neat, subdued outfits. It seems to Raven that everyone in the store is very politely disregarding her.

"Yes," says the assistant, who looks 15 years old. She has the translucent skin of a baby newt and bright cherry lipstick. "I think there might be a problem."

She brings out the huge helium balloons. There are a hundred of them.

"I see," says Raven. Who on earth orders one hundred helium balloons?

Together they manage to wrestle half of the balloons into the car, losing three to the greedy sky and a further three to *ad hoc* explosions. The squeaking of their latex skins sets Raven's teeth on edge. She's about to drive away when the assistant reminds her to pay.

"Jess hasn't paid for them? Are you sure?"

"Absolutely."

Raven is half expecting a glossy reptile tongue to shoot out of the woman's mouth.

"Don't you have her card details on file or anything?"

The newt is patient with her. "No."

She rings up the hundred balloons. A cheerful figure of R3,000 appears on the machine.

"R3,000?" whispers Raven. "For party balloons? Are you joking?"

The other customers turn their backs to her, not wanting her to be embarrassed.

"I have to charge you for the ones you're not taking. Sorry."

"R30 for a balloon?"

"They're long-life balloons. They have a special gel inside. They last a week."

Who needs a balloon to last a week? The little brats just pop them with their teeth, anyway, don't they? She scrubs her forehead with a fist and hands over her card. She takes a complimentary sucker from the counter. She thinks they're complimentary. They had better bloody well be complimentary.

"I'm sorry," says the lipsticked newt. "Your card has been declined. Do you have another one?"

"Jessica!" she yells into the phone. She can hear kids playing in the background. Carnival music. The party has already started. "Send me your card details. For the balloons."

"Oh for heaven's sake," she says, "I've got my hands full here. The face-painter has just arrived and I…"

She's interrupted by a squealing child. It sounds like she drops the phone on the floor. "Just pay for them yourself and I'll pay you back."

Raven's cheeks burn. She hisses into the phone, "If you want these bloody balloons send me your card details right now."

Her phone buzzes with photos of both sides of the card. The transaction is successful.

On her way out the assistant calls after her, "Be careful! They can pop in the car."

Raven drives carefully to Jessica's house, a veritable mansion beribboned by emerald green lawns. The Bryanston property sits nestled behind a ten foot high wall topped with glittering electric wires. A security guard waves and opens the electric gate for her. The driveway is tiled with luxury German SUVs. She parks her matchbox car between a Porsche Panamera and an oversized BMW, checks her crowded reflection in the rearview mirror and takes a deep breath, grabs as many balloons as she can hang on to and lets herself into the house. There is excited shrieking coming from the back garden. She leaves the balloons to bounce on the lounge ceiling, kicks off her sandals and goes to find Rebecca.

"Rabby!" says Matthew, and reaches for Raven.

She picks him up. "Hello Monkey. Having a good time? Where's your sister?"

His fingers are orange with chip dust. He tries to poke out her eye. She kisses him and puts him down again. He toddles off and tumbles in the direction of the children's snack table.

"Finally!" says Jessica.

"The balloons are in the lounge. More in the car."

With a flick of her head, Jessica dispatches Thabisa to fetch the remaining balloons.

There is a mob of kids on the lawn. They are smashing a pony-shaped piñata and being rewarded by raining sweets. There is a face-painter, a magician and a candy-floss sculptor.

"Pony theme?" asks Raven.

"Rainbow Ponicorn."

"What now?"

"Ponicorn. Mash-up of pony and unicorn. It's the 'Latest Thing'."

She sees one of the kids is using the ponicorn's own broken-off horn to gouge out its insides.

"Violent creatures," says Raven. The kids scream in delight.

"They're just playing."

"I rest my case."

A particularly barbaric child gets carried away and hits the smaller boy standing next to him. The victim's face sours into a red mask. His mouth opens in a silent cry and beetles of half-chewed candy fall out. He takes a few steps but is blinded by his tears and falls. The mob pays no attention to him. Raven glances over to where the parents are standing, gabbing and drinking fruit Pimms with diamond-flashing fingers. They don't notice him either. Jessica catches her eye and acts as if she hasn't seen the pint-sized tragedy; wipes imaginary sticky handprints off her dress. Raven supposes she should comfort the boy, even though she doesn't want to. She makes a move forward but Jess steps in her way.

"Why don't you come have an aperitif? I'll introduce you to everyone."

"I can't stay," says Raven. "I'm just going to find Becks and wish her happy birthday."

The ponicorn piñata is finally knocked clear off its leash and lands with a thud on the grass. The children converge on it like hungry hyenas, ripping its candy innards out.

Raven makes her way over to Rebecca who has avoided the gory game her friends are playing. She's standing in her princess-themed wendy house, banging some pans on the wooden stove.

"Hello, birthday girl."

"Raven," says Rebecca, "I didn't think you'd come."

"I had to come. I have something for you."

The girl sighs. She's tired of opening presents. "What is it?"

Raven hands her a book wrapped in grey and a chaplet of rosebuds. "It's a very special book."

She turns back to her play cooking.

"I'm not good at reading."

"That doesn't matter. You don't have to be good at reading for this book."

She turns back to Raven, takes the book tentatively. Peels open the paper. Inside is an old, black, leather-bound book.

"A Bible?"

"Of sorts. Open it."

Inside are pictures of circles and candles, crystals and pentacles. She traces a crescent moon with her finger.

"Is it about magic?"

"Yes. It's a beginner's guide to witchcraft. It's over a hundred and fifty years old."

Rebecca drops the book as if it's burned her. "It's evil."

Raven picks it up. "Magic is the opposite of evil."

"I don't want it."

"It's natural for you to want to deny your destiny. I did the same."

"I thought you always wanted to be a witch," says Rebecca. "Mom said you were always one."

Jessica used to hate Raven's childhood sorcery: her dandelion potions, wax crayon spells scrawled on walls.

"That doesn't mean that sometimes I didn't want it." She touches Rebecca's cheek and the girl flinches. "Being different can be hard."

The flock of parents seem to be watching them. Suspicious eyes dart in their direction.

"Anyway, you don't 'become' a witch. You either are a witch or you aren't. Deep down you know the truth. Just like deep down I knew the truth when Brenna had this exact same talk with me."

"Granny Brenna gave you this book?"

"On my seventh birthday. And her aunt gave it to her when she was seven."

The parents are still looking over, gossiping over their dripping drinks.

"Brenna was a witch?"

"Your great-grandmother was the best witch I knew."

"And she said that you were a witch?"

"She reminded me that I was a witch. She reminded me I had power. Just like you do."

"I don't know." Rebecca bites her lip, not sure whether to accept the gift or not.

"You don't have to know anything. You don't have to do anything. This book is just a tool and it will be here for you when you are ready for it."

Her niece stares at her, barely blinking. Raven puts the chaplet around her neck, takes her hand, can feel her power pulsing.

"You don't become a witch, Becks, you just remember who you are."

14 / LUCK FAITH LIBIDO

Raven looks at her to-do list while she eats the popcorn she purloined from the party. There aren't many hours left in the day but she's sure she can get something done before passing out. The cats are out exploring, Jake and Bill are snoring open-mouthed in their baskets and Eli is perched on her shoulder, sharing her snack. Occasionally he makes her jump with a 'Jesus Christ!'.

She won't write any more today. This morning's effort has vacuumed all the words from her brain. The scarecrowess is done. She wonders if it's keeping the pigeons away but doesn't get up to check, doesn't want to be side-tracked. She must choose, then, between some spell-crafting for cash and dealing with the Wicked Witches. She thinks of the Vimeo video and the images flash in her mind: the grainy, naked bodies painted by moonshine, the chanting. Like some bloody Blair Witch revival, some American Horror story. She taps out a Whatsapp message to Luella, clicks 'send'.

It's late and the dusk light is pulling at her. She wants nothing more than to curl up in her oak tree with a baby bunny on her lap. She's been up that tree a hundred times, a thousand times. She could climb it in her sleep. Being up there — surrounded by leaves and fresh air — is like being hugged by Brenna. Her grandmother used to tell her that oak trees were the most magical of all: "Oak in the forest towers with might / In the fire brings the gods in sight". She had told her that an oak wood fire-warmed house would keep illness away and that carrying an acorn in your pocket was always good luck; druidic rituals would only ever take place in the shade of an oak and that the Oak Fairy brings courage and a stout heart.

Benjamin had made a simple tree-house for her — just a platform, really — in the canopy, with some planks spiralling up the trunk so that the dogs could bound up there with her. She can't imagine losing her oak tree.

"It's settled, then," she says. "Spell-crafting it is."

Raven pours herself a long overdue glass of coffee pinotage and opens her laptop. Logs into her Turning Tricks website, where customers can order spells from her, online, and pay with their credit cards or eBucks. She has 124 straightforward spell requests which just require her to cut and paste the relevant details into the reply emails. Wanted: the usual suspects — love; money; happiness. Easy money, but brain-numbing. It takes her two hours and she racks up R12,400. Next, the more complicated spells and another glass of wine, then on to 38 triple-cast pentacle spells which require more work. Luck; faith; libido - R9,500. The next level up cannot, unfortunately, be performed via email. These require from-scratch spells, fresh and original. Bespoke spells come at a premium, at R1,500 an hour. This is her real work. The rest is just marketing. These are the spells she has been avoiding - her greatest source of procrastination.

She has always loved her work. What has happened lately?

It's 2 a.m. and she can hear the inhalations and exhalations of the animals and the house.

Is it really ironic? Raven asks the dark space around her.

What?

Well, you know. People are always getting it wrong. Irony. They confuse it with bad luck.

That's Alanis Morisette's fault.

I think it IS truly ironic.

I still don't know what you're talking about.

My… situation.

And what's that?

Come on, you know what I mean.

Not precisely. Your thoughts do tend to jump around a bit.

Don't everyone's?

Probably.

My situation! My 99 problems. My shadow-struck state of mind.

Okay.

Do I have to spell it out? You know that I don't like saying it out loud.

This isn't out loud. It's all in your head.

Fine. It's about time I admitted it. I've been in denial for long enough.

Tick-tock, Miss Kane. Spit it out.

This is my situation. Are you ready?

Yes.

Then here it is: I'm burnt out.

Yes, that's a good example of irony. Well done.

Is that all you have to say?

What else is there to say?

Do you understand why this is such a big deal?

Yes?

Because a witch can't afford to be burnt out. I need energy. I can't do magic without energy. Magic IS energy.

Your problem is that you keep giving your energy to everyone else.

Yes, well, that's an occupational hazard.

I guess so. Still, as a job, it beats bomb disposal and lion-taming.

I don't know. I think I'd make an excellent lion-tamer.

I'm sure that's what they all think; you know, before they find themselves bleeding down the cat's gullet.

A lion wouldn't eat me.

You're probably right. You're too skinny. You'd get stuck in his throat. There's no... there's no human bacon on you.

Human bacon? That's disgusting.

You do realise that you've just called yourself 'disgusting'?

Go to bed, says the voice.

Raven puts her head down on the desk. I can't. I need to make the lump sum payment tomorrow. Tomorrow is the last day. I only have R20K in my bank account.

It's late.

I'm out of time.

Not yet. You're not out of time yet.

15 / TREMBLING HEART

Bishop is at the gate. Raven has had less than five hours sleep and her eyes sting in the morning light. How can it be so hot already? It's not even 7 a.m. She tries to rub the grit out of her eyes but realises there is nothing there but accumulated exhaustion. Makes a mental note to not rub out her actual eyeballs. She can't get up. Her body is being kept down by imaginary forces. She imagines herself as a giant tied down by the tiny people in Gulliver's Travels. Phantom loops of miniature rope like dental floss. Fierce little people the size of Lego men cheering and making obscene gestures.

The doorbell rings again. That's it, she thinks. I'm disconnecting that doorbell today.

"Miss Kane!" she hears him call. "Miss Kane!"

"Oh for Christ's sake," Raven hisses. The invisible ropes disappear and her quick anger lifts her out of bed. She is still wearing last night's clothes. When was the last time she had actually changed into pyjamas? Does she even own pyjamas?

She yanks open the gate in her usual greeting to Bishop.

"It's 7-bloody-o'clock," she says. "I was sleeping."

He's holding his shield again. Perhaps one day she'll greet him with a crossbow and that Bible will finally serve its purpose. She sees him, spread-eagled on the pavement, an arrow a mere inch from his trembling heart. Delivered by the Good Book. As Eli likes to say: "Jesus Saves!"

"Miss Kane."

"Father Stephen."

He peers behind her, watching for the dogs, but they're still dreaming of juicy bones and pretty poodles.

"I couldn't help but notice that your perimeter fence has not yet been repaired."

"I'm working on it. My carpenter is working on it."

"I was wondering. May I have a word with him?"

Why did he need to talk to Benjamin? In case Raven had not made it clear that the fence needed fixing? In case she had, as a woman, not grasped the dreadfully technical aspect of nails driven through wood?

"It's Sunday morning, Bishop. He's not here."

"Perhaps you'd be kind enough to share his contact number with me."

"Okay," Raven sighs. "Is that it?"

"What do you mean?"

"I mean, is that it? No complaint today?"

"I thought my complaint was implied by my observation of your decidedly un-mended fence."

Good fences make good neighbours.

"Thank you, Bishop. Good day." Raven closes the gate.

After a large brain-blasting coffee and fresh-egg pancakes with gooseberries, courtesy of the chickens and the now pigeon-free potion garden, Raven feels her spirits lift. She isn't going to let Bishop spoil her Sunday morning especially after such a constructive day yesterday. Her *scarecrowess* is looking striking, her book is almost finished and she had mowed through her work last night. She still had the bespoke spells to do but they could wait till Monday. Let him spoil his congregation's morning instead, with his hellfire and brimstone speeches. She had her own version of hell to deal with today.

Why do you have such a chip on your shoulder? says the voice.

Me?

Do you see anyone else in the room?

I don't have a chip on my shoulder.

You do. It's a giant chip, and it's in the shape of...

Yes?

...I don't know. A — a Christian.

It's in the shape of a Christian? So, basically in the shape of a human?

You know what I mean.

Go home, voice, you're drunk.

What did they ever do to you anyway?

You know what they did!

Tell me.

They executed thousands of us. *Malleus Maleficarum.* The Hammer of the Witches. They hanged us and drowned us. They dragged us down and lit us up. They orphaned children and widowed husbands just because we didn't fit into the narrow little stories they kept telling themselves about what women should be, or how women should act. Have you ever seen the Scottish witch's bridle?

It was a different time, says the voice.

Yes, it was a different time. Now they target little boys.

You can't judge a whole religion by what a minority of the believers do.

It's what people do. It's human nature. In fact, let's take a look.

Raven gets her laptop.

A look at what?

She opens her browser, finds Twitter, types in #wickedwitches. A video comes up that has been retweeted over a hundred times.

Raven clicks 'play'. At first she thinks it's not working because the picture is black, but then she sees a pale hand moving in the corner. What is it doing? It looks like some kind of stuttering sign language, too fast to read. Is it a secret code? Some kind of message?

The video cuts to one of the coven members, Morgan, with a wand in her hand. She is reciting a spell under her breath. You see her lips moving but the words are difficult to make out. Despite this, Raven can tell it's a hex. There is a certain energy that is required for dark magic and it's all over the witch's face. Her chanting gets louder but the words are still not clear. Other voices join in, swelling the spell. The camera tracks backwards to show that the woman is surrounded by her coven sisters and they are all speaking as one. Then the subject of the hex is revealed: a big, brightly-lit building with a water feature outside. The Terrors have added red dye to the water making it look like blood. It's the Jo'burg Stock Exchange.

The gesturing hand is back.

"Neo-Pagan *Femmes*," whispers a voice off-camera. "We are the Neo-Pagan *Femmes*. We are the Dirty Thirteen. We are the Diabolical Disciplettes.

Luella's face appears in a jump cut, wearing her usual dark make-up and candy-cane coloured hair.

"They thought they could drown us," she says to the camera, eyes flickering, "but they didn't know we were sponges."

You see? says Raven.

See what?

Wait until this video goes viral. Then we'll see who's judgemental.

Raven types an email to Lavinia:

Dear High Priestess

I've summoned the Wicked Witches to a meeting at the Moon Chapel tomorrow night. Luella confirmed that she'd be there along with the rest of the coven. Join us? Blessed be.

Raven

Outside, in the backyard, Raven sits in the dappled light with the

Grimm Brothers. She's sitting as far away as she can from the one clock she has in her house. She was tired of it tick-tocking at her with its mean face. D-Day, it is saying. Lump-sum. Pack-your-bags. Would this be the last time she sat under this tree? What would happen to the animals? She wouldn't be able to take Fred, Toby or Applejack with her. She can imagine the peacock screaming his lungs out in their new one-bedroomed semi-detached with paper thin walls. The tortoise alone would take up half the house. And her? Without her magic she would certainly melt into a hot puddle of self-doubt and depression. It can't happen. She can't let it happen.

She knows that her idea is dangerous but she can't see any other solution if she wants to keep Colborn Manor. She stands up and puts the acorn she was polishing into her pocket.

The Universe supports action. She has work to do.

Raven uses her ritual knife to collect the herbs she needs from the potion garden. She harvests cassia, wild parsley root, civet and sorrel. She also gathers some dried powders from her witch's cupboard — Calamus, Alderbark and Musk — and she begins to formulate the spell in her mind. It's never easy to write a spell for yourself, especially if you're not good at asking for help. There is also the perennial problem of Imposter Syndrome. Is she really a witch? Is her magic good enough? It's always difficult at the beginning of the process. She wishes she had an online resource for excellent spells. A Wiccapedia. A Tinder app for witches. Swipe right for Spells.

She puts the nagging cynicism aside and sits quietly. The spell comes to her slowly, line by line, as if from another source altogether. She wonders if Brenna has anything to do with it.

You always say that money spells are problematic.

They are.

You say that the money may come, but at a cost.

Yes, that's how it works. You pay for the money in other ways.

So you're not nervous about what it will cost you?

I don't have time to be nervous.

Raven moves all her lounge furniture to one side and rolls up the oriental carpet. Lily Lightfoot and Cocoa, intrigued, sit on top of the bookshelf and watch her work. To clean the space, she sweeps the timber floor and burns a smudge-stick of wild sage and sandalwood. While waiting for the sweet white smoke to clear, she stands back to admire it.

Dance floor? asks the voice.

Ha ha, says Raven.

She casts a wide circle in chalk and sits in the middle of it, wand on her lap. She gives her wolf's head amulet a rub, then grounds herself and incants the spell she has designed.

I do not ask for diamonds or gold

Silk and saffron have no hold

I want nothing of silver domes

I just need enough to keep this home.

Save the house, in a flash —

That's all I ask for, please send cash.

She knows that it's a good spell: one of her best. It ticks all the boxes: original; specific; playful. But her reserves are so low so she doesn't know if the flame will take. She doesn't feel the hum of power in her body, doesn't feel the magic current running through her veins. All she can do is perform it to the best of her ability and hope for the best. Lily Lightfoot comes to curl up on her lap and they sit there like that, in silence.

PART II

AIR

17 / NEVERMORE

Just as Raven finishes clearing up and replacing the furniture, the doorbell rings. The Grimm Brothers launch themselves up and out of the front door like bloodhounds that have sniffed out a fox.

Oh dear, says Raven. Bishop again. The rabbits have probably moved into his kitchen now. They've probably figured out how to open his fridge. Perhaps they are, at this very moment, helping themselves to his mint leaves and baby carrots.

"Pillage, rob, loot, raid," he had said. "Ransack, strip, fleece, ravage," as if they were pirates, or vikings, instead of adorable little pom-poms whose racing heartbeats you could feel in the palm of your hand.

The dogs jump up against the gate, barking excited greetings. Hello! They're saying. Hello! Come play!

"Get back, you devil hounds," she says in her deep voice and they jump and smile at her. Play! Play!

She tries to rein them in.

She opens the door expecting to see Bishop, but he's not there. In his place stands a cocoa-skinned woman with a severely yellow aura and glasses that are too big for her face. Pink lipstick and a darting glance.

"Hello," says Raven to the hummingbird.

"I'm sorry to just show up here like this."

Raven holds the Grimm Brothers back. "Can I help you?"

"Yes," she says, and waits a beat. "Please tell me that you are Veronica Kane."

Raven stops. She hasn't heard that name in years. "Not anymore."

"Nevermore!" yells Eli from inside the house.

"Excuse me?" says the slip of a woman.

"I was born Veronica Kane. I changed my name. Who are you?"

"Oh, Miss Kane!"

"Raven."

"Raven, I am SO glad to have found you."

They sit at the sun-bleached table on the verandah. The woman, Wandile Mphikilele, sits across from her and unpacks a sheaf of official-looking papers. Raven holds her business card in her hand and plays with it. LAWYER, it says, in handsome copperplate. Despite the warmth of the morning, she turns down Raven's offer of a drink.

"We've been trying to find you for over a year," she says.

Max is lying on the floor on his back with his legs open, showing them his down-soft tummy. He's never been known for his elegance. Raven strokes him with her toes.

"We?"

"Direko & Associates," she says, gesturing towards the card in Raven's hand. "The company I work for."

"I've been here all along."

Fred screams, making Mphikilele jump.

"Don't worry," says Raven. "It's just the peacock. I know it can be disconcerting. Do you often work on a Sunday?"

"No," she says. "No. But we've been trying to find you for so long and we were running out of time."

"For what?"

"We sent you a dozen letters."

"Oh," says Raven. "I don't open mail."

The lawyer looks at her. "You changed your name and you don't open mail?"

Raven can tell that the lawyer's mind is darting around, trying to figure her out.

"It's a long story."

Veronica. Ravenna Blackbird. Raven.

"Eventually we tracked down your sister, who gave us your number, but then we tried phoning and we couldn't reach you."

"I don't have a landline."

"I guessed as much. We didn't have any luck on your cell phone either —"

"Why?"

"I don't know, I tried at least —"

"No, I mean why all this? What do you need from me?"

"Oh! Well, we need a certified copy of your ID and your FICA documents."

Raven grunts and rolls her eyes. Why was she being punished in this way?

"I've brought my portable scanner so we can do it right away. And we'll need your bank details, of course."

"Bank details?"

"You… DO have a bank account, don't you? Please tell me you have a bank account?"

"I have a bank account."

"Ah," she says, smiling. Her yellow aura glows.

Raven stops stroking Max. Why would they need all this?

"You said this was about Sheldon Bond's estate?"

"Yes. We've processed all the documents and the estate is close to being wound up. The only detail which was missing was you. To be honest, I'm surprised that no one from the Bond family has contacted you to tell you about the settlement."

"I thought he might leave me something small. Sentimental. He was a very kind man."

"Nope," says Wandi. Raven can tell she wants to laugh. She scans Raven's proof of residence and her ID card.

"No?"

"What Sheldon Bond left you is neither small nor sentimental."

Raven feels a punch of adrenaline.

"You must have been close," she says.

"Not really," says Raven. "He was a client of mine."

"He must have really," she clears her throat, "appreciated your services."

Raven narrows her eyes at the lawyer. What was she up to? What was she saying? Mphikilele finishes annotating a document and slides it towards her.

"This is the acknowledgement of who you are, and that you are accepting the funds from the Bond estate. Please sign on all the Xs and initial every page."

Raven speed-reads and signs.

"Wonderful, thank you. Here is your copy. This is mine. The money will be transferred before the end of play tomorrow."

"How much?" asks Raven.

The hummingbird stops smiling. "You really don't know?"

18 / BARE SKELETON OF BROWN COINS

Can this really be happening? she asks Eli.

Eli, for once, is quiet. Maybe he is thinking.

Is it in yet? The money? asks the voice.

Not yet. I'll get a text message when the transfer is done but I can't help checking my account. If I refresh this screen one more time I think it might crash altogether.

She chucks the phone onto the couch and sucks at her asthma pump.

Have you called your bank manager? The one who wants the lump sum?

No?

Why not? Call him! Tell him to stop the repossession.

What if the money doesn't come? What if it's just a dream? Now that I think about it, yesterday did feel completely surreal.

It is real. You still have the papers. The business card.

I'm worried.

I'm sure it will reflect any minute now. Don't worry.

I'm worried because it's so much money.

Why? How much did you ask for when you cast the spell?

It doesn't work like that. There's suggestion. Intention. I asked for just enough. There was no number.

Now there are a whole lot of numbers. Most of them are zeros.

Raven's phone tings with a text message. She dives to the couch, breaks into an instant sweat. She wipes her hands on her jeans and picks the phone up with shaking hands, logs into her Atlas banking profile and into her account. She chokes on air. Can it be true? Can it really be true? There, in her personal account, which usually reflects a sad dearth of funds; a bare skeleton of brown coins: sits a handsome and irrefutable eight million rand.

It's there, pants Raven. Holy Hecate, the money is there. And my bank account didn't explode.

You thought it might?

Yes, I thought it might.

Raven immediately transfers the R100,000 lump sum to her homeloan account and sends the proof of payment to the bank manager. Please, Goddess, she thinks, let it not be too late.

Next, she sends R100,000 in the direction of Benjamin's account, but an error message in red tells her that she has reached her daily transfer limit. She'll have to pay him tomorrow.

"Thank you, Sheldon Bond Senior," she says out loud, "wherever you are. Thank you."

She feels like lying on the floor and staring at the white ceiling for a while but then she glimpses the clock on the wall: she's running late for her meeting with the Wicked Witches.

19 / TAGLOCK TERRORS

Raven's Morris Minor zips from Colborn Manor to the Moon Chapel in Melville in record time. Her mind races alongside it. All the zeroes she has seen in her bank account are crowding her head, as if a bubble machine has been at work. She feels different. Is this what it feels like to be rich? Her car feels more powerful, her wallet feels fat. Nothing material has changed but everything looks different. She can feel her stress evaporating. So many problems can be solved with money. Beloved haunted house falling down? Money. Old car problems? Money. Need time off to finish your book? Money.

She allows herself the reprieve the settlement grants her and ignores, for now, the whirring in her head, the soft tap-tapping inside her skull — *tok-tokkie* — that is warning her that life is not as simple as this.

She turns in: advances through the open gates and hurtles along under the black pines until her feeble headlights illuminate the weather-stained ivory walls of the chapel. She parks between seven other vehicles including Lavinia's Vespa. She is late.

She uses the torch function on her phone to make her way through the tall weeds and over the fallen branches and the litter of pinecone chips. Candlelight flickers in the broken windows. She can hear the drone of low voices coming from inside.

"Greetings," she says, slipping in past one of the heavy wooden doors. Every time she visits this chapel she wonders why the thieves don't take the doors. They have stripped the church of everything else, from the pews to the roof. Maybe they're too heavy.

"Raven," says Lavinia. "You made it."

"High Priestess," says Raven and nods towards the woman in her regal robe.

The interior is painted with flame.

Luella stops talking and walks up to Raven, grips her shoulders, kisses both cheeks. "Welcome." She picks a blackjack off Raven's cloak.

Morgan, Luella's second, presses a goblet of wine into Raven's hand. Another witch casts a large circle on the concrete floor, which has seen its share of winter bonfires and other rituals.

"Let us sit," says Raven, and they do. She looks up at the sky and finds the moon.

"May the moon bless our gathering here tonight."

The other witches repeat after her.

Luella says, "May life thrive, now and always. The circle is ever open, never unbroken. May the Goddess awaken in each of our hearts. Merry meet and blessed be."

"Wicked Witches," says Raven.

"We are going by 'The Taglock Terrors' now," says Luella.

"Very well." Raven shifts in her place. Next time she must remember a cushion. "The Taglock Terrors."

"We have found that consistently changing the name of our coven is very effective in avoiding unwanted attention from the media."

"It confuses them," says Morgan. "It makes us… slippery."

"Unwanted attention?" says Raven. "I was under the impression that everything you are doing is to GET attention?"

"Only on our terms," says Luella. "We want the communication to come directly from us so that the message doesn't get distorted."

"The mainstream media distorts everything," says a red-haired witch called Sonja.

"But you do understand that the media will report your stunts?"

"They're not 'stunts'," says Luella. "They're protests. We're subverting the *status quo*. We're starting a revolution."

The other witches chime in with their agreement. Raven waits for them to quieten down. It takes a while.

"A revolution?" she asks.

"A revolution," says Luella, determination setting her bones. "Against patriarchy. Against abuse. Against religion."

"Against misogyny," says Sonja.

"Against corruption," says Morgan, and the rest of the coven take up the chant. Against rape. Against xenophobia. Against consumerism. Against animal cruelty. Against bullying. Against violence.

Raven holds up her hand to stop them. "Okay."

"Okay?" says Luella.

"I get it," says Raven. "I get it. I know what it's like to be young and idealistic."

"You don't take us seriously," Luella says. "You're patronising us."

"I take you very seriously, or I wouldn't be here tonight."

Luella looks at Lavinia. The High Priestess's face gives nothing away.

"Why are we here tonight?"

Lavinia speaks in a calm and measured tone. "To discuss the — unintended — consequences of your protest actions."

"There will always be fatalities in a righteous war," says Luella.

"Stop," says Raven.

"It's true —"

"Just stop," she says again. "We are not at war. And there will be no fatalities."

Morgan wants to argue but Lavinia shoots her a warning glance.

"Luella," Raven says. "I need your word, and the word of your coven, right now, that you will not incite any kind of violence. Those videos were bad enough —"

"What was 'bad' about them? We saved over a hundred animals from that evil place."

"That ritual —"

"Why shouldn't we share our rituals? Share our Craft? Should we not be spreading the word of Wicca?"

“Don’t act naïve. You know just how dangerous that clip could be in the wrong hands.”

“We refuse to be ruled by fear.”

Raven scoffs. “How very young you are. Don’t you realise that The Burning Times were only four hundred years ago? That’s nothing.” She clicks her fingers with a spark. “That’s a blip in time.”

Luella drums her feet but keeps her mouth shut.

“You are welcome to continue your ‘protests’ but please do so responsibly. Those videos were reckless and I don’t want any more of them, do you understand?”

The witches sit in a steaming sulk. Lavinia seems satisfied.

20 / BREAD

Raven wakes up in her own bed, dressed in pyjamas, after ten uninterrupted hours of sleep. She can't remember the last time this happened. The animals are confused. Why had she been unconscious for so long? What did it mean? Most importantly: where was breakfast?

She yawns and stretches, cuddles up to a purring Lightfoot. Looks out of the window at the Granadilla trellis. Her granadillas. Her trellis. Her window. Her house. The late Sheldon Bond's bequest has proved to be a potent sleeping-potion indeed. What is there to worry about when you have just short of eight million bucks in the bank? What would she ever have to worry about? No wonder she had been out for the count. The house is sorted; the pigeons dispatched; the book is almost finished; the Wicked Witches — the Taglock Terrors — have been reined in. Ten hours of sleep! She feels so rested. No, it's more than that. She feels rejuvenated. She feels like singing. She feels like that Facebook meme of Julie Andrews in *The Sound of Music* where she fires automatic rifles in her twirling hands.

"Watch out, world," she says. "This zombie has a pulse!"

What are you doing? asks the voice.

What does it look like I'm doing?

It looks like you're getting ready to go out. But I know you better than that.

I'm not a complete hermit, you know, says Raven, brushing her hair.

Is that a new dress?

Kind of. I haven't worn it in years. Does that count?

Raven makes her way through the front gate and runs, doubled-over, on the pavement until she is out of sight of Bishop's house. When she is sure he can no longer spot her, she straightens up and enjoys the rest of the walk up to the village strip. She heads into her favourite coffee shop — *Vovo Telo* — where they have a steaming double-shot latté ready for her before she's finished browsing the artisanal baked goods. The staff greet her, tell her they've missed her. The aroma of fresh bread and pastries sits like a warm cloud inside the restaurant. Her appetite is back. She feels like she could eat everything on the rack in front of her. Pastry pockets of warm cinnamon apples; fat pecan tarts; triple-glazed brioche. She steers clear of the rye bread — a long-running joke that only witches understand. She selects a warm loaf of olive sourdough and a *pain au chocolat* and pays with a credit card that is not declined.

On the stroll home she is fantasising about cutting two thick slices of the soft, crusty bread and slathering them with room-temperature butter. The coffee cup gets too hot in her palm and she has to swap hands. When she is half a block from her house she sees a man in filthy clothes rooting through the municipal rubbish bin. He's not a man collecting recyclables for cash: there is no trolley. His only luggage is an old Checkers plastic bag knotted to his belt.

Raven sighs, hugging the warm loaf to her for the last time. She supposes it would be mean to take the pastry out, so she reluctantly leaves it inside and hands the lot over to him. The man is not sure what's in the brown bag. He peers in, then looks up at her.

"Bread," she says.

Instead of feeling good about the gesture, she feels ridiculous for giving a homeless man artisanal, stone-ground-flour bread. She taunts herself: why not give him a tin of beard wax next time or a designer bowtie? He seems half-pleased, but doesn't smile. They stand in each other's space: it's an intimate act, sharing bread.

What does he want from me? she wonders. The bread will be a bit dry without anything to spread on it. She wishes she had some take-away tubs of butter that you get in Portuguese restaurants and hotel restaurant buffets. He looks at her coffee which has just stopped burning her hand. She gives him that too.

She arrives home empty-handed. Her fridge is vacant. Her larder is a desert. Her stomach starts to gnaw at itself. She'll go pick some fruit from the garden. There are people out there who are hungry all the time, she thinks. They don't have a garden like mine; an organic supermarket. Next time she goes to that coffee shop she'll buy double. Triple. It will be like that story in the Bible when Jesus magically multiplies the fish and the loaves of bread. That will just be the beginning —

Slow down there, Tiger, says the voice. *You're being more blasphemous than Eli.*

Why? says Raven.

You're comparing yourself to Jesus Christ.

Why not? Jesus was a pretty good witch, too.

Please don't ever say that in front of a Christian.

She laughs out loud. Why? Don't Christians have a sense of humour?

Just don't.

How else do you explain the water-into-wine? The healing of lame legs? His coven? His persecution? How do you explain his resurrection? Not only was he a witch, but he was on top of his game!

The voice doesn't answer. Maybe he's given up on her. Maybe he's a closet Christian.

Are you a closet Christian? she asks. No answer. She leaves him alone.

21 / WHITE STONE

A Google alert points Raven in the direction of a fresh newsclip. As Raven had predicted, a journalist with a reputation for being sensationalist has picked up on the Wicked Witches' online videos and has been milking the scandal for all it's worth. The post mushrooms before her eyes, popping up on Facebook, Tumblr, Reddit. The journo, Jeremy Devereaux, has a receding hairline which shows off his very shiny forehead. He has beautiful eyes and teeth which he shows to maximum effect with a wide, shit-eating grin.

"These 'witches'," he leers to the camera, not bothering to hide his enjoyment of the scandal, "these dangerous women have broken into private buildings, stolen property and defaced government establishments." The shot cuts to the naked women raising their arms to the sky, chanting; black irises for eyes. "All the while performing some kind of Satanic ritual." Cuts to a bare-breasted Morgan with red dye splashed on her chest. Raven can't bear to watch the rest of it. She slams her laptop closed.

"You see?" she says out loud to the room. There is no answer.

While the voice is giving her the silent treatment and she is feeling jumpy with anxiety, she heads out again, this time in her car. She sees Bishop run down his path with his hand up, wanting her to stop, but she pretends that she doesn't see him from behind her dark glasses and puts her foot down.

Her idea is to go grocery shopping but the Morris Minor has other ideas. Its old engine rumbles along the Jo'burg streets, farting out carbon monoxide, faded roof absorbing the hot sun. It stalls at a yield sign and Raven thinks, as she turns the key in the ignition, that maybe she can treat herself to a new car. Something more environmentally friendly. An electric car. It's the responsible thing to do.

She lands up on a leafy avenue in Bryanston: rattling to Jessica's house.

Why have you brought me here? she asks the steering-wheel. The guard recognises her and calls the main house while he opens the gate. Raven shows him her palm in acknowledgement and drives up the steep driveway, parking in the shade of the Pin Oak. She's hardly out of her car when Jessica comes flying out of the front door. A screeching bat. A banshee. She is so furious that she seems to leave a trail of light behind her.

"How DARE you?" she shouts. "How DARE YOU?"

Raven freezes.

"Don't act as if you have no idea why I'm angry."

Oh, thinks Raven. The book.

"Are you cross about the gift I gave to Becks? Is it about the book?"

"Do you even have to ask? Of course it's about the book!"

"Can I come inside? Can we talk about it?"

Raven starts to walk towards the house but her sister steps in her way.

"You don't realise what you've done," Jessica says.

"I'm sure you're going to tell me."

"I found her studying it. After bedtime. Under the covers."

Raven is impressed.

"But that's good. She's showing an interest."

"That's GOOD? Are you insane? She's seven years old!"

"She's the same age as I was when Brenna gave that book to me."

"I always hated that."

"The book?"

"The book. The weedy flowers. The special attention she gave you."

"She gave you things, too. Things that you liked. Dresses. Shoes."

"Always the fucking favourite. Always."

"That's not true."

"Spare me the bullshit, Raven. We both know it's true. Even my… even my husband prefers you!"

Jessica is crying now. Despite the sisters' natural beauty, they are both ugly criers.

"You're still angry that Brenna left Colborn Manor to me."

Mascara spills down her cheeks. "As if it wasn't clear enough that she loved you more."

"Jess. Brenna left me a crumbling house that has cost me my life savings. She left you all her money, all her jewellery. Your settlement was far more valuable than mine."

Jessica sobs. "I'm just not good enough, am I? I've just never been good enough."

"This isn't about you, Jessica. Where is Becks? Can I speak to her?"

"Absolutely not."

"Why?"

"Rebecca is grounded."

"Grounded? Why?"

"I caught her drawing satanic symbols on her wall."

"Do you mean pentagrams?"

"Whatever. That satanic star."

"The pentagram is NOT satanic. It's a symbol of power —"

"There will be no witchcraft in this house!"

"You don't want me here?"

"I don't want you two seeing each other anymore. Tim agrees."

"What do you mean? I'm her aunt!"

"You're a bad influence."

"I'm a bad influence?"

Matthew crawls out through the front door and down the steps, stands up and toddles precariously towards them. He's holding the scarecrow poppet that Raven gave him. It looks grubby and well-gummed, as if he hasn't let it go since the party.

"Rabbie!" he says, beaming. "Rabbie!"

"Go inside!" shouts Jessica, pointing at the house.

Matthew is confused. He whimpers.

"Don't shout at him," says Raven.

Jessica speaks through clenched teeth, "Don't tell me how to raise my kids." She spots the poppet in the baby's hand and snatches it away from him. "Filthy thing!" she says. He wails, silently, with a wide-open mouth; he wants it back, but she won't give it to him. He turns red and then purple.

Breathe, baby, Raven wants to say.

Thabisa, the nanny, comes running. She scoops Matthew up and takes him inside, clicking and cooing into his neck.

Raven looks skywards, and catches sight of a small moon in the upstairs window: a round, pale face. A smooth white stone. Raven waves, but Rebecca doesn't wave back.

Well, that escalated quickly, the voice says, as Raven fumes all the way home.

That bloody woman! Sometimes I can't believe we're related. Can you believe we're related?

I don't know. I guess so. You certainly have your differences.

A *bakkie* cuts her off. She wants to hoot at him but the horn isn't working. She punches it and hurts her knuckles. She just catches her curse in time.

Can you believe she said that? About me being a bad influence?

What did you expect?

What is that supposed to mean?

What did you expect, giving Rebecca that book?

I can't *not* foster Becks's gift just because I might rock the boat.

Rock the boat? More like: tank the Titanic. All you were missing was a string quartet.

Where were you anyway?

I was there.

I could have used some back-up.

I'm not here for that.

What do I do now? About our relationship?

Jessica will come back. She always does. Much to my disappointment.

Don't be so horrible.

She's horrible.

She's infuriating, but she's still my sister.

She's a vampire.

You don't believe in vampires.

I mean she's an energy vampire. You're better off without her.

What about the kids?

Bygones. You don't even like kids.

The car stalls again. Raven closes her eyes and lowers her face to the steering-wheel.

"I like Rebecca and Matthew," she says, and begins to cry.

22 / SHOW ME AN ELF

As Raven pulls into her driveway she sees Bishop waving at her in the rearview mirror. She parks and closes the gate behind her. She will NOT indulge him in his moaning today. She will NOT. He can just take his dog collar and shove it up his —

The doorbell rings. She ignores it. She goes to her bathroom and washes her face with cool water, rubs at the spilled eyeliner under her eyes.

Why do I let her upset me? she asks her reflection. I should know better. Goddess knows I should know better. But she knows why. It's because she's alone in this world. Mom and Brenna in the grave, Dad the glowing epitome of the Absent Father Figure. Who else does she have? The menagerie, of course. But sometimes she needs more than fur and feathers up against her. Sometimes she needs hot human skin. A cheek. A palm. A pulsing chest. Sometimes she just needs —

The doorbell rings again. Raven glowers at herself in the mirror. Electric eyes.

Don't do anything rash, she tells herself. Don't do anything stupid. Just ignore the pterodactyl.

The thing about mirrors, she thinks, is that you think you're seeing yourself, but you're not really, you're seeing your reflection, which is quite different to seeing the real thing.

She remembers, at 6 years old, the Brownie Girl Scout initiation ceremony at primary school, where the Brown Owl had set up a pond — the 'pond' being an oval mirror placed on the scuffed hall floor — eyes closed, she had been spun gently by the shoulders: "Cross your little fingers / Stand upon your toes / That's a bit of magic / Every Brownie Girl knows". Then Raven had to say, "Twist me and turn me and show me an elf, I looked in the water and saw myself" and Raven had opened her eyes and looked down and felt as if she had seen herself for the very first time. Herself, but not quite herself. It was a Veronica with promise, with power. What she didn't realise was that Veronica was already falling away and giant black wings were sprouting: she was becoming Raven. She had grown out of Brownies within the year, but what had stayed with her was the new knowledge of the inherent magic in rituals.

Perhaps other parents — less distracted parents — would have recognised the warning signs: a child who talked to the fairies in the garden, who made potions from dandelion seeds and rainwater, who lit illicit fires to boil leaves and flowers, who spoke to birds and cats. How grateful she is now to those wholesome Brown Owls and their innocent spells. How charming she found it that those sweet Brownies turned out to be her gateway drug down the dark and glittering road to witchcraft.

The doorbell rings and a cord in Raven's head snaps. She has absolutely had enough of Father Stephen Fucking Bishop. She marches through the house and snatches her wand off the kitchen counter. Anger is beating through her whole body. An invisible line has been crossed. She no longer tells herself to keep calm. She has to dispel this fury. She has to dispel Bishop. Her spellstick tingles in her hand. She can feel the magical current moving through her body. Is her magic coming back? Or is it just the anger that has whipped her energy into sharp focus? Raven stomps down the path and smashes the bolt across, wrenches the door open, holds her twitching wand aloft.

But there is no dog collar, no Bible-shield and no Bishop. Instead, before her stands a tall man with an outspread chest and a fine face. He seems at first puzzled by her flaming cheeks and the wand in her hand, and then vaguely amused.

Hello, says the voice.

The man peers into her face.

"Raven Kane?"

She nods. She likes the way he says her name. He is certainly not unattractive. There is something especially appealing about his eyes, which are kyanite blue.

"I'm Captain Kruger."

Captain Kruger? she thinks. What is he, a pirate?

He opens his wallet, shows her his South African Police Service identification.

"I'm going to need you to come down to the station with me."

23 / PACIFIC ISLAND DEVIL MASK

"The station?" says Raven. Her brain is not computing.

"The police station," says Kruger. "We have some questions."

They don't take their eyes off each other. Raven lowers her spell-stick and tucks it into the top of her skirt.

"Usually we just phone people," he says. "We phone them and ask them to come down. But —"

"But I don't answer my phone," says Raven.

"Yes."

They understand each other. A witch and a pirate. Raven's knife is sheathed secretly, snugly against her thigh. Kruger's revolver rests plainly in his hip holster.

"Is it necessary? To go to the police station? Or can we just talk here?"

"It depends," he says, "on whether you have any decent coffee."

Raven leads him through the front door. He is a Detail Man. She senses him taking in all the little things: the Pacific Island Devil Mask clock, the mantelpiece goats'-hoof candlestick holders, the medieval astrological chart that is framed on the wall, the antique illustrations of bees that have been on the wall for as long as Raven can remember. The giant pentagram, drawn in charcoal and ash, where Raven has forgotten to replace the canvas that usually covers it up for polite company. Although she isn't yet sure if this man is polite company. She puts the kettle on, pulls out cups, cream, ground coffee and her glass plunger.

He walks up to a vintage print of a woman on a broomstick, swirling thunderclouds behind her, a black cat in the foreground. She has a black halo of hair and a wild look on her face.

"Relative?" he jokes.

"Probably," she jokes back. They try not to smile at each other.

He studies the photographs in their dusty frames: Raven, as a toddler, riding Toby the tortoise. Jessica, four years old or so, wearing one of their mother's dresses and pearls. Brenna and Jack on the verandah, sipping tea.

Eli swoops in and greets the visitor with a "Jesus Christ!" which makes Kruger's eyebrows shoot up. A baby rabbit is asleep on the kitchen counter. Raven sets up a tray while the coffee is brewing. Kruger sneezes.

"Blessed be," she says.

Kruger sneezes again, and again. The man has a violent sneeze. Raven tries to swallow her laugh.

"Are you… all right?"

He sneezes again.

"Cats?" he asks, looking around for evidence.

"Cats," she says. "Dogs. Birds. Rabbits."

He nods, and keeps sneezing. His eyes are watering.

Raven opens the glass doors out onto the verandah. Sets the tray on the table.

"Come out here. It'll be better in the fresh air."

"I'm allergic," he says.

"I can see."

He walks out onto the stilted porch and looks into the garden. Tries to blink away his tears.

Raven quickly pours some lavender lemonade and 10ml of anti-histamine syrup in a cocktail shaker. She mixes it and pours it out in front of him in a tumbler.

"Drink this. It'll help."

He doesn't ask what it is. He just flattens it like a 15-year-old at a high school social. They stand, awkwardly, waiting for the next sneeze. The Grimm Brothers' ears prick up in their sleep. Did they hear a new voice? Someone to play with? They stumble over sleepily and show Kruger their tongues.

"Hello, boys," he says, and they pant at him. "I've always loved dogs but I've never been able to keep any."

"They especially like people who are allergic to them," she says, motioning for him to take a seat.

"They're huge. They're like grizzly bears."

"They like fresh salmon," says Raven.

"And fresh human, by the looks of things," he says, as Jake chews gently on his calf. Kruger's face is clear. The potion has worked. Raven pours the coffee.

"I assume that you're here because of the Taglock Terrors," says Raven.

"The who?"

"I mean, the Wicked Witches."

"The Wicked Witches?"

"The Twisted Sisters?" says Raven. "The Sick Wiccas?"

Kruger frowns at her.

"The protests? The breaking and entering at Xosmetix?"

Stop talking, says the voice.

"Are you saying, Miss Kane, that you know the people who broke into that building?"

"Not personally," she fibs. "But they're witches. I'm a witch. I assume that's why you're here."

"I'm just here for the coffee," he says, and strokes Jake with his foot. "And the company."

"And?"

"And… because I have a few questions about a… client of yours."

"I don't discuss my clients with strange men."

"I'm a policeman."

"I especially don't discuss them with policemen."

"I'm afraid you'll have to bend your rule in this particular case."

"We'll see about that."

"I don't want to have to drag you down to the station." Kruger takes a sip of coffee. "If you co-operate, we can keep this very civilised."

"God Almighty!" shouts Eli. "Mother of Christ!"

"Shoo, Eli," says Raven. "Shoo. Go find some grapes or something."

Uncharacteristically obedient in the face of the law, the African Grey flies in the direction of the grapevines.

"A blasphemous parrot?" says Kruger. He seems to be — again — vaguely amused.

"He doesn't mean to be blasphemous. He just spends a lot of time with the neighbour across the road."

"The neighbour enjoys blaspheming?"

"Quite the opposite. He's a retired Catholic priest. Eli listens to him practising his old sermons."

"Let me tell you why you're on our radar," says Kruger.

"That sounds exciting. Am I a 'person of interest'?"

"In a way," he says, still stroking the bear-headed Rottweiler. Jake looks up at him with complete doggy-doration. "We wouldn't have connected you to the victim at all, if it wasn't for his son."

The peacock screams.

"Wait," says Raven. "You were talking about a client of mine. Now you're talking about a 'victim'?"

"A *late* client of yours," he says.

Raven gets a fright. "What? A client of mine died?" Her hand is over her heart.

"You could put it that way," he says, putting down his still-warm, empty cup.

"Is there another way to put it?"

"You could say that a client of yours died. Or you can say that you killed him."

Fred keeps screaming. The Grimm Brothers get up to investigate.

"It's not boring around here," says the policeman.

"You're telling me," says Raven. "I want to know everything."

"I was hoping that you'd be the one filling me in."

"Who is it? Who *was* it?"

"Do you need a name?"

"Of course I need a name. How else will I know —"

He holds up a hand to stop her. "Mrs Kane, do you make a habit of killing your customers?"

"You're rude," she says.

"You're deflecting," he says.

"Of course I don't make a habit of killing clients. It wouldn't make much business sense, would it?"

"On the surface, the answer would be 'no'."

"I think the answer will always be 'no'."

"Unless?" Kruger says, rubbing his stubble.

It's good stubble, thinks Raven. He has a good face. He may even be described as handsome, in a kind of rugged, dirty-cop way. Although she can tell he's not dirty at all. Compared to her, he is positively gleaming.

"Unless you somehow convince the unlucky client to leave a substantial amount of money to you in his will."

Oh, thinks Raven. Oh. Shit.

"Sheldon Bond," she says.

"Sheldon Bond," he says. "Welcome to the conversation."

"Why now?" asks Raven. "Sheldon's been dead for over a year."

"It seemed that he died of natural causes."

"Cancer," she says. "Bowel cancer."

"Yes. But now that they've wound up the estate some new information has come to light."

Uh-oh, thinks Raven.

Keep calm, woman, for the love of God, says the voice. *Don't give yourself away.*

"Bond's son," says Kruger, "also by the first name of Sheldon —"

"I remember him! He's such a little shit!"

"Then your feelings are mutual."

"You've spoken to him?"

"He's the reason I'm in your house."

"Do you know," says Raven, "that in the last two weeks of Sheldon Bond Senior's life, when I was practically living with him — "

Kruger sits up straight. "You were living with him?"

"I was nursing him."

Kruger writes this down.

"He was in the end stage of his disease. He had days left to live. I phoned his son every day asking him to come and see his father. Twenty minutes, I told him. Just a twenty minute visit before he dies."

"He didn't come?"

"He didn't come. He didn't so much as send a get-well card despite living in the same city, in the same part of the same city. That didn't stop him from drawing on his father's income, though, the entitled little shit!"

"Did he go to the funeral?"

"Of course he went to the funeral. There are appearances to be kept up."

"Did you go to the funeral, Miss Kane?"

"No."

"No?"

"It was a church funeral. I don't do churches. They make me sweat."

"How about weddings?"

"I don't do weddings, either."

"And here I thought you were a romantic, with your goats'-hoof candlestick holders and Pacific Island devil mask."

"How did you know it was Pacific Island?"

"How did you know Sheldon Bond Senior?"

"He was referred by another client of mine. That's mostly how my business works."

"Referrals and Twitter," says Kruger.

"Yes."

"Is that particular client alive? The one who referred him?"

"Yes," says Raven. "Of course. I mean, I think so. I don't see why not."

"You didn't knock him off, in other words?"

"I didn't knock him off."

"Hey," says Kruger. "I've stopped sneezing."

24 / 93 MINUTES

When Raven finally closes the door behind Kruger, she leans her back against the door and tries to keep her breathing even. Adrenaline has been pulsing through her body for the last hour and now she allows herself to shake. She walks towards the kitchen, breathing and shaking. Breathing and shaking.

Do you need your asthma pump? asks the voice.

What do they know? she asks. What do they know?

They know enough to come and pay you a ninety-three-minute visit, says the voice.

"Ninety-three minutes," says Raven. Holy shit. She pours herself a whisky and downs it. Fire in her throat. She pours another one.

They'll need proof, says the voice. *Is there proof?*

There's always proof, says Raven.

Were you careful?

Of course I was careful. I'm always careful.

But you broke one of your rules. You phoned a relative.

I had to. The poor man was desperate to see his son. He didn't have anyone else. He wanted a hand to hold in those last moments of shadow. He wanted to see that his life wasn't meaningless. Besides, he would have found out anyway.

But you didn't tell the son who you were. How did he know?

Raven finds her asthma pump and breathes in the medicinal mist.

Because I got the money.

Of course.

I got the fucking money. I knew it would come at a cost.

Raven's skin starts tingling. She knows what it means. She fills a jug with ice from the ice-machine and pours it into the bath, starts running the cold water. Cracks out all the back-up frozen trays she has for times like this. The tingle becomes an itch: a burn, as if someone is holding a blowtorch to her limbs. She follows her well-rehearsed routine without thinking; climbs into the freezing water, feels the shock of cold: the immediate relief. But her skin is too hot and the ice melts away before it can reverse the burn. In front of her eyes, patches of red blossom all over her pale body, like fast-forward bacteria spores multiplying and mushrooming. Raven catches what is left of the ice and holds it to the worst parts of the rash, but it doesn't stop it from erupting into blisters.

" Holy shit!"

What's happening? asks the voice.

I don't know. It's never been this bad before.

It's stress. Stop stressing.

'Stop stressing'? That's useful advice.

You need more ice.

I don't have any more ice.

Where is that dithering bartender when you need him?

25 / SUBTLE SILVER SCARS

Raven walks around the house naked to keep her skin cool. The attack is over, now she just has to deal with the after-effects — an unsightly rash and weeping blisters. In a few days the broken tissue will be replaced by a shiny new epidermis and then subtle silver scars. The most upsetting thing about the attacks is that they make her distrust her body. She thinks of the inflammation as treason: her own cells fighting against her. She despises disloyalty.

In witchcraft, the body — especially the female body — is an expression of the sacred being. Raven is not in the mood to celebrate her particular temple today.

She gets a jar of home made ointment out of the fridge; oak bark essence and honeybee propolis. She smoothes it over her angry skin with a spatula. The coolness of the cream is balm in itself.

Eli looks at her strangely.

"What?" says Raven and he looks away. She must look like some kind of Amazon woman warrior. Eli's not used to that kind of thing. The dogs don't mind. They think it's some kind of game. They lick her fingers and try to pull her outside towards the garden. How she loves the canine mentality. If only humans also saw life for what it is: a game. A messy, complicated, rule-impaled, red-taped game. But a game nonetheless. Points for happiness, points for health, points for success. Extra points for hard work and good deeds. Negative points for general life fuck-ups. What most people forget, including her, is that you don't get to take your points with you to your next life. That's the cosmic joke.

The coven who seem to keep this in mind, however, are spending their points with gay abandon. Raven's phone beeps with a Google alert that they've posted a new video online.

Did we not agree that they would NOT post any more videos? she says.

YOU may have agreed. I didn't hear them agree.

But our meeting at the Moon Chapel, I told them to stop.

And you thought they would? The coven who call themselves the Taglock Terrors and are unapologetically radical feminists and revolutionaries? You thought they'd listen to an authoritarian figure? Ha ha.

But I explained the danger. I explained —

Somehow I think that they don't mind a little danger. I think a little danger is exactly what they're looking for.

Jeremy Devereaux's face appears on her screen. "Call them what you will," he says, "but the Wicked Witches are back and they are hellbent on bringing evil into our lives."

Oh, how Raven would love to slap the man.

The video cuts to the now familiar black screen with the hand gesturing in the corner. Then you see the women arming themselves: swords, ritual knives, crossbows. Raven's blood runs cold. We're seeing the shaky amateur footage of someone's GoPro. Under the cover of night the witches jump over a high wall and run up a path of a private residence. They use a crowbar to prise open a side-door, setting off the house alarm. They make it inside — you hear heavy breathing and hurried footsteps — and rush into what looks like the main bedroom where they handcuff a man in his sleep. He moans. You see flashes of blades and arrows.

"Holy shit," says Raven. "Shit, shit."

Devereaux is back. "Businessman Gavin Burke was abducted last night from his home in Bryanston and has been missing for almost twelve hours. A photo of a beautiful blonde woman wearing sunglasses comes up. "Mrs Burke could not be reached for comment."

Luella comes back on screen. "You thought you could blow us away," she says. "You didn't know that we had wings."

"As you can see," says Devereaux, "these so-called witches are getting more dangerous by the day. Where is Gavin Burke? What have they done with him? We'll do what we can to get an answer for you soon."

"Damn it, Luella," says Raven into her phone. "I thought that I had made myself clear."

"I didn't do it," says Luella.

"What do you mean, you didn't do it?"

"I mean, of course we did it — the abduction; the video — but I didn't post it on Vimeo. I don't know who did. It wasn't any of us."

"Who the hell is this Burke? What have you done with him?"

"The less you know, the better."

"Holy Hecate, Luella, I hope this is all a show!"

"A show?"

"A stunt. I hope that this man is in on your crazy plan, that he's playing along, that you're doing this for eyeballs."

"He's co-operating. After some persuasion."

"So you've done it with his consent?"

"I didn't say that."

"Luella."

"Look. Burke is not a good guy."

"And how is that any of your business? Or the coven's business?"

"We're tired of sitting around."

"You've hardly been sitting around. Xosmetix. The JSE building."

"We're tired of the indifference shown to the abuse of women. It's time to fight back."

"What?"

"Burke. He's a serial abuser. Wife and kids. They've all had their bones broken. He put her in hospital on a ventilator for a week last year."

"How do you know?"

"How do you think?"

"Is that some kind of, I don't know, breach of your professional protocol?"

"Raven. Hypocritical much? You're the one who uses my position as —"

"Okay. You're right. Forget it. But what about Burke?"

"He'll be delivered to the police station as soon as he's ready to confess."

"What about the weapons in the video?"

"I know you don't want to hear this but we're arming ourselves. We want to send a message."

Raven sees the flash of swords, the crossbows.

"It's a mistake," says Raven. "Violence is never the answer."

"It's not violence if it's self-defence."

Raven scrubs her head with her knuckles.

"So, you're not saying that you didn't post the video online, just that you didn't post it on Vimeo."

"Yes."

"Where? Where did this anonymous poster get it from?"

"We thought it would be a safe place to post it."

"WHERE, Luella?"

"On Nevermore."

"What the hell is 'Nevermore'? Send me a link."

"I can't."

"What do you mean, you can't?"

"It doesn't work like that. It's part of the... dark web. That's why we thought it would be okay."

"Holy Goddess! Do you not think my life is difficult enough? Managing you lot is like... trying to herd cats on acid!"

In fact, I'd much rather be herding hallucinogenic cats, she thinks. There is a pause in the conversation.

"With all due respect, Raven," says Luella, "It's not about you."

26 / BLUNT

What are you doing? asks the voice.

What does it look like I'm doing? says Raven, out of breath.

It's the middle of Summer. It's 32 degrees in the shade.

I don't care.

You planning a communal braai? A bonfire? A funeral pyre?

Nope.

Seriously, that's a lot of firewood. What's the plan?

There is no plan. I like chopping firewood. It feels good. Satisfying. Okay?

Okay. You really do cut that wood with a vengeance.

Is that a compliment?

An observation. It's ironic that you are a treehugger AND a tree hacker.

Leave me alone.

Okay. Please don't chop off any vital body parts.

What if I chop off non-vital parts? Will that be okay?

No need to be shirty.

How about a toe? How about my little finger?

The wood is dry and splits easily despite the glinting axe being blunt. The voice doesn't answer.

27 / THE SPIRAL DANCE

"Lavinia, I'm in trouble," says Raven. She looks up at the facade of the Rosebank block of flats; thinks please let her be here, please let her be here. Taps her feet.

The gate buzzes and Raven jumps forward to push it open. She bounds up the old concrete stairs to the third floor and knocks on the High Priestess's blue door. Lavinia paints it a different colour every year, on the eve of Beltane.

"I'm sorry to just arrive like this," she says when Lavinia opens the door. "I was just driving around and Morris brought me here."

"Then I shall thank Morris," says Barkridge. "Your visit is weeks overdue." She's wearing a raw silk blouse overflowing with giant stitched-on sea creatures: translucent anemone, urchin shells, gossamer blue-bottles.

Raven collapses on the couch, under the watchful eyes of Lavinia's many paintings. Her flat would look like an art gallery — if an art gallery crammed framed works into every square inch of available wall space and didn't mind if Dali consorted with Da Vinci, or Tretchikoff with Tobias.

"Shall I make some tea?"

"Do you have anything stronger?"

"How bad is it? Chardonnay spritzer? Tequila Sunrise? Double brandy?"

"A glass of wine please. Red, if you have it."

A goblet of ruby wine appears in Raven's hand, despite her not having seen Lavinia pour it. Indeed, the High Priestess is already sitting adjacent to her with her own glass in her hand, and is helping herself to a handful of roasted almonds from a bowl on the coffee table.

"Tell me," she says.

Raven hesitates. Does she really want to involve Lavinia?

"I don't actually want to talk about it," she says. "Being here, with you, is enough."

She always feels better at Barkridge's house. It's perennially cosy and smells of just-baked biscuits.

"Have you been baking biscuits?" asks Raven.

Lavinia hands her a saucer of peanut butter biscuits. Where did she get them from?

"My dear," she says. "What happened to your hands?"

Raven covers them up, self-consciously, but the High Priestess takes one of her clammy hands in hers and puts her cool palm over it. The irritation seems to be soothed.

"My hands are the least of it," Raven says. "It's all over my body. Burnt and blistered."

"You had one of your attacks."

"It's never been this bad before."

"We have to do something about it."

"I've been applying oak-bark tincture. It helps."

"I mean," says Lavinia, "not to treat the symptoms, but to avoid the attacks altogether."

"You make it sound easy. It's not. I've had this condition for as long as I can remember. I've tried everything."

"What triggered the first episode?"

"I don't know. I was young. Too young to remember anything."

"Maybe that would help. If you try to remember."

"I think it runs deeper than that. I don't know. I feel —"

But what was the point in talking about it? It wouldn't change anything.

"You should tell me. Maybe I can help you."

Raven drinks her wine. Chews on a warm biscuit. Already she can feel her muscles relax, her jaws unclench. Lavinia looks deep into her eyes as if she might find the answer there. It's such an intense gaze that Raven has to look away.

"Perhaps," says the High Priestess, "we just have to accept that what gives light must endure burning."

"Gives light? I don't give light."

"Oh, but you do, Raven dear. You just don't see it."

"I feel like a fraud," says Raven.

"Everybody feels like a fraud," says Lavinia. "Imposter Syndrome. It's the human condition."

"Not like this."

"I think you'd be surprised. What did Shakespeare say? 'All the world's a stage,/ And all the men and women merely players;/ They have their exits and their entrances,/ And one man in his time plays many parts'. It's all acting, really. Always has been."

"But Shakespeare was a writer who could write. I'm a witch who can't do magic."

Saying it out loud hurts. She puts her goblet down, puts her hand over her heart.

"Of course you can do magic. You're the most talented witch I know. The hardest battle you'll ever have to fight is between who you are now and who you want to be."

Raven blinks away some tears. They sting. "It's fading. My magic is fading. Something has happened. Something has short-circuited. I try to cast a spell now and it's like — the sparks won't leave my fingers."

"But you've done some powerful work recently. I can tell."

"But it's like I can't *feel* it."

"Everyone has their ups and downs, just as the earth has her seasons. You know the warp and weft of life. The spiral dance."

"I fear it's worse than that. I feel… different."

"My dear Raven. Magic never disappears. You know that."

"What I know and what I feel are at odds."

"You're burnt out. You need a holiday."

"I need a lot more than a holiday."

"You need a holiday," says the High Priestess, "and you need to get laid."

Raven almost chokes. "Lavinia!"

"What?" the old lady says, eyes glittering. "It's very good for your magical charge. You know that."

Raven laughs out loud and then can't stop. The hysterical laughing winds down into a sob. Lavinia comes to sit next to her, pats her back.

"There, there," she says. "It's going to be okay. Have another biscuit." And she does.

Three glasses of wine later Raven is feeling almost cheerful.

"Can Morris sleep here tonight? I think I'll have to Uber home."

"Of course," says Lavinia, who has kept up with her, glass-for-glass.

Between them they have come up with a plan to rein in the Taglock Terrors; to liven up the next PaganCon; to encourage a common friend to come out of the broom closet; and (theoretically) to save the world. What they have not done is come up with a plan to save Raven.

"Is there anything else you want to talk about, dear?"

How did Lavinia know? Lavinia Always Knew.

"There is one other thing," says Raven, and hiccups.

"Just one thing?"

"Well. Many things. But one... pressing thing."

"I'm listening." Lavinia lights her rum and maple pipe and settles back into the padded couch.

"I had a visit from a man."

"That sounds promising," giggles Lavinia.

Raven has never heard the High priestess giggle in the 20 years she has known her. The moment takes on a surreal quality. The paintings seem to be winking at her.

"A policeman," says Raven. "A captain, actually."

"Oh?" says Barkridge, smile fading.

"It appears that I'm a 'person of interest' in a case he's working on."

"What kind of case?"

"A murder investigation."

Lavinia sits up straight. "Murder?"

"A late client of mine."

The High priestess is quiet for a moment. "Well?" she says at last, "How did you do it?"

Raven puts down her empty glass. Hiccups. "Don't you mean: 'DID you do it?'"

"You wouldn't be here," Lavinia says, "if you didn't do it."

28 / DESSICATED BRAIN

Wake up, says the voice. *Wake up.*

Leave me alone, groans Raven. Her stomach turns and the room turns with it.

You drank far too much last night.

Thanks for clearing that up. The Karoo sand in my mouth had me confused.

I did warn you to stop after the third drink.

Well, you should know better than that.

I *should know better?*

You know how rebellious I can be. Especially after three glasses of wine. When you tell me how to behave it makes me want to misbehave.

So your hangover is... my fault?

Yes. So it would have been considerate of you to let me sleep in a little, to recover.

I did. It's 11 a.m.

Oh.

You need to get up. The menagerie needs to be fed and you need to go shopping.

Shopping! In my condition? No way.

Your condition?

Desiccated brain. Lacerated skin. Very little will to live.

Your kitchen is officially empty.

It can't be that bad.

It is. You're out of bread and yoghurt and rusks.

I can do without.

You're out of coffee.

Raven lifts her head off the pillow. It's smudged with eye make-up.

Then shopping it is.

Morris is waiting obediently in the driveway for her.

Oh no. I didn't drive home. Did I?

Don't worry, says the voice. *You did no such thing. I wouldn't have let you, even when you are trying to drown me out.*

How did Morris get here?

I assume Lavinia arranged it.

How did an 89-year-old woman become my best friend?

You're hardly a spring chicken yourself!

You're right. I feel 89 on a good day.

Raven wanders the aisles of the small Woolworths near her house, leaning on her trolley for support and wearing her sunglasses. She sweeps an entire shelf of salted crackers into her wire car. She finds a mocha milkshake and downs it where she stands, then takes another one for sipping as she shops. She laughs out loud at the price of organic gooseberries. A few people shoot her interested looks.

"You would think," she says, "that with all this powerful magic swirling around, there would be a quick cure for a hangover. Maybe it's a business opportunity." She uses the dictaphone function on her phone and records the thought for later contemplation.

"Hey," says a woman with a basket resting on her arm. She's wearing chapped lips and a beige cotton dress that is two sizes too small for her. It has the unfortunate effect of making her look naked and trussed up. A pork loin.

Raven lowers her dark glasses to get a better look. "Do I know you?"

"Are you the woman on the news?" the pork loin asks.

"I doubt it," says Raven and keeps walking. She still needs to visit the cheese section.

"You are!" the woman says and paces to keep up. She puts her hand on Raven's trolley to stop her. "You're that witch. You killed someone!"

Raven stops, as does all the activity around them. The man stocking the dairy shelf looks particularly perturbed. Good Goddess, Raven thinks. Has the world gone mad? She moves up close to the woman, pictures her roasting in an oven; says in a low voice, “Do you make a habit of walking up to murderesses in grocery stores?”

“No?” quavers the woman.

“And do you wish to stay alive?”

The woman hops a step backwards, out of Raven’s way, as if the trolley has shocked her.

“Thank you,” says Raven, and finishes her shopping.

On the way back to Morris she walks past a hardware store, and remembers that she needs more rechargeable batteries for her solar security lights. She selects a value pack of 12. At the counter there is a display of new tools that have just arrived. She admires the electric drill and matching screwdriver.

“What’s this?” she asks the man behind the counter.

The shop smells like new plastic, oil and sawdust.

“It’s a nail gun,” he says, “200 watt. Just arrived.”

“Is it a good one?”

“Top of the range.”

“I’ll take it.”

When she gets home there are a few reporters milling around outside her house with notepads and big black cameras. One is talking to Bishop, one is balancing on a rock, trying to glimpse through a hole in the fence.

“This is private property!” she shouts at them.

Bishop looks anxious. He’s probably worried about his immaculate lawn getting trampled.

When the press spot her they run over for a comment.

"Mrs Kane," the one in the peak cap yells, "can I have a moment?"

It's MISS bloody Kane, she wants to say. "No, you bloody well can't!"

"Give us your side of the story," the other one says, aiming his video camera at her.

"Get off my property," says Raven, "or I'll set the devil hounds on you!"

On cue, the Grimm Brothers begin barking and growling. They do know how to play the part. She's glad that she's bought them some extra treats. Morris screeches into the driveway and the gate shudders closed. She sees the reporters peeking through the fence. She really needs to get it fixed.

She paces around the house, agitated. She tosses dog biscuits up in the air and Jake and Bill catch them. She stands on Max's tail by accident and he hisses at her.

"Sorry!" she says to him, but he shirks her off. She craves a cigarette, even though the last time she smoked was at a 1999 New Year's party in Bathurst, where she and a friend had shared a bottle of Old Brown Sherry under a giant pineapple, before skinny-dipping in the sea. It had been her last cigarette and her first gay kiss. Salt water. Moonlight. The unexpected softness of —

Can we focus here please? says the voice. *In case it has escaped your attention, we've got serious problems.*

I'm thinking, says Raven.

We need a lawyer.

I don't know any lawyers.

Best change that.

Her phone beeps with a message. It's from the cop.

Raven. I need to see you.

Her insides jump. She had been thinking about him, too.

Where? she types.

At the station.

Oh.

You're disappointed? asks the voice. *You thought he was texting you about a date?*

Well, not a 'date' *per se.*

Per se?

I wasn't expecting dinner.

Raven. He's building a criminal case against you! He is not your friend. He is certainly not your —

All the more reason to win him over then, don't you think?

No.

What about that old chestnut - keep your friends close and your enemies closer?

I'm not sure that's actually ever worked out for anyone. Look at Caesar, for one.

I was hoping, texts Raven, ***that we could meet somewhere else.***

Her heart beats staccato as she waits for his response.

I didn't want to admit it, she says, but there's something there. Between us.

A police badge?

No. I mean… a zing.

A zing?

A zing. Right up inside my body. Didn't you feel it?

It's not my job to feel.

Her phone beeps.

Sure, comes Kruger's response. ***Next time. But this time I need you at the station.***

29 / ZOMBIES IN UNIFORM

Ten minutes after arriving home, Raven sneaks out of the back entrance. She can't risk taking Morris so she climbs on her black bicycle instead. Miraculously, both tyres are still inflated. There is a sticker of a broomstick on the side, a keepsake from her varsity days when she had started her very first coven. She was still finding her way, then. Playing with popular — but not always realistic — images of witchcraft. Taking cues from urban legends, novels and movies in the absence of legitimate literature or Craft elders. Firstly, they had called themselves 'Besom Buddies', then 'The Bristles' because it had seemed cooler. They had thought it was edgy for its time. Now the Diabolical Disciplettes were the edge.

It takes her half an hour to cycle on her broomstick to the Norwood Police Station despite it being just a few kilometres away. The neglected bike is still in good condition but she's a bit rusty.

The police station is a squat row of bricks and windows. Worse than bland. It's like some kind of culture vacuum. As if, if you stood before it for too long, it would suck all the aesthetic appreciation out of your soul. It looks like it was designed by someone who was clinically depressed. It reeks of institutionalism. There may as well be an eleven-foot wall glittering with barbed wire and electric currents for the amount of foreboding Raven feels. She doesn't want to go inside. She's worried that once she steps through the door she will never be the same person again. Which, she thinks, must happen here quite often.

My hat, you can be melodramatic.

Can I? I'm wanted for murder and I'm standing before a building full of handcuffs and patriarchy.

Go on, says the voice. *It won't bite.*

How do you know? says Raven. She locks her bike up outside and makes her way inside.

Kruger welcomes her like an old friend. He seems genuinely happy to see her and leads her down a corridor of scuffed blue enamel paint and into an interview room that is brighter than Raven expected. He's taller than she remembers. His eyes are exactly the same, probably because she has been picturing them often since they last met.

"You didn't bring your wand," he says.

"The dogs chewed it up. They think it's a fetch-stick."

"Does that happen often?" His eyes are smiling.

"At least once a month. It's my fault, for leaving it out."

Kruger pulls out a chair for her and she sits. He sits right next to her, which makes her feel a jab of excitement.

"So," he says, putting a handsome hand on the table between them. "You have a high wand turnover."

"Occupational hazard."

"Do you have a lot of those? Occupational hazards?"

"Yes," says Raven. "Any worthwhile job does. Yours, for one."

"Indeed," he says. His eyes don't leave her face.

She looks away. "Any sneezing since our last encounter?"

"None. I remain impressed by your potion-making skills."

"That was so 101. I have elixirs that can —"

Careful, says the voice.

Kruger gestures for her to continue. "That can?"

"Never mind," says Raven, re-crossing her legs. "Why am I here? What questions do you have that can only be answered in this hallowed hall of zombies in uniform?"

"You think that the police force are… zombies?"

"Do I think they are mindless agents who follow orders and don't hesitate to prey on others? Mostly, yes."

"You have a persecution complex," he says.

"Wouldn't you if you shared my history?"

"It's not your personal history," he says. "The witch trials happened hundreds of years ago."

"Believe me, I take it very personally."

Raven is acutely aware of her warm knife against her thigh. How can they let people just walk in here with concealed weapons? But then she realises that every person in the building is armed, so metal detectors would not be a viable solution. Still, her *athamé* seems to be asserting itself. Does it feel danger in the air?

Or is it just the close proximity of this man to her leg that is causing the nerves in her thighs to jig?

“I want to know about being a witch,” he says.

“How long do you have?”

“Twenty minutes,” he says, without looking at his watch.

“What do you need to know?”

“Let’s start with what you think I need to know.”

“What do you mean by that?”

“Sometimes, it’s the most revealing information.”

“I still don’t understand why I have to be here - in this place. Could we not have done this over the phone? Skype? I mean, you haven’t even asked me a proper question yet.”

Isn’t it obvious? says the voice. *It’s not about the questions. It’s a strategic move getting you in here. It’s to show you who’s boss.*

“Look,” Raven says. “I understand the whole power-play thing. You’re the man with a shiny badge and an army behind you. I’m a lone woman with a questionable past with no one in my corner.”

He looks at her. Nods. “Okay.”

Raven sits back. Shakes her hair out of her face. “Twenty minutes isn’t going to cut it. Why don’t we do this properly?”

“What do you mean?”

“Why don’t we meet somewhere more comfortable when you have a little more time.” She uncrosses her legs.

“You’ll answer all my questions?”

“I’ll tell you everything you need to know.”

"I'll take you up on that."

"Tonight?" says Raven. "At 8 p.m.? I know a place."

30 / ILL-FATED KNITTING

Raven speeds away on her broomstick bike as fast as her legs will take her. She can't face going to Colborn Manor, not with the reporters on her pavement who she's sure have multiplied faster than her rabbit colony. When she is far enough away from the police station, she relaxes and starts to enjoy the ride. She passes landscapes of bright street art: robotic rats; bejewelled and glowing skulls; topless manga girls made out of shiny candy. She rides past broken windows like buildings' rotten teeth, battered dustbins overflowing with litter, trees topped with shivering clouds of leaves. She thinks she may ride all day. It's such a welcome reprieve from the cluster-fuck her life has become. The just-warm breeze lifts her hair, the sun is on her skin. She could be anyone right now. She could be a schoolteacher; a librarian; a veterinary surgeon; a mathematician; a wife on her way home to her loving husband and pigeon pair children; a woman on her way to visit a friend with freshly baked muffins. She allows herself to daydream of the parallel lives she might have had if she hadn't been born with her power. The sweet, dull lives of women who have never had to live up to their potential, who have never experienced the burden of such a deep and demanding promise.

Soon the stained buildings and pocked streets are behind her, replaced by avenues shaded by solid maple canopies and homes hiding behind bold walls. The houses get bigger and bigger and then there is the oasis of a large park, a vast verdant carpet of lush grass and leaves. Raven slows down and hops off her bike. She chains and locks it to the darkly varnished, thigh-high, gum-pole fence that hems the greenness in. An upright railway track. A keloid scar.

Raven's not sure she knew that this kind of park still existed in South Africa. The parks in her neighbourhood are small, with patchy dry grass and neglected playground equipment, scrawls of amateur graffiti: layers of declarations of schoolyard love and vulgar slogans. Phone numbers. Skateboard half-pipes shined by the trousers of the kids who slide down them. Wire fences rusted and pulling apart like someone's ill-fated knitting.

This park is entirely different. This park is seeded with real money; private money. Its maintenance is not left to the municipal squads of serial underachievers. Gardeners are employed here; real gardeners, who know when the bulbs should be planted, when the roses should be pruned, when to cut the lawn right down, when to protect the roots by leaving it just too long, which is where it is at the moment. Raven walks over the *kikuyu*, a woolly rug, and inspects the various flower beds. She sees bees greedily stacking their legs with pollen from the pink inca lilies and feels like leaving a love letter for the caretaker. What a glorious place, she wants to say. What a haven. It's a shame she has no idea where she is — how will she ever find her way back here? She keeps walking, following the dozens of different scents. How she'd love to see this park in its different seasons. She is sure that, even in Winter, it is a wonderful place to be.

Raven finds a bench and sits down. Her hangover is ebbing away. Her legs are feeling the fatigue of the previous adrenaline. She takes off her shoes, closes her eyes, angles her face up to the dappled light, catches some warm spots of sunshine on her cheeks. Tries to relax her rigid jaw muscles. Her bare feet are cooled and comforted by the soil beneath the grass. As she feels the earth all around her, she thinks: this is where magic could happen. She feels her mind floating away when a figure stalks towards her, throwing her into shade.

"What the hell are you doing here?" says an angry man.

Raven opens her eyes, squints, tries to make out the face of the silhouette before her.

"What do you mean?" says Raven. "Who are you?"

"Who am I?" The man laughs: an angry, bitter cough. "Who am I?" His fury sucks all the colour out of the surroundings.

Raven stands up, draws herself up almost to his height, tries to shade her eyes from the light.

"You have no right to be here," he says to her. He looks ridiculous in a lycra sports outfit. What is he? A cyclist? A runner? A half-drunk beaker of what she guesses is a protein shake dangles from his hand.

"It's a public space," says Raven. "I'm a member of the public."

"You shouldn't be."

"What is that supposed to mean?"

"If I had my way you'd be thrown into a cell. You'd never see sunlight again."

Raven blinks, moves a little more to the side and then the confrontation makes sense. Although she has never met this man she recognises the curve of his chin, the set of his eyes. She reads the golden plaque on the bench, which says: *In Loving Memory of*

Sheldon Bond. She remembers that Sheldon didn't want a gravestone — a 'tomb' he had called it. He had wanted a peaceful place with trees. He had wanted this place, and, without knowing it, she had felt his spirit here.

She knows now that the man standing before her, the one whose anger is bleaching the gardens around them, is his son, Sheldon Bond Jnr.

And Raven knows that he knows that she killed his father.

31 / PISS ON THE FLOWERS

“You ran away?” says a distracted-sounding Lavinia on the other side of the phone.

“Of course I did.”

Raven is still out of breath. She’d sprinted out of the park, tripped over the grass, fallen flat on her face, jumped on her broom and cycled off, leaving a red-faced Sheldon shouting after her.

“You should have stood your ground.”

“No way! You didn’t see how angry he was. He was clenching his hands as if he could imagine them around my neck. I could imagine them around my neck. There wasn’t anyone else around.”

“You think he would have hurt you?”

“You didn’t feel the force of his fury. He *is* going to hurt me. It’s just a matter of time.” Raven hears music on Lavinia’s side. Footsteps.

"He was wearing this ridiculous outfit. I think he was on his way home from rock climbing or something."

"What was he doing there, anyway?" asks Lavinia. "If he didn't visit his father while he was alive, why visit when he's dead?"

"I don't know. To piss on the flowers."

"He sounds like a charming individual." Now Lavinia is the one breathing heavily.

"What's that in the background? Are you at a concert or something?"

"I'm learning a new dance," says Barkridge. "It's coming along very well."

Raven hears a male voice purring in the background. Spanish?

"The funny thing is," Raven says, "I don't think he really cares that I… completed the job I was contracted to do for his father. In fact, I probably did him a favour."

"Well. You did, in a way."

"He's only angry about the money, that I got the money."

"Does he need it?"

"Goddess, no. He's absolutely loaded. I think it's the principle of the matter. He probably sees me as a charlatan who conned his family out of eight million rand."

Under the cover of darkness Raven is able to unlock the back door of her house, which looks like it's part of the fence. Immediately the Grimm Brothers attack her with slobber and kisses. They almost push her right over, into the bushes.

"Okay, boys. Okay. Okay," she ruffles their pelts. "I know I've been away too long. I deserve that."

Under the moonlight she checks on the other animals. Applejack gives the ground a happy kick. Fred, the peacock, is uncharacteristically quiet. Toby is still alive. She walks around the side of the house to her potion garden and listens for the tell-tale cooing of the pigeons, but all is still. It seems that the scarecrowess is doing a sterling job.

"Shit," she says, catching a glimpse of a clock inside. It's 7:30 p.m. and she's supposed to be meeting Kruger at 8. She chucks food in the general direction of the menagerie and launches into a pre-date grooming routine at double the speed. Washes her hair, shaves everywhere, moisturises her just-healed skin. Conditioner, serum, body butter. Perfume, eyeliner, lip balm. She chooses lingerie that she thinks will appeal to him. Sexy, but understated.

"Not too kinky," she says. "Not yet, anyway." Who knows what he's really into? That's one of the best parts of getting to know someone. Prodding the boundaries. She feels a zip of sexual excitement up the front of her body. She'll play it safe, for now. She doesn't want to scare him away. She climbs into a little black dress that she knows she looks beautiful in. Her reflection reminds her how well she cleans up, but she knows the look isn't right. She shakes the dress off, puts on jeans and a hoodie. Washes off her perfume. Musses her hair.

An Uber driver collects her a block away from her house. He watches her from his rearview mirror.

"Eyes on the road, buddy," she says and puts her hood over her head.

32 / UNBOIL AN EGG

Raven is twenty minutes late. Kruger doesn't seem perturbed. If anything, he seems a little surprised that she has turned up at all. Or maybe it's the dark cave of the setting, maybe it's the ghoulish bartender, the topless vampire waitresses.

"Interesting choice of venue," he says, standing up to greet her.

"I thought, after this morning, we needed the extreme opposite."

"This is the opposite to zombies in uniforms?"

"This is the opposite to sitting in a white room with bars on the windows."

"I guess it is," he says.

He's drinking whisky. She orders him another and the same for herself. The vampire winks at her. Raven recognises her hazelnut nipples and winks back.

"I see you come here often," says the cop.

"Come on, Kruger, You can do better than that."

"Just trying to break the ice."

"You broke the ice when you told me that I'm a 'person of interest' in your murder case. Believe me, the ice is very much broken."

Kruger has a particular look that he almost always wears. It's as if he's trying to sum her up. She can tell that he has a hundred questions. What is he waiting for?

"Have you eaten?" she asks.

There is a skeleton bending an elbow at the bar with a cigar clenched in his teeth. He's naked except for a top hat. He turns green, then yellow, then pink as the stage lights catch the dry ivory of his bones.

"No. Would you recommend the food here?"

"No," she says and he laughs.

"Who cooks it? Werewolves?"

"No. No werewolves here. Apparently they make terrible employees."

"I thought I saw something about werewolves on the menu."

"That's the Wolfsbane Sling. A cocktail. Personally I prefer the Corpse Reviver."

"Wolfsbane?" he says, his eyes on her Fenrir amulet.

She rubs the silver wolf's head, warm from her chest-skin. "Extremely poisonous. The real stuff, I mean, not the drink. I don't know what they put in the cocktail."

"Tell me more," he says.

Raven hesitates. "So you can laugh at me?"

"It doesn't sound like a laughing matter."

"It's a Saturn herb. Classic to garden witchcraft and sacred to Hecate."

"Why would you want to poison someone?"

"It's not used to harm people. It's for protection. It's said to reverse shapeshifting, among other things."

His eyes sparkle at her. She's not sure yet if it's interest or mirth.

"In our folklore, flints dipped in Wolfsbane juice could be thrown at the enemy. They're called elf-bolts."

The band take up their positions. Three skinny women wearing white vests and crimson lipstick. You can see from the way their slight breasts move under the fabric that they are not wearing bras. The bassist and the drummer have short silver hair; the lead vocalist: mermaid blue. They start playing a song: slow, mournful. The lyrics are incantations. "Catch the Fire," she croons, "catch the Flame."

Raven lets her amulet drop and she and Kruger watch each other over their whisky glasses.

"Who are you, Kruger?"

"You know who I am."

"I don't mean the badge. I mean, who are you, really? Too English for your Afrikaans surname. Too educated to be in the police force." Goddess, he is good-looking.

"Too good-looking not to be on the cover of a magazine," he says.

"Well, I wouldn't go that far!"

"That's what you were thinking."

"That's not what I was thinking."

Cops shouldn't be allowed to be this attractive. It puts them at an unfair advantage.

"Besides, you'd never make it as a supermodel," she says. "You have that scar on your lip, for one thing."

He touches it. He has beautiful lips. "I thought it added to my allure."

"You see? That's exactly what I mean. Cops don't use words like 'allure'."

"Tell me," he says, his leg so close to Raven's that she can feel his body heat. "How have you gotten away with this for so long?"

"With what?"

"With what you do."

His hand is on the table. It's almost touching hers.

"I don't 'get away' with anything. I'm a responsible, law-abiding citizen."

"I think we both know that's not true."

"Okay. I'm an irresponsible, mostly-law-abiding citizen. I follow the laws of the Universe."

"You don't see yourself as a criminal?"

"Why would I?"

"That's what us zombies call people who break the law, which you seem to make a habit of."

"Have you ever thought that perhaps the laws are the problem?"

Kruger laughs. "I knew it from the moment I met you," he says. "You're trouble."

A vampire in stilettos brings them another round.

"Luckily," she says, "you seem to like trouble."

"Tell me about your magic."

Raven has to cross her legs. Her whole pelvis is buzzing. "It's not my magic. It belongs to everyone. To anyone who wants to access it."

"It belongs to everyone? So it's communist magic."

"You like to put everything in a box."

"It's neater that way."

"Magic doesn't work like that. Magic is not a tidy concept."

"How does it work?"

"Like electricity."

"Like a current? An electric charge?"

"It's just there. In the walls. In the invisible wires. Even though you can't see it and you're not exactly sure how it works."

"It's energy," he says.

"Exactly."

They sip their drinks.

"It's interesting, actually," she says.

"Indeed."

"I mean it's interesting, because, in a way, actual electricity is magic in itself. It's a great example because it works both ways."

"Now you've lost me."

"Think about it. Someone, somewhere, in a power plant, burns a black lump of coal - coal that's been created by the earth itself. And that burning, hundreds of kilometres away, means that you can flick a switch right here and the room will be filled with light. A lump of coal! Is that not pure magic?"

"Yes," he says. "You could call it magic. Or you could call it science."

"Magic *is* science and science is magic. What is not magical about vaccines and antibiotics and ..."

A couple of elves begin slow-dancing in front of the band.

"... blood transfusions. Heart transplants. Technology is also magic. Do you know that they have figured out how to un-boil an egg? How to print a kidney?"

"I've always thought of magic as more... natural than that."

"Science is the study of nature."

"I mean, more down to earth."

"It's that, too. At its core, it's earth magic. Pregnancy, birth: there is nothing more powerful than that. Why do you think women have the most magic?"

She can tell that Kruger wants her. It's the way he moves his body around hers without touching her; the way he is so highly aware of her, despite the darkness and the drink. It's how deliberate he is.

"The best kind," says Raven, "is not obvious. Magic doesn't wear a witch's hat. It's in your refrigerator. In your medicine cabinet. In your blood."

Her urge to feel his body is intense. Her breathing deepens. He moves his fingers next to hers; his warm hand that is so close to her. He doesn't touch her.

"Just because we're used to it or not aware of it, doesn't mean it's not there. We take magic for granted, like a fish takes water for granted. It becomes invisible because it surrounds us all the time."

The band starts packing up. Amps are unplugged. The drum-kit disassembled. They don't call last round. They don't flicker the lights. It's not that kind of place.

"Can I give you a lift home?" Kruger says. He is reluctant to leave.

"Already? I was just getting started."

"It's 1 a.m. I'd love to stay but I have court in the morning."

"How different our lives are."

"How different we are," he says, standing up. "Conservative Cop vs. Wild Witch."

"I don't know," says Raven. "I think we have something." The dim light hides her blush. "Something in common, I mean."

"Really? What's that?"

"I have a feeling we'll find out."

He parks outside the back entrance of Colborn Manor, as per her instructions. Switches off the engine and turns to her.

"It was a most edifying evening," he says.

His lips, she thinks. His lips. His mouth. His tongue. "There you go again. Using non-cop words."

He laughs.

"Am I still your 'person of interest'?" Raven asks.

"Very much so," he says. "More than ever."

The sexual tension in the car is unbearable. It threatens to blow the windows out. Kruger gets out and comes around to her side to open her door.

"Thank you," she says, stepping out, gate keys in hand. "See you soon."

"That you will."

They part ways without touching.

33 / SHAKING OFF THE RIGOR MORTIS

Raven climbs into bed naked but can't sleep. Her pelvis is still murmuring with sexual radiation. She lies there finger-tapping her hipbones for a few minutes and then throws the covers off and gets up. It's 2 a.m. She throws on a white robe and puts a pot of coffee on the stove.

"Brenna!" chirps Eli, making her jump.

"Jesus, Eli," says Raven. "You gave me a fright."

How does Eli know Brenna? asks the voice.

"Oh, Brenna!" wails Eli.

You're up, too? asks Raven.

Of course.

Checking up on me? On my date with Kruger, I mean?

Just observing.

You didn't say anything while I was with him.

I'm a polite third wheel.

A chaperone.

Yes.

"Well," says Raven, pouring cream into her coffee. She breaks open a box of chocolate biscuits. "I thought I'd be all alone in a dark house when I got up, but look at us! We have almost enough people for a party."

There is no reply. Eli has gone back to sleep.

Raven makes her way to her office. She switches on her green glass desk lamp. Max blinks bleary eyes at her then closes them again. He's curled up on the bookshelf: it's his happy place. He feels safe here. Whenever there is a thunderstorm or a Guy Fawkes celebration, he'll be here, between *Ancient Spellcrafting* and *The Beekeeper's Almanac*.

Raven opens up her laptop, switches off her wifi and her phone and reads through the last few pages of what she has written. It's surprisingly good. Or maybe that's the whisky talking. Either way she is inspired enough to start typing. The first few sentences come slowly, but soon her fingers are flying all over the keyboard. A thousand words. Another cup of coffee. Two thousand words. Where did all those biscuits go? Three, four, five thousand words. A fresh pot of coffee. Rusks and a green apple. Ten thousand words. And then a magical thing happens. She types 'THE END'.

Raven laughs out loud. Spins her chair around to look outside as the molten sun is rising, coating her backyard and oak tree in an orange syrup. Her limbs are stiff, it hurts to stand; but she doesn't care. She stomps around with her frozen limbs like a zombie trying to shake off rigor mortis. Which, in a way, she has. She's finished the thing.

The proposal for the project is already with a few agents and publishers. Raven had sent off some query letters in an unusual (and as it turned out: unfounded) burst of optimistic sentiment a couple of months ago. She had thought it might help her finish the manuscript. She had thought that if someone, somewhere, showed interest in publishing it then she'd *have* to finish it, but no one had responded. Not one. No form rejection letters. No 'please remove me from your mailing list'. Not even a chocolate ice-cream emoji. She imagines her sample material crumbling to dust at the bottom of slush piles all over the world while designer-bespectacled agents swill martinis and laugh in shrieks.

But now: now she has finished it. She's finished the book she's been writing for 15 years, for 200,000 words. And she knows that it is good. She tries to save it to her iCloud but it says that it's full. She saves it to her desktop instead and makes a mental note to sort out her Cloud as soon as she's had some shuteye. Raven's mind travels to the night before, with Kruger, and she feels the throb return. Thinks of his face and his hands and feels a weakness in her knees. What is this sorcery? She can't remember ever wanting someone so much.

Despite the caffeine and adrenaline Raven is ready to fall into bed. She's going to sleep and sleep until —

What's that noise? asks the voice.

What noise? I don't hear anything.

It's like... it's a like a swarm of bees. Outside your house.

You're imagining things.

Go and check the windows.

You're being paranoid.

Go and check the windows.

Raven opens the curtains and peeks through. There are people camped outside her house. They are packing up their tents, switching off torches. Handing out tea in plastic cups. She can count thirty heads.

What the… ? More reporters?

Reporters. Lurkers. Rubber-neckers. Trouble-makers.

Why?

Check your phone.

34 / COLD SLABS OF JELLY

Raven switches on her phone. It's gone mad with messages, the screen is wallpapered with Twitter and Google alerts. What happened? Has there been a major news event? An earthquake? A tsunami? A terrorist attack? Over a thousand tweets addressed to her and they don't look friendly. Shouty all caps. Exclamation marks poke her eyes like needles.

@Turningtricks YOU SATANIST YOU WITCH YOUR EVIL.

Funny, how trolls never quite get their grammar right.

DEVIL WORSHIPPER YOU DESERVE TO DIE!! @Turningtricks.

Raven feels their hatred hot on her face as if they are in the room and breathing on her, slipping their cold hands under her clothes, squeezing her.

MURDERER!!!!!!!!!!!! @Turningtricks COLD BLOODED BITCH!

The wheel turns @TurningTricks and I hope it flattens you.

She starts to feel a bit short of breath. She looks for her asthma pump, doesn't find it, goes back to the messages.

YOU KILL INNOCENT PEOPLE YOU"LL BURN IN HELL. ONLY GOD CAN TAKE LIVES @turningtricks.

Well, says the voice, *that escalated quickly.*

A WhatsApp message from Lavinia: ***I saw the newsclip and some of the articles. Terrible. Are you okay?***

Raven slams her phone on the kitchen counter and steps away from it. What the fuck? What the fuck has happened? The Grimm Brothers wake up and start barking at the front door. They whine and wheedle to be let out.

A tweet comes into her head even though her phone is no longer in her hands.

@TurningTricks Evil women like you need to be taken care of and I am the man for the job. I know where you live.

She lets the dogs out and they sprint to the fence to bark at the unwelcome visitors. Her airways start closing up. She searches again for her medicine. She finds it and gives herself a double dose.

Relax, Raven, relax, she tells herself. This is not the time for an attack. But the more she tries to get air the more difficult it becomes to inhale. Her lungs turn into cold slabs of jelly incapable of oxygenating blood. Her throat starts to make a gasping sound, a terrible, dry, sucking sound, the opposite of heaving. She puts her hands around her neck as if her touch will somehow bring back her ability to breathe. She becomes dizzy. She needs a paper bag to breathe into. She needs a humidifier. Eucalyptus. She needs —

Light batters her line of sight. If she can only take one breath —

She can't feel her legs. And then there is nothing.

35 / WRONG CARPENTER

"Raven?"

Someone is standing above her. He shakes her. "Raven? Can you hear me?"

He presses his fingers against her wrist, feels a pulse. Pulls an eyelid up and checks the dilation of her pupils. Her mouth is swollen and dry, her head hurts. She assumes it's from banging it when she fell. He picks her up as if she weighs nothing, lays her gently on the couch. She wants him to stay with her but he walks away. She hears the tap running in the kitchen and he comes back with a glass of water. She smells sawdust and wood varnish.

"Are you okay?" he says, sitting next to her. "What happened? Shall I call a doctor?"

"Jesus," she says. He is illuminated by the morning light. He is wearing a crown of sunlight. His pure goodness is radiating off him.

"Not quite," he says. "Wrong carpenter, I'm afraid." He leans forward and his halo disappears. She sees his face.

"Benjamin."

"I'm going to call a doctor. Do you have a doctor?"

"I don't trust doctors."

"Shall I call your sister?"

"Don't you dare."

"I'm glad I have a key. You could've been lying here for hours."

"I think I was," says Raven, rubbing her back.

He looks at his watch. "I don't want to leave you like this, on your own."

"Why? Where are you going? Aren't you working today? I need the fence fixed. It's a security risk. Have you seen the people outside?"

"I'll send someone over. Someone I trust, to fix it."

"I don't want someone else. I want you to do it."

"I can't."

"Okay, so you're busy today. Come tomorrow."

"I can't. Look, I didn't want to have this conversation with you in your state…"

Raven sits up. "What conversation?"

He rubs his face. "It's… difficult."

"For Hex's sake, Ben, spit it out!"

He doesn't.

"Is it about the money? Didn't you get it? I transferred a hundred thousand rand to you. Is it not enough?"

“It’s not about the money.”

“Did you get it or not?”

“It hasn’t come through but that’s not the reason.”

Those fuckers! They’ve frozen my account.

“I can’t work for you anymore, Raven.”

Ben has been a constant in her life for years. There is always something at Colborn Manor that needs fixing. She can’t imagine not having him around.

“I hope you’re kidding.”

“It’s Karen. She doesn’t like me working here. She never has.”

“Karen? Why?”

“I don’t know.”

“You don’t know?”

“It’s because you’re a… witch. She doesn’t even like it when we talk. She says when I am here I need to just keep quiet and do the work as quickly as possible.”

“Well. You *are* very efficient.”

“I like you, Raven. I really do. I’ve always valued our relationship. And I enjoy working on this house. But my marriage comes first.”

“Of course,” says Raven, picturing Karen in her head and slapping her across the face. She pulls her robe tighter around her.

“She was willing to put up with it till now, but then you were on the news last night and—”

“So that’s it? You don’t care about my side of the story? About the truth? Do I think you killed someone?”

"It doesn't matter."

"Of course it matters!"

"Not to her."

Raven stands up. Wobbles a bit. She is still light-headed. He puts a steadying hand on her arm and doesn't remove it. Their decade-long friendship stands before them like a husk, outwardly solid-looking, but, on closer inspection, it can be seen that the insides have long since been demolished by termites. It turns out that a breeze is enough to carry the shell away. Were they ever really friends? Raven likes to think so, even though it makes this hurt more.

"I brought you something," he says, and hands over a bright, shiny fire extinguisher.

"A parting gift?"

"Something like that. I… worry about you. Here, alone, in this big house."

"I'm not alone," says Raven.

Ben is awkward. He touches his ear-pencil, runs a calloused hand through his hair.

"You should go," she says, but he doesn't move.

"I can't leave you like this."

She shakes her arm free of his grasp. "I don't need a knight in shining armour." She says it more to convince herself than anything else. In truth she feels as small and vulnerable as a just-shucked oyster.

36 / NARROW-MINDED MEAT-BAGS

The Grimm Brothers are unsettled. They lope around Raven in anxious loops. Lightfoot and Cocoa are hiding in the cupboard like they do when there is a thunderstorm. Max is on his bookshelf. Eli has spent the morning blaspheming to high heaven and is now helping himself to an early lunch in the potion garden.

The buzzing sound coming from outside is relentless. A swarm of bees, the voice had said. She goes to the window to have a look; parts the curtain slightly and peers out. Not only are there press teams and camera crews, but a small crowd has gathered too. Raven thinks they must be concerned neighbours — she spots a few faces she recognises — and curious bystanders who look innocent enough, but then she sees a banner. White splashed with red. 'KILLER' it says. Another poster says 'WITCHES NOT WELCOME'. As Raven watches, new people join the crowd.

"No," says Raven. "This can't be happening."

It was just a matter of time, says the voice.

Really? I'm finding it totally unexpected.

I don't think you are. They've always been in the back of your mind.

These blank-faced narrow-minded meat-bags? They have not.

Raven lets the curtain fall closed.

Who do you have in mind when you talk about persecution? It's one of your favourite topics.

I don't know. Those crazies who approach me in public restrooms. They're lone lunatics, though. They wouldn't be able to organise a crowd, to mobilise whatever is going on down there.

Think again. Think of religious fundamentalists.

They're also mad, says Raven.

And their mobilisation skills?

I guess it takes a whole lot of charisma to persuade an 11-year-old to strap on a suicide vest.

Bingo. You don't need to be sane to lead an army. In fact, as world history proves, it probably helps if you're a little off your rocker.

Raven throws some clothes on and locks the Grimm Brothers in her room with water, toys and treats. It seems to settle them, but their ears still prick up at the sounds outside, so she puts some classical music on for them too. Wonders if she should sedate them, but doesn't. At a loss as to what to do Raven goes back to her computer. She doesn't go near Twitter or Facebook, but searches for the newsclip that has everyone so riled up. It's been shared on so many news networks and personal blogs that the first five Google results pages all seem to shout her name. She hesitates and then, with a clammy finger, she clicks 'play'.

"You may never have heard of Raven Kane before but be prepared to see a lot of this particular witch's name." He flashes his famous white teeth. "You heard me correctly," he says. "Raven Kane is a practising witch. In other words she's been tricking people out of their hard-earned cash for almost fifteen years. Do you need some help with your love-life? Or your love-handles? Because Raven Kane will help you out with that! She'll wave her wand and… R500 will disappear magically from your wallet!"

"Bastard!" she says. "I've never swindled anyone."

A picture comes up. It's a screen grab of her website: her price-list. The image fades, and is replaced by a pentagram on a black background. The canned sound-effects fade in to show that the mood of the piece is now getting serious.

"But that's only half the story," Devereaux says. "As they say in literature—"

What the hell does someone like him know about literature?

"…the plot thickens. This 'charming' woman—"

The visual cuts to the video of her leaning out of her car to shout at the press.

"Get off my property," the Raven on screen yells, "or I'll set the devil hounds on you!"

The journalist pretends to clear his throat in surprise. "This charming woman is wanted for murder."

That is just not true, says Raven. She can't stand looking at his plastic-looking face anymore, his rubber lips. She stops the video and quits Google.

It's kind of true, says the voice.

It is not. I'm a suspect. I am not 'wanted for murder'. He makes it sound like there is a bounty on my head.

The crowd outside gets louder.

It's absolutely reckless with those sheeple out there.

"We have established that she is linked to the women who call themselves the Wicked Witches, the Taglock Terrors, the Twysted Sisters, who have, in the past few months, been responsible for multiple counts of vandalism, theft and abduction. These are not the kind of women we want in our neighbourhoods."

Raven clicks off. The people outside start chanting. Raven can't make out the words but their intention is clear. They want Raven gone and there seems to be no shortage of civilians who wouldn't mind achieving this.

37 / BLEEDING IN A BUSINESS SUIT

You need that fence fixed, says the voice.

"Jesus Christ!" chirps Eli from right behind Raven, making her jump a foot in the air. She puts her hand to her chest. This is not good for her health.

The doorbell rings. Since when do Pitchforks ring your bell?

Maybe it's not a Pitchfork.

"Hello?" says Raven into the intercom.

"You're expecting me," says a male voice which is muffled by the noise of the crowd around him.

It must be the new carpenter, the one Ben has sent to fix the fence. Although there is a hint of an off-purple aura of familiarity. Someone she's met before?

"Who is it?" she asks, but there's no response. Her finger hovers over the pedestrian gate button. Not wanting him to be eaten up by the crowd she presses down.

No! shouts the voice.

No?! You wait until AFTER I have pressed the button to say no?!

I didn't think you'd actually press the button!

Raven runs to the front door. Locks it. The man approaches. She sees his silhouette through the stained glass panels.

"Hello?" she says. "Who is it?"

An explosion of coloured glass. A well-polished black brogue is sticking through her door. It's attached to a leg. Raven screams. The foot disappears and is replaced by a clutching hand. She picks up the heaviest thing she can see — the poker from the fireplace — and smashes it down on the hand. There is swearing from outside the door. The hand emerges again, bleeding from the stained glass shards and before Raven manages to hit him a second time, the hand's owner manages to unlock the door from the inside. It swings open and exposes a man in a business suit, bleeding.

"So," Sheldon looks at the poker in her hand. "You were expecting me."

The dogs! Why hadn't she gotten the dogs? They are barking and scratching, trying to get out of her room.

"Get out," says Raven. Her voice sounds wrong.

"I'll leave after I get what I want from you."

They stand, full-bristle, eyes alight.

"You're not getting anything from me."

"I'm not a man who likes to hear 'no'," he says, dripping bright blood onto her pine floor.

"Get out of my house."

The Grimm Brothers are going ballistic. Raven takes a step towards her bedroom. If she can only reach that door.

Sheldon jumps at her. She tries to raise the poker to strike a blow but he wrestles it away from her. His strength is terrifying. She scratches his face. He drops the poker behind him and grabs both her wrists. She tries to knee him in the groin but he moves away in time, pushing her backwards, into the kitchen table. He pushes his whole body up against hers to keep her still. Raven tries to move, to kick, to bite, but she is pinned to the table.

"What do you want?" She tries to stay calm, not to panic, to think.

"What the fuck do you think I want?"

He is close. Too close to her. All over her. His warm breath in her ear makes her ill.

"The money," she says.

"Ah. The money. That's right. The money you stole."

"The money your father left to me in his will."

"The inheritance you swindled."

"I'll give it back to you," she says. "I'll transfer it right now."

"It's not enough."

"Eight million rand is not enough?"

"I want you to pay for what you did."

"You pressed charges. I'm under investigation. The law will follow its course."

"I want them to find every single person you have killed or maimed or cheated."

"I haven't cheated anyone. I run a legitimate business."

Sheldon laughs. Black marbles for eyes. His face is a mask.

"You're a slippery little bitch. You know what you need," he says, "you need a man to show you who's in charge."

"I know who's in charge," she says, "and it's not a man." She tries, again, to wriggle free but he slams her backwards and a shock of pain runs up her back. Sheldon bellows in anger and rips open her top. Ugly streaks of blood on milk-pale breasts.

"No!" shouts Raven. "No!"

"I'm going to show you," he says. Sheldon transfers both of her wrists to his non-injured hand and starts to unbuckle his belt.

No no no no no!

Raven screams as loudly as she can. He tries to muffle her but she bites his hand. He hits her, hard, across the face. She sees stars. She can feel his blood smeared all over her cheek. His belt is off, his pants open.

"Don't do it," she says, "You don't know what you're doing."

"Trust me," he turns her around, slams her stomach into the table, winding her. Forces open her legs. "I know exactly what I'm doing."

Don't panic, says the voice. *You are stronger than him.*

She feels his hand reach in, under her skirt and tear her underwear aside. His grip on her wrists loosens slightly as he prepares to enter her from behind and Raven takes the opportunity to wrest her right hand away from his. She snaps her black-hilted knife out of the harness and plunges it into the straining muscle of his thigh.

Sheldon yells and in his shock he lets go of Raven. She wrenches her *athamé* out of his leg, spins around and kicks him backwards.

A swift ninja kick so that he can't catch her foot and pull her over with him. Already off-balance in his pain, he falls, sprawling on the floor on his back and elbows.

"You little bitch," he hisses, trying to stand up, but she points her dagger at him in warning. He grabs hold of his punctured quadricep and roars in anger.

"Nema! Livee morf su revilled tub noishaytpment ootni ton suh deel," chants Raven, bringing the *athamé* to the centre of her chest with both hands. The blade is freshly painted in his blood.

"What… what are you saying?"

"Suh tshaiga sapsert tath yeth vigrawf eu za sespsert rua suh vigrawf." She can feel that her face is bleached by her previous terror and she knows that it's smeared with blood. She uses every ounce of power she has left to finish the spell.

It's Sheldon's turn to be terrified. His erection shrinks as she finishes the chant. "What have you done?"

Raven seals the spell with a three-fold crossing. "Only what you deserve." She gestures towards his groin. He shuffles away from her towards the door, pulls up his boxer shorts and pants as if to protect his manhood from her magic.

"You'll never be able to use it again," says Raven.

"You're lying." Sheldon stumbles into an upright position. "Don't think that this is the end of it."

"It's certainly the end of something," she says and watches him limp away.

Once he is gone she drops her tough act and falls to the floor and weeps. The Grimm Brothers seem to be launching themselves at her bedroom door trying to knock it off its hinges. She crawls, crying, over to them and opens the door. They rush right past her to follow the intruder's trail, fangs bared, barking viciously. Raven sits in her hallway, puts her arms around herself and sobs.

Once the dogs are back and climbing all over her, she gets up and finds her phone.

I need you, she types to Kruger. ***My house.***

She washes the blood off her *athamé* but it doesn't remove the negative charge. She'll have to consecrate it before she uses it again.

Her phone beeps.

I can be there in twenty minutes.

Raven starts crying again.

Bring a rape-kit.

38 / DAMAGED MANNEQUIN

Kruger gets to her in ten minutes. He breaks into the house via the back door and calls out in order not to frighten her with his sudden presence. Raven walks towards his voice.

I will be strong, she says to herself. I will be strong, but then Kruger sees her torn top and mess of a face and Raven sees his shock and they collapse together right there on the floor. Her face in his hands.

"What happened?"

She can't stand the close scrutiny. "Don't look at me," she says, twisting her head away from his searching gaze and begins crying again.

"What the fuck happened?" His voice is hoarse.

Raven is not ready to talk. They sit, entwined in each other. They hear the crowd chanting outside. The Grimm Brothers, calmer now, saunter in and lick Kruger. He sneezes, stands up, walks out of the room. Raven hears the water in the pipes in the walls. He's running her a bath. He comes back, opens up the box he has brought with him. Sneezes again.

"Hang on," she says, getting up. She fetches the antihistamine syrup from the kitchen and passes it to him. He takes a swig, then carries on unpacking the rape-kit.

"I don't need the swab," she says. "I stopped him before he could—"

Kruger closes his eyes. Relief. He sighs. Raven offers him her hand and he scrapes under her fingernails, takes a sample of the blood on her face and her palms. Transfers what he gets into an evidence bag. Seals the box, writes on it, puts it away, out of sight. He twists her hair up into a loose bun, secures it with a clip from the bowl on the table. Slowly, slowly, he undresses her. Pulls her torn shirt off as she stands there, motionless - a damaged mannequin, as if he is undressing a child. Inspects her for damage with light fingers. Photographs her swollen face, stained breasts, bruised back. Unbuttons the top of her skirt, lets it fall to the floor. He is so very gentle with her. The way he touches her tells her that he is there for her, he can protect her, but that she is still in charge.

Once he is finished with collecting evidence he sweeps her up and carries her to her bathroom. He unclasps her bra, removes her torn panties and helps her into the warm water. The underwear goes into another plastic bag which he labels with a sticker. She thinks he will leave her now, but he doesn't. Kruger gets some cotton-wool pads off the dresser. He soaks one in the warm water and uses it to wipe her face. Once it is brown with blood he bins it and wets another one. Raven lies back and closes her eyes. She says nothing; thinks of nothing. All that is in her mind is the sensation of the warm cotton-wool and the nearness of Kruger. She counts seven pads to get her skin clean.

When Raven opens her eyes all she sees are hundreds of empty bathroom tiles. She climbs out of the water and wraps herself in her gown. Has Kruger left? Is she alone? She starts to feel the beginning of panic. Ribbons of yellow adrenaline reach for her bowels. She can't be alone. Not like this. And not with all those Pitchforks outside. She rushes to her bedroom which is empty and then back through the house to the empty couches in the lounge. Her lungs threaten to close.

"Raven," says Kruger. He's in the kitchen. Steam floats out of the spout of the just-boiled kettle. He has two mugs out and honey. A tea-towel over his shoulder. It's one of a pair, with a matching apron, picked up at a recent craft fair. It says, in an old-world font: A BUN IN THE COVEN.

"Kruger."

Has she ever been this grateful for another person's presence in her house?

"I didn't know which one to use," he says, gesturing at the various teas and herbs on the counter. He picks up a sachet of small sticks, labelled, in her handwriting, as Linden Flowers. "And I didn't want to accidentally put a spell on you."

"I thought you had gone."

Kruger leaves the tea and turns his whole body towards her. "You're not getting rid of me that easily."

Raven steps closer to him. She wants his arms around her. She wants to smell his skin. He doesn't move. She gets closer, and closer still until their thighs are just touching. Raven shakes her gown off; it falls in a pile.

Kruger looks at the birthmark on her chest. He traces the edge of its leaf-shape. Nothing is rushed. He puts his hands in her hair, looks at her eyes, her lips.

"This is a terrible idea," he says, and kisses her long and tender.

It begins as a comfort: his lips; stubble; hot fragrance. His wide chest and undemanding mouth. Un-rushed. It's so beautiful and real and soft that Raven wishes she could crawl up into this moment and never leave. How could a simple kiss, a speechless act of mouth, be so perfect, so all-encompassing? They luxuriate in it and Raven wonders how she has ever thought life was complete without this: this moment, this act, this man.

But then there is a shift: a falling forward. There is a dark rolling thunder that is bowling towards them. It smacks their bodies together and their affection evaporates, sublimates – blasted away by light and stardust. In its place is pure desire. A red beam of purpose. Kruger's grip on Raven tightens.

They kiss and clutch towards the bedroom. The world tilts sideways. She winces at the twinge of a bruised wrist. Kruger stops. She sees the conflict of his hunger and his restraint. She wants him inside her.

"I want you," she says, breathing hard. "I want you now."

"Are you sure?" He touches her bruised eye.

She moves his hand from her face down to her breast. She won't have Sheldon in this bed.

"Yes. Yes, yes, yes," she says as she moves her body against his. Kruger growls, pins her down with a hard kiss, then moves his mouth to her breasts. She arches her back in pleasure.

Yes, she wants Kruger's hands to obliterate Sheldon's vile handprints. Yes, she is reclaiming her body and her sex. But it's more than that. It's apart from the violence. She wants Kruger more in this moment than she has ever wanted anything in her life. He moves his tongue down past her stomach and she moans loudly, bites her lip. Yes, it's more than that, so much more than that: it is its own exploding star. Yes, yes, yes.

"You were right," says Raven, as they lie, skin-to-skin, in tangled white sheets.

"About?" Kruger strokes her hair.

"It was a terrible idea."

They smile at each other.

He shakes his head. "How did we get here?"

"It was just a matter of time," says Raven. "I knew that when I met you."

"You knew we'd be in this... position?"

"This position and many others, I hope."

Kruger turns onto his back, looks at the ceiling. Raven expected this, too. She sees his scars then. Two unhappy marks — she guesses of bullet origin — one varnishing his ribcage, the other tucked into his stomach. She moves to touch them, but he catches her hand.

"Now is when you tell me that this can never happen again," she says.

"This can never happen again," he says. "How did you know?"

"I'm a witch, remember?"

"You've seen the future?"

"In a manner of speaking."

"And... does it happen again?"

Raven rolls on top of him. "Of course it does."

39 / PETTING, HYPNOSIS, BLADE

"You can't stay here," Kruger says, pulling his shirt on and buttoning the front.

"I don't have a lot of other options."

"I'd take you to my place, but —"

"But it wouldn't look very good, shacking up with the main suspect in your high-profile murder case."

"Why don't you go to a hotel? Somewhere close, but… low-key."

"Only if you promise to visit."

He stays quiet for a while as if trying to work out how to let her down gently. He clears his throat. "I should say no, of course — but I'm not sure I'll be able to keep myself away."

They look at each other. There is still longing between them.

"What about the Grimm Brothers? The cats? The rest of the zoo?"

"I'll come around. Check on them. Feed them. I've grown quite fond of the devil hounds."

"Have you seen how many cameras are out there?"

"You have a point. What about a friend?"

Raven shakes her head.

"Family? Neighbour?"

She shakes her head faster. "No. I'll arrange a pet-sitting service."

Kruger picks up the rape-kit. "I don't want to leave you here on your own."

"I'll be okay."

"Let me give you a lift."

It will be difficult to get Morris out of the front entrance with all the Pitchforks there.

"Okay," she says, and gets her travel bag out of the cupboard, throws in a couple of dresses, a handful of lingerie, a toiletry bag and her laptop. Zipping it up, she slings it over her shoulder, grabs her laptop bag. "I'm ready."

"Any particular preference?"

"Hmm?" Raven is half out of the car window trying to see what is happening at the front of her house while they idle around the back.

"You want to take a look? At the front?"

"Yes," she says, scuttling back inside.

He reaches around to the back seat, grabs a cap, puts it on her head. She already has her sunglasses on.

"You could be movie star," he says. "Incognito."

"Look at us. A movie star and a supermodel. In the same *bakkie.*"

"This is NOT a '*bakkie*'. It's a Toyota Hilux."

She sinks down lower in her seat. They cruise around the block and Raven is reminded of how badly the perimeter fence is in need of repair. The replacement carpenter hasn't shown up —

"My God," says Kruger.

"You sound like Eli."

"That is a large crowd."

"You'd think they'd get bored standing around."

"Nah. It's probably the most exciting thing on their calendar."

"Is that… is that a refreshment table?"

"Even stupid people need to snack."

"Incredible."

"Is it?"

"I mean, it's incredible how our generation is so time-poor, but here are fifty people who are just hanging around on a pavement on a Friday, shooting the breeze, painting banners and eating biltong and pretzel sticks."

"I'll talk to a colleague. Get a team to disperse the crowd."

She doesn't want rubber bullets and teargas on her account.

"You shouldn't. It's a free country. They're not doing any harm."

She spots a poster that says DEVIL WOMAN. Didn't they know that the devil was a recent Christian invention?

"Besides, it might incense them."

They drive away. There is an official-looking envelope in the dash console. A bill, or a notification of some sort. Raven can just make out the company name on the logo — BigBuild — and the last part of his address. Hyde Park Heights.

"Any preference with regards to a hotel?"

"*The Regent,* in Rosebank. They don't mind witches there."

"I won't ask how you know that."

"It's where we have the PaganCon every year. They are very... accommodating."

"They let you slaughter chickens in the conference room?"

"Something like that."

She knows he's joking, but she has slaughtered her fair share of chickens in her lifetime. She does it as humanely as possible, of course. Petting, hypnosis, blade. People might think it's barbaric, but she finds buying pre-chopped animal flesh in white styrofoam containers a great deal more problematic, morally speaking. At least her chickens have led a good free-range life, free of growth hormones and antibiotics.

"You okay?" says Kruger, putting his hand over hers.

Raven nods.

"I feel like I lost you there."

"I was thinking about the chickens."

Kruger's radio crackles. He puts his earphones in and calls in to the station.

"Uh-huh," he says to them. "Uh-huh. Uh-huh."

When he disconnects he says to Raven, "Your friends are causing trouble again."

"Friends?"

"Your Taglock Terrors."

"They are not MY Taglock Terrors."

He keeps quiet.

"Why are they calling you about them? What do you have to do with them?"

"I asked to be kept informed."

They travel in silence for a few minutes. Raven's curiosity gets the better of her.

"What have they done?"

"They erected some kind of banner. At the courthouse. Or, more likely, wrapped the building up, like a Christo & Jeanne-Claude installation."

"What does a South African police detective know about Christo installations?"

"I've been to one. Switzerland. '97."

"You keep surprising me."

"The feeling is mutual."

"So the Wicked Witches are now installing public art?"

"Not quite. They graffiti'd some political slogan all over it."

Raven checks Twitter. Sees an Instagram photo of the building that is being circulated with the hashtag #MolefeMustGo.

"Who is Molefe?"

"He's a judge," says Kruger. "Known for his inappropriate rulings."

"What do you mean?"

"He's got a reputation for being too lenient. He sees a lot of cases of abuse. There have been NPOs who have tried to get him removed but it never seems to work."

She zooms in on the image.

#LastWarning. #LockUpMolefe.

Another spraypainted slogan says: *You thought you could bury us. You didn't know we were seeds.*

It's a Mexican proverb. Raven thinks of her guerrilla gardening, her rainbow-coloured wildflower seedbombs. How mild her own rebellion is compared to these renegade witches.

"That doesn't sound too bad," she says.

"It's bad," says Kruger. "You shouldn't threaten judges. Not when they're so clearly in someone's pocket."

They arrive at the hotel and Kruger looks for the parking-lot.

"Just drop me off in front," says Raven. "I know you need to get away." She gestures at the evidence he needs to take in to the station.

"You'll need to come in to the station, you know."

"*Ja*, I don't think I'm going to do that."

He slows to a stop, rubs his stubble.

"You need to report the assault. The attempted rape."

"They wouldn't take it seriously."

"I'll take it seriously."

"They wouldn't believe me."

"That's what the evidence kit is for."

"It's hardly conclusive. It proves that I scratched his cheek, that we fought. Nothing more."

"It's something."

"It's my word against his. A successful businessman with a lot to lose versus a delinquent witch with a criminal record."

"But he did it. He needs to be held accountable."

"He will be," says Raven. She knows that it's true.

Kruger doesn't want to leave her. "You'll be okay?"

"I'm a big girl. I'll be okay."

He touches her cheekbone where the swelling has gone down. A patina of purple.

"How is your face?"

"Fine. Healing."

"How is… everything else?"

She doesn't know the answer. Numb. Traumatised. Angry. Anxious. Still tingling from Kruger's touch. She leans forward and they kiss.

He gets her bag and goes to open her door but she beats him to it. She waves as he drives away, and only remembers when she turns to go inside that she is still wearing his cap.

PART III

EARTH

41 / THE REGENT

"Sorry, it's still not going through," says the receptionist at the Regent. She's flustered. She fixes her twitching eyes on the terminal in front of her.

"I can't think why," says Raven, smiling. "I just used it a moment ago. Why don't you try it one more time?"

Raven knows that The Regent's policy is a deposit upfront or no access. They may be accommodating in many ways when it comes to a large annual conference, but this particular rule is never broken, as if they make every employee write it in their own blood.

"I don't think it will—"

"Just try it," says Raven. "Please."

The woman purses her lips and tries to put the transaction through one last time. It's declined.

Bastards! Raven knows her account is frozen, but her credit card? Now it's her turn to be nervous. Her cheeks bloom pink.

The receptionist hands her back the card. "We also accept cash," she says, hope dawning on her lavishly made-up face.

Raven punches the desk.

"And EFTs!" the woman says, then gathers herself. "And EFTs. The bank details are on the invoice."

"Wonderful," says Raven.

The receptionist gets her room key-card ready for her, but doesn't hand it over. There is no way Raven will be able to transfer the money electronically.

"On second thought," says Raven, smoothing out the invisible hair on her arm, "let me use my other card."

She takes out her phone and scrolls to her photo album. Finds the pictures of Jessica's credit card.

"May I have the card?" asks the woman.

"I don't have the actual card on me," Raven smiles, "but I do have the details. Can you process it manually?"

The receptionist hesitates.

"Look," says Raven. "I'm a regular guest. I pay my bills. You can check my records."

The woman squirms. Looks around for help. No one is there apart from an ancient cleaning lady pushing a vacuum cleaner around the balding maroon carpet of the lobby.

"I'm sorry," she shrugs, "It goes against our policy. I'd lose my job."

Raven takes off her sunglasses. The receptionist's eyes widen as she sees her bruised face. She takes Raven's phone and dials Jessica's card details into the merchant device; it prints and spits out the receipts. She pushes the room key-card along the counter.

Raven dismisses the porter's offer of help and carries her bags up to her regular room. Closes the door. Lies down and stares at the pressed ceiling. This bed may have been slept in by a thousand different strangers but at the moment it seems like it's all hers and no one can hurt her here. She imagines black water rising from the floor and covering everything but the bed. Drowning everyone but her on her freshly ironed cotton island.

There is a knock on the door.

"Go away!" shouts Raven.

Well, sighs the voice.

Where the fuck have you been?

I've been here. I'm always here.

I needed you.

No, you didn't.

How do you know?

I'm here when you need me. Even if you think you don't. That's how it works.

Tell me how it works.

I'm your rational mind. Your Voice of Reason.

No you're not.

Okay. Fine. I'm your intuition.

Raven laughs out loud.

You wouldn't know what intuition was if it bit you on the arse.

I'm hurt and offended, says the voice.

Typical.

I don't follow.

Bloody typical that I get the intuition that doesn't believe in magic. I'm a witch, for Goddess's sake. My intuition is supposed to be the thing pointing me *in the direction of magic.* Witches are witches BECAUSE OF THEIR INTUITION. No wonder I'm so conflicted.

Are you finished?

Yes. For now.

Good. We need a plan.

This hotel is my plan.

They're going to kick you out in 23 hours.

Good point.

Where will we go?

I don't know. I'm tired and hurt. I need to recover. I just want to lie here and forget about everything that's happened.

We need a safe place to stay. And money. And, most importantly, we need to prove that you didn't kill Sheldon Bond Senior.

Well. That will be difficult. Seeing as —

Okay, we need to get rid of evidence, then. Before it's discovered.

Raven sits up on the bed, reaches for the hotel phone. Dials a number. It rings three times before being answered.

"Raven," says the person on the other side. "I've been expecting your call."

42 / DEMONESS

"How did you know it was me?" says Raven.

Luella chuckles. "I'm a good witch."

"A proficient witch, anyway," says Raven.

"*Touché.*"

"Can we chat online, somehow? In a… secure environment?"

"Nevermore?"

"I still don't know what that is," says Raven, feeling a hundred years old.

"Are you on the dark web?"

"No."

"I'll send you a link and an encryption key. Let me know your identity when you have it and I'll make contact with you. Don't use your real name or any username you've used in the past."

"Okay."

"Don't use your email address or anything that can be linked back to you."

"Got it."

Raven opens her laptop and follows Luella's instructions. She spirals into the virtual onion that will hide her IP address. When prompted, she calls herself Lone_Wolf and sends the name to Luella via WhatsApp. Soon, an avatar named Demoness pops up.

[Demoness has joined the conversation]

Demoness> Greetings.

Lone_Wolf>> I need your help.

Demoness> This isn't about the Twysted Sisters?

Lone_Wolf>> Why?? What have you been up to?

Demoness> Nothing. *Whistles*

Lone_Wolf>> Jesus. As if I don't have enough to —

Demoness> Ah, relax. It's nothing.

Lone_Wolf>> Nothing? That makes me more worried.

Demoness> What do you need help with? More product? It's difficult at the moment —

Lone_Wolf>> I need to know how you get it. The Poppy.

Demoness> I can't tell you that.

Lone_Wolf>> I need to make sure that it can never be traced back to me.

Demoness> If anyone knew I was siphoning Poppy I'd

lose my job. I'd be arrested. I'd lose my licence. I'm very careful.

Lone_Wolf>> That's what I said. And now I'm being investigated.

Demoness> I know (!)

Lone_Wolf>> You and the rest of the world!

Demoness> Don't let the sheeple get to you.

Lone_Wolf>> It's difficult when they are camping on my verge like hobo pirates. Do you know that they have set up a refreshment table?

Demoness> You know you did the right thing. That's all that matters.

Lone_Wolf>> You're young.

Demoness> What's that supposed to mean?

Lone_Wolf>> Life isn't as simple as that. People get jailed for doing the 'right thing' all the time.

Demoness> What about running? Leaving the country?

Lone_Wolf>> I'm too old.

Demoness> You're not old.

Lone_Wolf>> I don't have the energy.

Demoness> We can help you. The coven, I mean.

Lone_Wolf>> I don't want anyone else brought into this mess.

Demoness> We don't mind getting into trouble.

Lone_Wolf>> I’ve noticed!

Demoness> Let us know if you change your mind.

Lone_Wolf>> What have you lot been up to? I need to plan my damage control.

Demoness> Gosh, is that the time? I need to go!

Lone_Wolf>> Don’t you dare!

Demoness> ...

[Demoness has left the conversation]

Raven snaps her laptop shut. Incorrigible, that witch, but she can’t help feeling a glint of affection for her. She drums her fingers on the table, wracks her brain for any kind of evidence they can use to arrest her. Sheldon’s body was cremated a year ago so there are no remains to exhume. There had been no autopsy, probably due to the advanced stage of his disease. So they don’t have a weapon and they don’t have a body.

What they do have is a motive, says the voice.

My motive was pure.

It was just a job for you.

It’s never just a ‘job’.

Your motive certainly doesn’t look ‘pure’ when you look at your bank account.

It was his choice. He wanted it. He contracted me to do it.

That doesn’t make it less illegal.

I am NOT going to prison. My magic will dry up in there for good. I may as well jump off a cliff.

Let's not get ahead of ourselves.

I need to get out of here.

No, wait. Where are you going? We need a plan.

I need a plan. A strategy. I need to know what they have on me.

Wait, says the voice.

Raven's cell phone rings: unknown number. Luella? Kruger?

"Hello?"

"I'm looking for Raven Kane," says a half-familiar voice.

"This is Raven."

"I am calling you to inform you that we will be doing an inspection of your animals today at Elderberry Lane. If their condition is found wanting we will be removing them."

"What the hell are you talking about? Who's 'we'?"

"The SPCA, ma'am. We've had numerous complaints and calls regarding the conditions of neglect of your pets."

"Conditions of neglect? Are you insane? Do you know how much a bag of *Kitty DeLite* costs?"

"They will be put in a place of safety pending further investigation."

"They will NOT."

It's probably that bloody Bishop.

"I'm sorry, but we are just following procedure."

"You can take your procedure and shove it up your—"

"Thank you for your time, Mrs Kane. The team will be there in about an hour's time."

"I'll be waiting for them," says Raven, "with a shotgun."

She wets the hotel handtowel with water and hand soap and scrubs under her arms. Drags a brush through her hair, then balls it up and hides it under Kruger's cap. Grabs her wallet, for all the good it will do her, and her laptop. Zips them into a backpack. Puts her hand on the hotel door handle.

What was that sound? says the voice.

What sound?

You heard it.

I don't know. I don't have time to think about it.

It sounded like...

Like a car arriving at a hotel. In a hurry. I'm sure that's not very unusual.

Look out of the window.

Are you mad? We don't have time to waste. We need to get home.

Look out of the window.

Raven swears loudly and goes to the window. Pulls the blinds aside. A car has parked badly right outside the reception. Two men jump out. They are in a hurry.

That's a police car, says the voice.

I don't see a flashing light.

It's a Toyota Corolla. Standard police issue. And those men are cops.

They do look like cops. I wonder what they are doing here.

Hmm.

What? You think they're here for me? But there's no arrest warrant.

That you know of.

I can't get arrested. The animals. My magic. I have to find out what evidence they have against me and get rid of it. I can't do that if I'm in jail.

There is a loud knocking on the door. Raven's heart practically jumps out of her chest like a cartoon character. She wants to run, to climb out of the window, to lock herself in the bathroom, but she is frozen to the spot. Her legs aren't obeying her simple commands. The door clicks and opens and she reaches for her knife, but it's not there.

It's the bartender from her previous visit. The one who brought her ice. The one who —

She's confused. There is urgency stamped all over his face.

"Come with me," he says, putting out his hand. "Come!"

Raven abandons her modest bag of clothes on the bed but grabs her laptop bag and follows him out the hotel room and into the emergency stairwell. He closes the door behind them and looks through the square pane of grubby glass.

"Follow me," he says and they run down the stairs. One flight, two flights. They open the door into the basement. It's cool and dark and empty. He jogs to the service gate and takes out a set of keys with trembling fingers, presses the worn button on a remote and the red gate slides open. Raven darts out and he presses the button again to close it.

"Take a *tuk-tuk* to get away," he says. "There's a pick-up point on the next block."

"Thank you," she says. She doesn't even know his name. She puts on her sunglasses and runs.

Safe and sweating in a *tuk-tuk,* Raven tells the driver to take her to Colborn Manor.

You're going home? asks the voice. *It's probably swarming with cops.*

I don't have a choice. They're going to take my animals.

You'll get caught.

There is no way I'm letting those people put my kids in cruel wire cages. Not even for an hour.

You're going to be put in your own wire cage. And it'll be for longer than an hour.

It's a chance I'm going to have to take. Also, if I'm going to be on the run, I'm not going to get very far without money or a car. I need to get Morris.

43 / A VIOLENT JIGSAW PUZZLE

I'm going to smile, let her in and let her do the inspection. When she sees that the animals are fine, she'll leave and I'll run.

What happened to you? asks the voice.

That is a very open-ended question.

You used to be a pessimist.

You preferred it?

It was more realistic.

Raven does a quick round of topping up the animals' food bowls. She gives the Grimm Brothers an abrupt brushing, and, realising that they are overdue for a bath, uses some Fabreze on their coats. She hauls out some new squeaky toys from the top of the pet supplies' cupboard and gives them one each. She throws them as far as she can into the garden at the back and closes the door to the verandah so that they won't be able to come into the house and jump up on the visitor. She'll take the SPCA representative outside once things have settled. The cats aren't around but she puts some catnip on their beds, just in case, tops up their filtered water.

"Eli," she snaps and Eli looks at her in alarm. She's nervous and tries to calm herself by speaking slowly. "We're having a visitor - an important visitor. Let's try to make a good impression, try not to blaspheme. Some people find it offensive."

"Salad," chirps the bird.

"Salad?"

"Salad," says Eli.

Surprised, she gives him a cherry tomato from the fridge.

He gets excited, *cha-chas* on his perch. "God Almighty!"

The doorbell rings. Raven looks through the gap in the curtains. A woman stands at the pedestrian gate. She is wearing a wide-brimmed sunhat; Raven can't see her face. The protestors, strangely, don't seem to be bothering her. They're not crowding around her and shoving banners in her face. It's hot and most of them have crammed into the small patches of tree-shade. One or two of them give the visitor a wave and a thumbs-up. Raven's instinct whispers to her to not let the woman in, but then she thinks of her animals, and presses the button that opens the gate. The front door is jagged with its missing pieces — a violent jigsaw puzzle — but the stained glass on the floor has been swept up. Kruger must have done it while she was in the bath. The door reminds her of her previous unwelcome visitor and she feels a shot of adrenaline stream through her body. Despite her foreboding, Raven opens it and stands aside.

The woman nods her way in, face still obscured. An unsettling familiarity trails with her through the door. Raven fake-smiles and tries to make conversation. Should she mention that she doesn't really own a shotgun? Offer lemonade? The woman wrings her hands.

"I don't know why YOU'RE nervous," says Raven. "I'm the one who —"

The woman takes off her hat and her face is revealed. Raven's veins solidify with dread.

"You don't remember me."

Raven stares at her. "Of course I remember you."

44 / EXODUS 22 VERSE 18

"You're not from the SPCA," says Raven.

"No," the woman says. "I'm not."

"But you phoned me —"

"My team said that you were out."

"Your team?"

"My people outside."

"You organised the picketing?"

"You give me too much credit. I didn't need to organise anything."

"Why...? The SPCA?"

"I didn't know where you were. It was the only way to get you to come home."

The woman lets go of the crucifix that hangs around her neck on a cheap, gold chain. Flea-market treasure. Raven remembers the pale, chunky neck; the shivering indignation.

"You're Celeste's sister." Raven can't understand why she's here. Eli coos.

"I have a name. But I didn't expect you to remember it."

"Danielle."

"So I did make an impression."

"How is Celeste?" asks Raven. "Is she okay? The baby? Is that why you're here?"

"Celeste is fine. My issue is with you."

"Could we possibly do this another time? As you can see, I'm otherwise occupied." She gestures towards the broken door and the Pitchforks outside.

"I am here in consolidation with The People. I've come to make you repent."

"Repent?"

"For your ungodly ways."

Raven laughs. She's relieved; her shoulders relax. Her animals are safe. "Have you met my neighbour? I'm sure you two will get on famously."

"For your evil-doing."

"My 'evil-doing'? Please elaborate. This'll be fun. Shall I get some popcorn?"

"I know what you did."

"What I did? I helped your sister conceive after six years of trying."

"Don't make it sound like a miracle."

"Well, 'miracle' is a strong word."

"I know what you did. It was a trick. A dirty, dishonest trick."

It's impossible that she knows what Raven did to get Celeste pregnant. Absolutely impossible. Unless —

"Holy Hecate," says Raven. "You're sleeping with the Orangutan!"

Danielle glares at her. "Excuse me?"

"Holy Hecate!" chirps Eli, making Danielle jump.

"The only way you could possibly know what happened," says Raven, "is if you're having an affair with your sister's husband."

"Rubbish!" she says, but her face and neck flush with the scarlet truth.

The Sumatran Orangutan is sleeping with both sisters. That's why he never wanted to talk to Celeste about their intimate relations. He wasn't being shy or conservative, he was being a bastard.

"You know you're fertile but you're not getting pregnant. That's how you know he's sterile."

"It's not true," Danielle says, going quiet. They stand there, stiff-limbed.

"Look," says Raven. "I don't care what you do with your personal life, it's none of my business. I'd appreciate it if you'd return the courtesy."

Danielle mumbles something and reaches into her bag. Another Christian pamphlet? Goddess knows this house is a magnet for them. But what she draws out of her bag isn't a magic ticket at all, but a small, stump-nosed pistol.

Raven takes a couple of steps back. "Whoa."

The weapon shakes in her unpractised hand.

"Danielle. You're not thinking clearly. Put the gun away."

"I'm thinking very clearly." She flicks the safety-catch off.

"You're a Christian. You're not supposed to kill people."

"Exodus 22 verse 18: 'Thou shall not suffer a witch to live.'"

"The Bible also says you should stone non-virgins and that slavery is cool, and not to wear polyester, which I'm sure you're dressed in right now."

"You think you're so *clever.*"

"Well—"

"Well, I'm the one with the gun now so you need to listen to me."

Are there bullets in the pistol? Would she really come over with a loaded gun? Or is it just a prop to scare her? It's a small gun. It could be a toy. But there are sparks in Danielle's messy bird's nest of an aura. It's probably best to assume the worst.

"Danielle, I'm willing to listen. I'll make some tea. Put the gun down."

"You are going to confess and repent, and then you're going to turn yourself in."

"Okay," fibs Raven. "I'll do that."

Mad yellow light in her eyes.

"Did you hear me? I'll do that. I have the captain's number on my phone. I'll call him and tell him I'm handing myself in."

"For murder," says Danielle. "For countless murders and acts against God."

"Yes."

"You need to make a list of names. You need to be made accountable. How many people have you killed? How many people's souls have you dispatched to the devil?"

"Witches don't believe in the devil. It's a Christian invention —"

"Don't get smart. How many?"

"I don't know."

Danielle blinks. "You don't know how many people you've killed?"

"No. I don't keep count."

"You are the very instrument of Satan."

"So I've heard."

"Satan!" chirps Eli.

She looks annoyed. "Only God has the right to take lives."

"Which he doesn't seem reluctant to exercise," says Raven.

Danielle is sweating now. She places her finger firmly on the trigger. "You're not taking me seriously."

"I'm sorry. I just... I'm finding it difficult to get my head around it all."

She knows she should be trying to appease her but Danielle's logic is making Raven's head want to explode.

"It's simple. Repent and stay alive."

"What I'm finding confusing is... I have a Christian in my home, who got in by lying, who is threatening to murder me... because... God is the only one allowed to kill?"

"Thou shalt not suffer a witch to live."

"So you keep saying."

"Repent!" she shouts, wild-eyed. "Repent! Let the holy blood of Jesus Christ wash you clean!"

"Jesus Christ!" shouts Eli and Danielle loses her temper. She swings the gun towards the African Grey and pulls the trigger. The pistol makes a popping sound. The bird erupts in a whump of feathers, but it's the fright that's done it, not the bullet, which lodges in the lounge wall behind his perch. He flaps his way towards the closed verandah door; flies hard into the glass and knocks himself out. He lies on the floor, quiet and unmoving.

"Bitch!" yells Raven going for the gun. Danielle shoots again and Raven feels the bullet whizzing by her ear. She dives at the woman but her weight is not enough to knock her over. Instead, there is a smashing of flesh and bone as Raven elbows Danielle in the stomach. Another bullet rips into the couch where Lightfoot usually sleeps. Raven manages to get her hands on the firearm and points it away from them at the lounge window, and, with a bang, that shatters too, raining crystals of light all over the floor.

"Stop it!" she yells. "Stop it before someone gets hurt!"

Raven refuses to be attacked, again, in her own house. She will not allow it to happen. She is not a victim.

"Devil woman!" shouts Danielle, as if possessed by some strange force. "Your evil ends today!"

Raven summons all the dark energy she can to wrestle with Danielle. They fall to the floor and roll and Danielle's bulk crushes the breath from Raven. The woman slams Raven's bruised cheek on the floor, exploding her vision with stars. Raven can't see, can't breathe. She grapples blindly for the hard metal of the gun between them; knows she has to redirect the barrel, but Danielle is so heavy and so strong. There's no way she'll be able to get control of the pistol. They struggle on the floor, rolling, gasping, groaning. Raven feels her strength fade; senses she's losing the fight. She knows that all Danielle has to do is pull the trigger and it'll all be over. She has to do something. She gathers all the power she can and, with a yell, tries to push Danielle off her. It doesn't work. Danielle heaves her weight up and down again, body-slamming Raven, knocking her head, sending a buzzing pain ricocheting inside her skull.

Raven pokes Danielle hard in the eye and she cries out. She does it again, much harder, so that it seems she will dislodge the eyeball if she keeps pressing. Danielle is forced to choose between her eye and the gun. She puts one hand up to her face to protect it, allowing Raven to get a better grip on the handle, but Danielle's trigger-finger remains firmly in place.

Raven growls. "Let… me… go!"

Slowly she edges the barrel away from herself. The deranged woman starts screaming.

"Never! I'll never let you go! You'll burn in hell! Burn in hell!"

The gun goes off and there is a popping sound between them. Despite the muted sound, it sends a shockwave through Raven's torso. She locks eyes with Danielle, their bodies clasped together, connected by the spinning force of life and death. Intensely intimate. They breathe each other's breath as hot fluid leaks between them soaking Raven's shirt.

In that moment they are one, as two people are able to become one. Sisters; lovers; friends. But they are none of these, they are opposites. They are yin and yang. The golden crucifix versus the silver wolf.

There is a look of satisfaction on Danielle's face. Has the woman killed her? She wants to look down but the shock has turned her rigid. Somehow she thinks that, if she can look down, she'll be able to tell from the colour whose blood it is. If it's red, she can lean into death - a tender exhalation of relief. If it's black blood then she has been lucky. Maybe the gun was her magic ticket after all.

45 / TWIN RORSCHACHS

Raven finally draws away from Danielle and they both lie, limp, on the floor, with matching bloodstains. Twin Rorschachs, in crimson. But Raven's stain doesn't flourish, not like Danielle's, whose polyester florals turn a clammy red. Her satisfied look changes into one of confusion, but only for a second, and then she loses consciousness and the pistol falls from her flaccid hand.

She's barely breathing and her chest movements become shallower.

She's still alive. I should call an ambulance.

But she doesn't move.

And the police. I should call the police.

Gradually, Danielle's twisted aura fades and then there is no more breathing at all. The finality of the situation starts to lose its blurry edges.

Holy shit. Holy shit. Holy shit. I've just killed someone.

Don't be so melodramatic, says the voice.

Melodramatic? Are you not in the same room with me? What part of a bloody corpse and a smoking gun appears to you as non-melodramatic?

I don't think that's a word.

Are you fucking kidding me?

You're always saying that death is nothing to be afraid of. That it's just a –

Yes, but… it's the violence. It's the violence of it.

It feels like her soul has an oily smear of black on it that it's never had before.

It's not like you killed her in cold blood.

Yes. Yes. It was self-defence.

In fact, I'm not sure that you were the one who pulled the trigger.

My finger was on the trigger.

So was hers.

I think I may have pulled the trigger.

No one has to know that.

No one has to know that? I'll know that! And how am I going to explain a dead body in my house?

You're not.

If you think I am capable of wrapping her up in a tarpaulin and dumping her body in a river somewhere you overestimate my talents.

I'm not saying you should hide it forever –

Hide HER. Hide HER forever.

— I'm not advising you to hide her body forever. It'll be a temporary solution. Just until the other thing blows over.

The other thing?

The other murder case.

Are we actually having this conversation?

It's not a dream, if that's what you mean.

How do you know?

I'm not in your dreams. It's no place for a voice of reason.

So I need to hide her. Where?

She looks heavy, which means your options are limited.

The attic would be a good place.

There's no way you'd be able to get her up there. Not on your own.

And it's not like I can call a neighbour for help.

Ha, says the voice.

What about the Grimm Brothers? They're really strong.

You want to tie a corpse to the Grimm Brothers?

Huskies do it.

With sleds. In the snow. Not up creaky wooden ladders into attics with 100kg worth of dead body.

I didn't really mean it. I'm just thinking out loud.

Well, if we can't take her up, then maybe we should be going in the other direction.

Hey?

What about the basement – á la Fritzle?

I don't have a basement.

You know what I mean - that space under the suspended floorboards where you and Jess used to play and come up covered with sand and spiderwebs.

Raven doesn't have many memories of playing with her sister but she does remember that. They used to raid the pantry for tins of strawberry Nesquik and Eno and spoon the powders into their mouths — home-made sherbet — and call it a picnic. By eight or nine years old they were too big to fit in that shallow space and Raven hasn't thought about it for over twenty years.

The trapdoor is in the hallway, under the oriental.

I know where the trapdoor is.

Raven pulls the Persian rug aside and there it is: a square of timber. A portal. She struggles with the rusty handle. Her arms feel weak. She gives it one really hard pull and almost falls over with it as it opens. She lies on the floor and sticks her head through the hole, into the dark, expecting to see a rusted tin of Nesquik, or an abandoned doll, but instead, there is a shoebox wrapped in brown paper and string. It says 'Stephen' on the lid, in Brenna's faded handwriting.

Raven reaches in and hauls it up. What on earth could this be? She wants to open it immediately, but there is a large Danielle-shaped carcass in her peripheral vision that reminds her that she doesn't have any time to waste. She goes to fetch the old metal trunk she keeps in her office, empties it of books and out-dated philtre recipes — eyes of newt are especially difficult to find nowadays — and drags it into the hallway. She lowers it through the trapdoor, hefting it inelegantly into the breathing space under the wooden floor. Ironic that it's called a breathing space, she thinks, when it is to become someone's tomb. She opens the lid and pours all the ice she has into the trunk and follows it with a two-litre bottle of bleach.

I see those episodes of CSI are finally paying off, says the voice.

Raven fetches her hand-mirror and kneels beside the body which seems to have shrunk in the last twenty minutes. She holds the mirror to Danielle's mouth. The glass remains clear.

"Right," says Raven out loud. "She's definitely dead."

She tries to bolster her courage to touch the corpse. She has to put her mind at rest that Danielle is well and truly departed. Already she can imagine the nightmares: Danielle waking up in the trunk, shivering, trying to scratch her way out. Danielle, with a black hole in her stomach, standing in her bedroom doorway watching her sleep while her dress drips on the floor. Danielle leaning over her chest with a sharp stake and a mallet.

The idea of Danielle trying to kill her (again) gives her the momentum to confront the body. With steady hands she grasps the woman's ankles but the sensation of the still, dead flesh makes her recoil. She takes a breath and tries again. The corpse is as heavy as she expects. She drags her along the floor in creeping inches. Eventually they reach the trapdoor and Raven musters all the strength she has to push and pull Danielle through the opening until she falls, head-first, onto the lip of the trunk. Then she climbs down into the space with her and contorts her limbs so that she fits into the metal chest. Human Tetris, she thinks, like one of those crazy Japanese game shows. Hopefully the abiding principle of Tetris now also applies: Fit In and Disappear.

Raven has to use brute force to thrust the woman's head down towards her body and she hears a snap as she does so — a chicken's wishbone cracking — which makes her feel ill. She turns away, on her haunches, to vomit, but the damp black air is like a cool facecloth on her cheeks and the impulse to retch disappears.

It's good, says the voice, *that you feel sick.*

What now?

It shows that you're still human. You're not just a homicidal maniac stuffing a body into a box.

Not homicidal, anyway.

She closes the trunk and covers it with thick dog blankets the same colour as the shadow sand.

I'm impressed. Seriously. You did a good job, says the voice.

Well, says Raven, dusting her hands. I am nothing if not a practical witch.

46 / COPPER, LONG-HAIRED STAR

Raven hoists herself up out of the shadows. She closes the trapdoor and replaces the Persian rug. She fetches a bucket of steaming hot water, detergent, a sturdy brush and begins scrubbing the bloodstain — a copper, long-haired star — off the lounge floor. As she's scouring she keeps seeing Danielle's face, angry and yelling, purple, then surprised and peaceful-pale, as if by bleeding she had been able to let go of her outrage, as if her rage had been a gradient of crimson; paint swatches in blood. Raven keeps replaying the skirmish in her head. Could she have reacted differently? Of course, but then would she be the one stuffed, crooked-necked, under the floorboards?

Could she have defused the situation? Told Danielle what she needed to hear? She could have, but she thinks that Danielle would have brought the gun out anyway. The woman didn't come here to hear a confession, she wanted some kind of skew justice. Still, Raven scrubs, and, as she scrubs, she sees Danielle's face over and over again, hears the gunshots. Sees Eli explode. Poor Eli who limped out of the house as soon as Raven opened the stacking doors onto the verandah and hasn't been seen since.

Even with the doors and windows open Raven can't get rid of the smell. Gunpowder; cheap fragrance; fury.

When she is finished sweeping up the glass she dusts herself off outside. She strategically places a throw cushion to hide the bullet-hole in the couch. With the lounge cleaned up and the body hidden it's almost as if the terrible thing didn't happen.

It happened, says the voice.

I know it happened, says Raven. It keeps happening. In my head.

You'll have to deal with it.

I know. I will. Just not now. I need to keep moving.

How many more people are out there waiting to attack her? She has to go. She has to clear her name before the next nut-job decides that it's his or her duty to remove her particular brand of evil from the earth.

The pistol sits accusingly on the kitchen counter, black as an oil-spill. An ugly, snubby thing, as if someone had chopped its nose off. What should she do with it? On one hand it may come in handy in her defence, that the madwoman arrived bearing a loaded gun. On the other hand, there is a dead woman under her floorboards and this is the murder weapon. If she could somehow, in the future, get rid of the remains and get rid of the pistol, then the police wouldn't have a body or a weapon. And if there is no body and no weapon, then was there ever a crime?

She can't decide whether to take it with her, for disposal or self-defence, or whether to leave it in the house. The crowd outside starts baying again. Raven picks up the gun, a .22 Beretta Rimfire, with a tea-towel and places it in an empty ice-cream tub from her Tupperware cupboard; puts the container in the freezer.

She's sure she'll never be able to eat *Double-Chocolate Hazelnut Swirl* again.

The crowd gets louder. This time it's a different chant, one she doesn't recognise. She squints out the window. Strains her ears.

"Give us back our leader! Give us back Danielle!"

Their leader? That deranged woman in a polyester shift? They have far more credibility now that she's gone, she wants to tell them. Their voices are growing louder. They start pushing on the fence in rhythm with their demands and it sways under their zeal. She starts to feel the beginning of panic.

"Give us back our leader! Give us back Danielle!"

There must be a hundred people out there who saw Danielle come inside the house. A hundred witnesses. She has to get out of here before they break down the fence. And she has to leave via the front entrance so that she can take Morris and so that the Pitchforks can see her leave, so that they don't break down the house. So that they don't scare the animals.

She tries to conjure up a protection spell but her thoughts are all over the place. Adrenaline tugs at her stomach. She can't think straight. She can't summon the concentration needed to focus the spell. The wrapped shoebox nags at her. Stephen.

You don't have time to open it, says the voice.

I know.

The butcher's paper is lacy in some places: eaten by moths.

You have to leave NOW, before the lunatics break down that flimsy fence.

"Give us back our leader, or we'll come inside to get her!"

Raven perforates the paper; lifts the lid off the vintage box.

47 / CAREFUL NAVY INK

The box is crammed full of envelopes and photos. It smells like old books and dry sand. She chooses a random envelope and pulls it out. 'Brenna' it says on the front in careful, navy ink. She pulls out another, and another, and they are all labelled in identical fashion. Letters to her grandmother. The strokes are distinctly male, but this is not her grandfather, Jack's, handwriting. She extracts a photo — black and white, grainy — of a beautiful woman standing in front of an oak tree. Her hands are behind her back, there is a cat at her feet. She is dressed in white as Brenna always used to be. The back of the photograph says *Brenna Stieg, Spring 1947*. It's the same script as the one on the envelopes. Raven finds more photos: Brenna in her famous garden, Brenna holding a steaming cup of coffee, leaning against a post on the verandah, smiling at Raven's mother. Brenna reading cross-legged on the checked tile floor. Brenna and Jack dancing the twist. Brenna holding a baby in a long white Christening dress. Brenna and Jack resting on the porch. A close-up of her, not smiling.

Who took these pictures? Who was privy to these intimate

moments? Brenna ages there in Raven's hands: her dark hair gets lighter and lighter, then is swept into silver highlights — the way Raven remembers her — and her eyes and lips soften. The babies grow into toddlers and then Jack disappears.

Raven opens one of the envelopes.

May 12th, 1992

Dear Brenna

This morning I was looking for inspiration. I took the bus to Melville and spent some time walking there, on the koppies, *as I do on occasion. Usually when I am surrounded by God's work — the acacias, the veld, the stubborn dandelion weeds that manage to propagate themselves in even the direst circumstances — I feel a renewed sense of purpose. Sometimes I find a new way of looking at something; a new perspective. Today there was no new message to be found. My mind was overcast despite the bright blue skies. My thoughts are tangled up in thorns.*

Oh, Brenna, how I love you. How my love is like that infuriating weed that just emerges everywhere it is not welcome. How I wish our circumstances were different.

Ever yours,

Stephen

July 27th, 1994

Dear Brenna

Sometimes I wish that Jack had never existed. I know that it's an evil thing to say but I need you to know my heart. How can you be so dedicated to a dead man, however much you loved him in life, when I am here in flesh and blood and my need for you burns me every day? How can you choose a memory, no matter how vivid, over me?

We have shared so much, we are so intimate. I live for our time together. Can we not take our relationship to its natural conclusion? I speak not of base pleasures, but everyday traction. I long to bring you tea in bed. I want to read Rilke to you while you polish your acorns. I ache to hold your hand when the moon is high.

My life without you is monochrome.

Yours, always —

Stephen

February 2nd, 1995

Dear Brenna

You have asked me to desist from my letter-writing and I understand why. I respect your wish as I respect everything you say and do, however my ardent heart instructs me to not lose faith. It's a foolish heart, as hearts almost always are. I wish I had a braver one.

Our conversations have exposed a deep part of me that I have never before had access to. Your thoughts have expanded mine. Before, I saw the night sky pricked by stars, now I see deep galaxies, stellar mosaics and supernovas.

Despite my weaknesses I must continue with my quest for your attention. Are we not the very tenderest of friends? Our relationship means everything to me and yet I need more. I know you say that you will never love anyone as you did Jack, but I am not asking for what you had with him. I know it is not possible. Yet, if I think of my future without you by my side, I wonder what the point is: of anything, of my vocation; of my life. Every moment spent without you seems wasted.

Yours, always —

Stephen

August 12th, 1997

Dear Brenna

It is agony, being so close to you but not being able to touch your skin. You will call me reckless, but I long to run my fingers through your hair. Living across the road — with you so near yet so absolutely out of my grasp — is a unique torture I wouldn't wish on the devil himself.

Do you know that I would do anything for you?

Yours, always —

Stephen

November 7th, 1998

Dear Brenna

I hate knowing that you are ill and that I am not right by your side to take care of you. Yes, I bring my paltry offerings of chicken broth and aspirin. I wash the tea-stained cups. I put ginger biscuits out on porcelain plates. I muddle by your side like a polite visitor instead of what I should be doing; changing the cold compress on your forehead, bathing you, reading you your favourite poetry: Plath, perhaps, or Auden. Lying beside you. How I long to lie beside your fevered body and hold you until you are well again.

My life's purpose has always been to be of service to God. How better to serve Him than to look after you, His most magnificent creature?

Yours, always —

Stephen

June 16th, 1999

Dear Brenna

I have given this hundreds of hours of thought and I have reached the only decision I am capable of making. I will leave the church for you, to look after you, to love you. I have made an appointment to see Father Flanagan of the Johannesburg archdiocese next week on Friday where I will be handing in my robes and my resignation. To think that my aspiration, before meeting you, was to inherit his post when the time came. I used to think it a lofty goal: now the scales have fallen from my eyes. Now when I think of that kind of life, that dry fog of loneliness, I can only worship you for giving me clarity. You have shaken my very soul.

I know you have urged me against this course of action saying that it will not change our status quo, but I feel that as long as I am entrenched in the church we can never be together.

How can I worship a God who denies my love for you? It is the only real thing in this cruel, prickly, hard-lined life. The only real thing.

I love you —

Stephen

There are no more letters. Brenna passed away on June 19th, 1999.

48 / RUSK CRUNCHER

Raven's foot is shaking making it difficult to operate the clutch. She's revving the engine, ready to dart out as soon as the gate opens. The crowd bays. The devil hounds are beside the car, barking their heads off, ready to snarl at any potential intruder who dares to attempt to slip in while she's getting out. Raven revs again, breathes, adjusts the wide-brimmed sun-hat on her passenger's head.

"Ready?" she asks, pressing the button on her remote, but the scarecrowess doesn't reply. Morris is ready and he screeches through the gate as soon as it's open wide enough. As soon as the tail is clear she presses the remote again. The protesters run towards the car, but jump back as they hear the Grimm Brothers. She had expected them to jump all over her car and bang on her windows, but the vicious barking is an extremely effective deterrent, despite the gate now being almost completely closed. Raven cheers and puts her foot down and Morris zips forward and away like a Maserati.

"Norwood."

Raven adjusts her phone between shoulder and ear and puts on the roughest Afrikaans accent she can muster. "I'm looking for Captain Kruger."

The man covers the mouthpiece and shouts for Kruger, who is not forthcoming. He shouts again. There is some shuffling and crunching in her ear. Perhaps he's eating a rusk.

"He's not in," says the rusk-cruncher. "Try his cell."

"He's not answering his cell," lies Raven. "And we need to get hold of him immediately."

"I can't help."

"We have an urgent delivery for him from a company called BigBuild. We need his address. It just says 'Hyde Park' on the slip."

"Deliver here. Norwood police station."

"It's specified for home delivery. I doubt you'd want what we have at your station. It's a cubic metre of crush."

"Crush?"

"Gravel. For his renovation."

"Renovation? He hasn't said anything about a renovation."

"Look," says Raven. "If we don't offload now then he won't get it this year. Next deliveries are in January. The team can't continue without this material. The captain will NOT be pleased."

"So you just need his address?"

"Just his street name and number."

He covers the mouthpiece and shouts again. Some metal cabinets are slammed. A female voice yells back at him. He repeats after her and she confirms.

"It's 111 Hyde Park Heights."

111. It's one of the most powerful numbers that exists. No wonder his energy is so strong. It practically leaks out of him like ectoplasm in a *Ghostbusters* film, if ectoplasm could be considered charismatic.

"Thank you. You've been very helpful." Her accent slips.

"Where did you say you were calling from?"

Raven ends the call.

I don't think this is a good idea, says the voice.

She presses all the buttons at Hyde Park Heights. Some people answer with "Hello?" while others just allow access. The door buzzes open and keeps buzzing. "Hello?" "Hello?" they call after her as she runs up the painted stairs.

There's no answer at 111, just as she knew there wouldn't be. It has nothing to do with clairvoyancy. Kruger isn't the kind of man who spends time in an apartment during the work day.

She tries to open the door with her credit card but it snaps in half. Good riddance, she thinks, but then realises that the one half has fallen through the crack in the door. She tries to retrieve it, but it's out of her reach. Anything she does will just jam it further into the crevice.

"Hex," she mutters. Of course it's the piece with her name on it and most likely covered in her fingerprints. She imagines Kruger coming home, opening the door and the card falling to the floor with a snap, right in front of him. It would be difficult to explain. Now there's no going back. She HAS to break in.

She looks left and right, then takes her *athamé* and starts using the tip to nudge the bolt back. It slips a few times, her hands become slippery with sweat and when she tries to prise it she almost loses a finger. She takes a break, looks up to the ceiling. A grey spiderweb patterns the boards.

"Blessed Goddess," she whispers. "I need a key. Open the door, so mote it be."

She jams the ritual knife into the bolt and tries to twist it. Her new approach of brute force and ignorance seems to be working. Just as she thinks she has it, she hears footsteps and has to let it click slowly back into place. She steps into the shadow between two pillars, holds her breath and waits for the person to pass. There is a jingling, a tinkling, accompanied by shuffling steps. The person is not in a hurry. Finally, a thickset man in blue overalls limps past her hiding place. The clinking is coming from a large silver ring of keys attached to his handyman belt. Is it possible? The Universe has sent her the resident handyman!

Or it's a coincidence, says the voice.

There's no such thing as coincidence.

It's one thing being sent the handyman, but another altogether to get your hands on the key for 111.

I'll look for the skeleton key.

You can look for it but how are you going to actually get it?

Oh ye of little faith.

You're going to get caught breaking into a cop's flat. I can't watch. I'm going to close my eyes.

Where's a cold pad of chloroform when you need it?

Okay, my eyes are closed. And I have my hands over them.

I'll give you a running commentary, then.

Don't.

The handyman stops and hacks into his handkerchief, wipes his nose and puts the fabric back into his pocket. Limps a few more steps.

Maybe it'll actually be easier to break in with the knife.

The voice doesn't answer her. Raven waits for another two minutes — which feels like an hour — while she watches the man fiddle with various tools and blow his nose. The ring of keys is looking less attainable by the second.

Finally, she glimpses an opportunity. The man clicks the ring off his belt, selects a key and uses it to open a supplies cupboard. He leaves the key in the outside of the door while he goes inside. Raven tiptoes out of her nook and steals towards the open door. She quietly closes it and turns the key.

"Hey!" says the handyman from inside his dark room. "Hey, I'm in here!" He knocks loudly on the hollow hatch. Raven finds the skeleton key and uses it to open Kruger's front door. She picks up the broken card from the tiles and puts it, along with its other half, in her laptop bag. She hears the muffled man yelling and cursing and considers unlocking the supplies' cupboard but it's too risky. Besides, with a roomful of tools, any handyman worth his salt should be able to jimmy the mechanism open.

49 / ROOM 111

Kruger's apartment is minimalist to the max, with stark white walls and tasteful natural timber finishes. The space is devoid of any kind of art, which troubles Raven. There is not so much as a sculpture or a hand-made ceramic dish. She can smell the complete absence of animals, too. It's clean, white, dander-free air — which makes sense, taking his allergies into account — but Raven still finds it disturbing. This isn't a home. It's a cardboard cut-out. It's a Hollywood set. It's a bachelor pad that has yet to be lived in. Perhaps this isn't Kruger's actual home. Maybe it's his getaway flat, his work-late apartment. Maybe his real home is far enough away — on a plot somewhere green — to warrant a *pied-á-terre*. There is no life here. This empty space is nothing but a vacuum.

It makes her think of that completely silent room in Minnesota. It blocks out ninety-nine percent of all external sound. No one can stay in the anechoic chamber for more than forty-five minutes without going crackers. In the absence of sound, your ears adapt and you become the sound. You can hear your lungs ballooning. You lose your balance. You have to sit down. And that's when the hallucinations begin.

But she's not in the Minnesota chamber, she's in Room 111. She moves through the space quickly — she knows that she doesn't have a lot of time. She finds his office as she knew she would. Kruger is the kind of man to take work home with him. That is, after all, why she is here. She had imagined a complicated mind-map on the wall with snowy surveillance pictures of her and untidy notes, different coloured strings tied around drawing pins to connect events to locations: Colborn Manor; Sheldon Senior's house; Jessica's mansion; the Moon Chapel. Yellow Post-Its covered in unintelligible scribbles.

She sits down at his polished desk and stares at the blank wall in front of her. It makes no sense at all that she's disappointed. She was worried that she would find something; she was worried that she wouldn't. She wants him to be obsessed with her, even though this is the very last thing she needs in her life. Will she always be this conflicted? Will her mind always be this fractured? It seems an exhausting way to live.

She starts rifling through the drawers, finds sparse stationery and empty notebooks, ink cartridges for a printer she can't see, a couple of unopened packets of travel tissues. A stapler and a sticky-tape dispenser. If Kruger ever sees her office, she thinks, he will have an immediate OCD attack. In the second drawer on the right she finds some files. Third in the stack (*third?* she thinks), is hers. It's a pretty powder blue that has her name printed in block letters at the top. She's about to open it when it occurs to her that she has not yet opened the last drawer. She has what she needs, so, in theory, it does not need opening, but Raven feels she won't be able to concentrate on the file properly if that last drawer is nagging her, so she decides to have a quick look. She's expecting paperclips, sorted into their respective colours and unopened envelopes of Prestik, maybe some extra paper for the ghost printer. But she's wrong. There's only one item in there: a framed photo turned face-down. She hesitates, then picks it up. The handsome silver border frames a picture of a smiling family. It looks like a scene from a lifestyle magazine — bright white smiles, happy eyes — but beneath that their true connection is made clear.

It's not the fact that he's married that hurts her. Or that he has a child. What is like a hot arrow in her heart is that she can see how in love he is with his wife.

50 / A COLD GLASS OF WATER

"I see you've found what you're looking for," says Kruger, leaning in the doorway, gun hanging by his side.

She doesn't jump; she has heard him creep in. She isn't able to unglue her hands from the frame.

"You're married," she says.

"You broke into my house," he says.

"Then we've both got some explaining to do."

"Come," he says, holstering his weapon and holding out his hand. He's not angry.

Raven stands up. She hasn't yet opened the file with her name on it. "How did you know I was here?"

"You tripped the silent alarm."

"You thought it was a burglar?"

Kruger laughs. He has nothing to steal.

They sit, straight-backed, in the room that pretends to be a lounge. Before, where there was coffee and whisky and topless vampire waitresses, an undeniable electric blue current, there is now a glass of cold water.

"If I set off the alarm why didn't the security company come?"

"I didn't want them to scare you. They carry semi-automatics. They can be a bit... forceful."

"You knew it was me."

"Of course."

"How?"

"Because I would have done the same thing."

"You would have broken into someone's property? Captain Kruger? My straight-laced cop?"

"I would have wanted to know," he says, scratching his stubble, "what evidence there was against me."

"Yes."

"You could have asked," he says.

"You could have told me," she says.

He stands up, comes around to her side of the room, sits on the couch next to her. She wants to crawl into him. She doesn't move.

"How are you?" he says. "How are you feeling?"

She gets the feeling he wants to touch the bruise that is fading on her cheekbone.

"I'm holding it together." She blocks the recurring images of

Sheldon's attack and Danielle's blue body in the trunk beneath her floor. "Just."

"You should be at the hotel."

"The hotel got… complicated."

"Being caught breaking into the police captain's home is more complicated."

"I wasn't planning on getting caught."

"Did anyone see you arrive?"

Raven shakes her head.

"You weren't being tailed?"

"Why would I be tailed?"

"They're trying to build a case against you."

"You mean YOU'RE trying to build a case against me."

"It's my job."

"That's what the *Schutzstaffel* said. That's what the Special Branch said."

"I said that it's my job, not that I follow orders blindly."

He runs a finger over her neckline.

Raven feels a bump of arousal. "It seems that we have a conflict of interests."

Kruger loosens the shoulder straps of her dress, lets the top fall down, exposing her bra. She unclips it, lets it fall to the floor.

"My God," his voice is gruff. "You're a magnificent creature."

He cups her bare breast, moves in to kiss her, but she stops him.

"First, tell me about your wife."

51 / SHALLOW POCKET

Kruger continues trailing his finger over her bare skin. Her whole body is thrumming.

"Tell me about the photo. The baby. Your baby. Your wife."

Her hand is on his sturdy thigh.

"Tell me who you really are."

Kruger gets onto his knees in front of her. He lifts the front of her dress and pulls her hips towards him. Pulls her panties down and off, slings her long legs over his shoulders. Buries his face in her pussy.

"Oh, fuck," she groans. "Oh, fuck."

She's so turned on that she thinks she will come immediately and tries to slow herself down. It is so delicious and so all-encompassing… she wants it to last forever, but the pressure builds and builds and she's shot into space. When the orgasm thunders inside her she hears herself shout.

Her eyes are still closed; she is not quite back to earth when he turns her over with rough hands, turns her so that her back is towards him and he can grip her ass. He licks her cheek, bites it, gives it a smack.

The aftershock of the orgasm is still rippling through when he penetrates her, wet and swollen and his hungry thrusts make her come again. She's falling down a mountain she doesn't remember climbing. He pounds into her spasms. He yells when he explodes and then melts away, but his grip on her is still firm. He hugs her towards him — she can feel his heart on her back — and inhales her neck as if she is the only thing in his world. Like they will never let go. Or like they will never touch again.

They sit on the carpet together. Raven's leg is outstretched and their feet nestle. Their glasses are empty. Raven is dressed as a cliché, wearing Kruger's shirt.

"My wife's name was Melissa."

Was.

"David was our baby boy."

His devastation, though no longer new, cuts through the room.

"You lost them?"

"I've always thought that's a strange phrase," he says. "Like I was careless. Like I wasn't holding on to them tightly enough and they just slipped away from me. Like they tumbled out of a shallow pocket while I wasn't looking."

Raven nods. Yes. There is a thickening in her throat.

"It happened a week after Dave's first birthday. We were so relieved to have the first year over. It was tough for us, having a small baby. The crying, the sleep deprivation. We were both professionals. We had neat lives. We weren't expecting it to be so messy, so all-consuming."

"It's a steep learning curve."

"Of course, now, I'd do anything to hold him again, just for one minute. I can see now that the sleepless nights were... inconsequential."

He takes a break, looks out of the window.

"He had just started walking. He was saying some words. He was a real little person. We went out one evening, together. To a family-friendly restaurant. Had dinner." He clears his throat. "In the parking-lot, the sun had just gone down. I was strapping him into his car-seat. I always hated that bloody car-seat. It was difficult to get both strap keys in the safety lock at the same time. My stupid fingers. Used to drive me mad. He was fussy, tired. It was past his bedtime. Then I finally got it to click and I looked up and there was a gun in my face."

Raven frowns; blinks at him.

"There were two of them. The one had grabbed Melissa, put a gun to her head. There was this... smell. The smell of them in our space. Sweat and smoke and something else. I don't know, but I'll never forget it."

"We knew what to do. Had spoken about it. Act calm, follow instructions, don't try to be a hero. I was going to give him the car key but I wanted to get David out first. The man was nervous, insistent, so I handed it over to calm him down and quickly unstrapped Dave, but he started crying and then the men started shouting. I had just lifted him out when the restaurant security guard came running up reaching for his walkie-talkie. He wasn't armed but they must have thought that he was. They just started firing. I saw these sparks, these small explosions, all around us. And the zinging of bullets. They got the security guard first, in the chest and then in the face. I couldn't see Mel so I thought she had tucked and rolled, exactly what she had been meant to do. I did the same, tried to cover my boy's body with my own. Hoped they'd just take the damn car now and leave. But then I'm down on the tarmac and I look over at her under the car and she's gone. I mean her body is there, but I can see — her face — that she's… gone."

He can't speak for a while. Raven waits. Her insides ache.

"David had stopped screaming so I was hoping that I wasn't suffocating him pushing him to the ground like that. One of the doors slammed closed. Thank God, I thought, thank God. The man closest to me took aim and shot me in the back, twice, then they drove off. After that I could hear the people from the restaurant coming out, shouting for ambulances and police. I rolled onto my side, I wanted to reassure David, check him, but before I could even look at him properly I knew something was wrong. He was completely limp. I shouted at him to wake up. I was sure that he hadn't been shot. I couldn't see any blood. I would have known if he had been shot. I would have felt it. But I was wrong. A stray bullet, they said, had glanced off the car."

"I am so sorry," Raven says. Her face is wet. "I can't even imagine —"

"I didn't let him go. I tried to crawl over to Mel. She was so close, I wanted to hold them both, together. But my legs weren't working. My arms gave up halfway. People started crowding around, crying. I woke up in ICU a week later. I was there for months. Sometimes I feel that I'm still there."

"You moved out of your family home. You resigned from your job."

"I used to be a state prosecutor."

"I knew you weren't an ordinary cop. I could sense you had lived… another life."

"It was. Another life."

"You had a breakdown? You must have had."

"Of sorts."

"Of sorts?"

"I got it into my head that I could find the guys who did it."

"Oh, shit."

"I saw their faces. More than that, I kept seeing their faces, every day when I woke up and every night when I fell asleep, or rather, didn't sleep. I became obsessed with finding them."

"I'm sure it's a natural reaction to what happened to you."

"I did everything I could for the investigation. I kept showing up telling them my ideas, but they got sick of me and the trail went cold. I kept on with it, on and on, until even the most sympathetic witnesses asked me to leave them alone. I followed up any lead. I cruised around Diepsloot on any tip from anyone.

"Then we got lucky. Against all odds the car was found in Quelimane, Mozambique. It had been stripped, but I paid for the best forensic detective to go out there and gather whatever he could. There was blood — an assailant's blood — on the ignition at the front of the car. The DNA matched a man with a criminal record. Moses Ramphele. He had been in and out of prison. They showed me a picture of the man he was known to work for — a gang member — and I recognised them both. The force put out an alert for the men and, within a week, an informant told them where the men were staying and they were picked up."

"So you got them."

"They were released after the docket went missing. Someone had been paid off or threatened. Whatever the reason, the evidence disappeared."

Raven covers her face with her hands.

"It was hardly a surprise. I knew the legal system, the inefficiencies of the police procedures and the courts. I tried to let it go. My psychologist tried to get me to let it go."

"Impossible," says Raven. "Not while they were still out there."

"I knew I had to get them or die trying." He rubs his stubble. "Sometimes I thought I wouldn't mind dying."

"So… you became a cop."

"I was too messed up to be a cop. I was drinking a lot. Forgetting to eat. All I cared about was Ramphele and Moletsane. Trying to let it go… denying my urge, denying justice, was just making it worse. The cops weren't giving it the attention it deserved. It was just another hijacking to them. A hijacking gone wrong."

"You went after them yourself."

"It wasn't the plan, but I found a story in the newspaper about a woman who was hijacked outside a well-known family restaurant. A mother with toddler twins. They all made it but I knew when I was reading it that it was the same gang. It was the same MO, targeting young families in big family cars when they're at their most distracted and most vulnerable. I knew it was just a matter of time before the next fatal shooting."

"You had to stop them."

"I tracked down the mother. Showed her the mugs. She confirmed it was the same pair."

"This time you didn't tell the cops. You went after them yourself."

He doesn't need to speak; the answer is clear. He absent-mindedly touches the scar on his lip. There was a struggle, but he survived. Raven is sure that Ramphele and Moletsane didn't.

"Then — afterwards — you became a cop."

"I thought stopping them would be enough. It wasn't. What about the next hijacking? The next home invasion? I used to hear those gunshots all the time. I thought they'd fade after… after what I'd done; but they didn't. I needed to get the bad guys."

"But you were a state prosecutor. You were putting the bad guys away."

"Not enough. Not nearly enough. In so many cases my hands were tied. It was too… frustrating. I saw people literally get away with murder. On my watch. It felt wrong to wear a business suit again. I needed… to get my hands dirty. That's where the work gets done - the real work. That's how you put people away for good."

52 / SPENT STAR

They make love again. This time, in bed, it's slow and tender and they look each other in the eyes. They trace each other's scars with soft hands. They're in a cocoon. All that exists are their two bodies and clean, white cotton on skin. Raven wants to heal Kruger with her touch. She is sure that she can help him; slowly erode his pain. She works on him with her hands and mouth. Her tongue. Feri magic. She gives him everything. She owns him and then returns him to himself. When they are finished, they lie, limbs and fingers entwined like old lovers. Slowly they float to the surface where the sun is shining and the world seems forever changed.

Suddenly Raven feels overwhelmed, as if she has been bowled over by a huge wave. The money and the violence and hope and uncertainty she has endured over the last few days, the last hour, just rises up and flattens her. She starts crying. Kruger holds her. He doesn't ask her what is wrong. Perhaps he knows that if she wants to talk about it, she will. She doesn't feel embarrassed. She's crying for herself, but she's also crying for him. For the trauma in the world, for the open wounds and the scars. For Melissa and baby David and also for her own children, babies that she knows she has lost in another life because she can sometimes feel them tugging at her skirt. The reminders not to have children in this life because losing them is too much to bear. She sobs and sobs and Kruger's full-body grip on her is unwavering.

When the tide retreats, so do the tears, and Raven is left exhausted. Kruger releases her, kisses her eyes, her cheekbones. Raven thinks she wants to stay here in the bed with him forever, but she feels the skin on her calf start tingling. She rubs her leg hoping it's her imagination but that just makes it worse. A shot of adrenaline shakes her into reality. This can't happen. Not now. She's being paranoid. It's nothing. It's just fear biting her leg. She ignores it, but it persists.

"Not again," she says. "Not now."

"What is it?" Kruger sits up.

The burning begins.

"Shit."

"What?"

The heat climbs quickly; quicker than ever before. She can feel that it's going to be a bad attack. The worst attack.

"Do you have any ice?"

"Did I hurt you?"

"No. Do you have ice?"

"I have a couple of trays in the freezer."

A couple of trays isn't going to cut it. She can't stay. She can't go home.

"Shit," she says again, launching out of bed. "I need to go." She scrabbles for her clothes on the floor. Slips her dress on backwards, then turns it around. Slings her laptop bag over her shoulder.

"Where?"

There's only one place she can go.

"To the emergency room."

Kruger speeds through traffic with his siren on, but by the time they reach the ER, Raven's skin is already blistering. Concerned that it might be a dangerous allergic reaction, the nurse on duty sweeps her in front of the young boy who has bitten through his tongue while falling off his skateboard and the middle-aged woman with white hair holding her wrist as if her hand will drop off if she lets go. Raven pulls her dress over her head and is helped onto a gurney, darted with an IV. The burning is intense. She cries out. Kruger holds her hand. More blisters stretch her skin.

The doctor arrives in a white coat and sneakers; a tall woman with a reassuring air of weary confidence. She doesn't say hello. Her stethoscope is beautifully cool against Raven's chest.

"Tell me," says the doctor.

"I need ice," says Raven. "It's what usually works. Ice bath."

"I'll get you ice," she says, nodding at the nurse, who leaves the room. "But what's causing it? We need to know."

"I don't know."

"Allergy?"

"No. I've been tested for everything."

"Your breathing," says the doctor. "Asthma?"

"Yes."

The heat is spreading up her body. She can feel it on her chest now, her breasts.

"Eczema," says the doctor.

"It's not eczema. It doesn't itch. It burns."

"There are over a hundred different kinds of skin conditions, eczema or eczema-related. Not all of them itch."

Raven isn't going to argue with her. She isn't going to tell her that she has seen over twenty different dermatologists in her life and that none of them could give her an accurate diagnosis. She isn't going to tell her that eczema has been ruled out time and time again by people who actually specialise in skin conditions. Raven has no desire to argue or to be right. All she wants is relief. She quickly tries to think of a spell to hasten the ice, but before she can start the nurse is back with an extra pair of hands and a trolley of ice-packs. They cover her in what looks like cling wrap and then pile the cold bags on top of her. It is good. It is so good. The doctor is back. She injects the IV with something, then something else and adds another smaller bag to the mix.

"Cortisone," she says. "Pethidine. Oritavancin."

Steroids, painkillers, antibiotics. As the pethidine warms her blood she develops a deep affection for the doctor. Why had she ever avoided the ER? The ER is a wonderful place. She will definitely be visiting in the future. Kruger catches her eye.

"Better?" he asks. He hasn't let go of her hand.

She wants to say: You're a wholly beautiful man. I would do anything for you.

She wants to say: As soon as I'm off this drip let's just get out of here. Let's run away together.

She wants to say: Kruger. I don't even know your first name but I am in love with you.

"Better," says Raven, and her consciousness shrinks and pops out of existence like a spent star.

53 / GUARDIANS

When she wakes up she is in a private ward surrounded by guardians. She blinks their halos away, recognises Kruger and Lavinia, but not the others. The others are in proper guardian uniforms. They have come to escort her somewhere. To the next dimension? She will finally get to see what it's like on The Other Side.

Raven! says the voice. *Thank God you're awake. You need to get out of here.*

"There you are," says the High Priestess. "Exactly as I saw you in my vision. Good to know that I'm not getting rusty."

Raven can't imagine Lavinia ever getting rusty. She can picture Barkridge at two hundred years old still having hawk eyes. Raven blinks some more and sees that her guardians are really minions in SAP uniforms.

"Don't worry about them," says Lavinia, waving her hand as if to dismiss the burly men. Kruger looks guilty.

"What?" croaks Raven. "What's going on?"

Kruger passes her the plastic beaker of water. A practised hand. A husband in another life. She takes a sip.

“Why are they here?”

Lavinia raises her eyebrows at Kruger. *Explain yourself,* she seems to be saying. *You traitorous imp.*

“Kruger?”

He sighs. “It’s not what you think.”

“Am I under arrest?”

“Yes.”

“Well then. It’s exactly what I think.”

“It’s not on my orders.”

“You’re running the case.”

“I’m heading up the homicide case. This — them — it’s a different case altogether.”

Raven thinks of Danielle’s body. Tetris in a trunk. They wouldn’t believe it was self-defence now, not when she hadn’t reported the intrusion, the gun; not when she had hidden the body like that. But they wouldn’t have found her. Couldn’t have. Not yet.

Don’t say ANYTHING, says the voice.

“I don’t understand —” starts Raven.

NOTHING, says the voice. *SAY NOTHING.*

“It was Jessica,” says the High Priestess, but that doesn’t make sense at all.

“Credit card fraud,” says Kruger. “You used her card at The Regent.”

"Fraud!" she scoffs. "She's my sister. It's a misunderstanding."

"That's what I told them," says Lavinia.

"My card was declined. My account is frozen. It was an emergency. I was going to pay her back. I didn't think she'd mind."

"When she got the bank notification of the transaction she must have alerted the police."

Had things really got so bad between them that she'd want her own sister arrested?

"A team was dispatched to arrest you at the hotel but you'd already left." Kruger seemed mildly pleased with this. "But it has complicated matters."

"Of course it has," sighs Raven.

"The fraud unit are now investigating you, too. It appears that it's not the first time you've used someone else's credit card or drawn cash from other people's cards."

"Oh, please."

"There are security videos of you. Most recently: various instances of you buying coffee and pastries with Sheldon Bond senior's card at a time when we know he was incapacitated. Also, drawing cash from his card."

That bloody Sheldon Bond junior. This is his doing.

"I don't see the problem. You've just said he was incapacitated. I was buying him the things he wanted."

"What about the cash?"

"The cash was for me."

"So you did take money from him."

"Yes," says Raven. "Obviously. He was a client of mine. Which means that I provided a service and he paid me."

"It looks bad," Kruger says.

"Of course it does. It's out of context. Anything can look bad out of context."

"And Bond isn't the only occurrence. They also got…" he pulls out his notepad, "Fitzsimmons. Solange. Mbete. And others."

"Of course they bloody do."

"Some of those families are also coming forward. Saying you didn't have their permission —"

"I didn't need their permission!"

"It looks like you —"

"I know what it looks like. It looks like I'm a con woman and I prey on terminally ill people."

"And then you kill them," says the High Priestess.

They both look at her. "What?" she says. "That's why we're here, aren't we?"

They keep quiet for a beat, glancing around.

"Did you ever have any kind of contract? Any written proof at all?" asks Kruger. "With the clients you —"

"Of course not," says Raven. "Euthanasia is illegal."

It's more illegal to kill someone without their consent. Maybe she should have thought of that.

"There's something else," says Kruger. Lavinia purses her lips. "A further… complication."

"It's the Taglock Terrors," says the High Priestess.

"I knew they were up to something," says Raven. "What have they done now?"

"They almost did something," says Kruger. "We caught them in time."

"Caught them?"

"Kept them from creating a far worse scenario."

"Just tell me what happened."

"Morgan and Elizar have been arrested for attempted arson," says Lavinia.

"What? Has the world gone mad?"

"They're looking for the others," says Kruger. "They found the plans and the devices. They've all been implicated."

"What the hex did they do?"

"Planted explosives under that courthouse that they vandalised. Apparently they were intending to send Judge Molefe a — stronger — message."

"My Goddess. It's like Guy Fawkes."

"They're all being investigated now. As you can imagine that's not good news for your case. It seems just a matter of time before they join the dots."

"I had nothing to do with that."

"Yes, but, you know — "

Raven knows all too well that Lavinia means the business connection between herself and Luella. If certain details come to light she will, without doubt, face life imprisonment.

"Yes," Raven says. "Of course."

"So what do we do?" asks Raven. She's had enough of lying in her hospital bed now. She wants to get up and do something. She sits up.

"The best thing you can do right now," says Kruger, "is to rest and get better. I gave Lavinia the name of an excellent defence attorney — an old colleague — who can start working on your case so long."

"Isn't that a conflict of interests?" asks Raven.

"I thought it would be clear by now," Kruger takes her hand under the starched white sheet, "that my interests remain extremely conflicted."

"What you don't understand," says Barkridge, "is that Raven isn't going to get better until she fixes this."

The policemen are statues.

"Fixes this? She can't fix it. It's much bigger than her, now. She has to be patient. Build an impenetrable defence. Trials can take months; years. There's no quick fix here."

Raven takes her hand away from Kruger. "Lavinia doesn't just mean my legal situation. Look at me," she pulls the sheet off to reveal her blistered body. "This is what I need to fix."

"You're in excellent hands here," says Kruger, covering her up again. "They'll treat you."

"They'll treat my symptoms," says Raven. "Until it happens again. And again. And every time it's worse."

"You're better off here than anywhere else."

"No," says Raven. "No. I need to go. Need to get out of here. I can feel it."

Kruger looks uncomfortable. "You… can't."

"Of course I can. Do you mean because I'm still on this thing?" she points at the IV in her hand. "I'll just get a nurse." She presses the button on her bed remote.

"No," says Kruger, shooting a look at the cops at the door. "Because you're under arrest."

Lavinia purses her lips. She is not impressed.

"And, while we're on the topic, there's something else. I need to take your computer."

"No," says Raven. "Absolutely not."

"I have to. I don't have a choice." He looks again at the uniforms at the door.

"My whole life is on there."

"I have a warrant. I'm sorry."

"I thought we were past this."

"Past what?"

"The power play. This is you telling me that you're still the cop. That you're still in charge."

"No. It's just me doing my job."

He looks pained as he picks up the laptop bag from the floor.

"I'll get it back to you soon."

"Kruger. Don't. Please."

He shrugs. He's sorry, but he's the cop, after all.

"If I don't take it in they'll send someone hairier to get it. Take care of yourself. I'll see you soon."

His easy betrayal stings her. Raven wants to yell at him. Throw her plastic cup after him. Instead her mouth hangs open a little. She's reminded of a quote. Elizabeth, before she was queen: *I trusted you and learnt from you that no one can be trusted, least of all lovers.*

"Don't worry," he says, winking, on his way out. "I'm not very good with computers. I probably won't find anything."

A nurse arrives in Kruger's place. She is shorter and has less stubble.

"Get this IV out of my hand, please," says Raven. "I need to go."

The nurse looks from Raven to Lavinia to the cops at the door, shakes her head.

"You haven't been discharged yet," she says. "And I can't take the drip out without orders from your doctor. And you can't be discharged while you're still on a drip."

Raven has had enough of people obeying orders. For Goddess's sake, can't they think for themselves? Barkridge dismisses the nurse with an authoritative nod, pulls a chair towards the bed, sits down close to Raven. The uniforms seem to take a step closer, too. If the two witches are going to talk, they're going to listen.

Raven begins to yank the IV line out. The High Priestess stops her. Raven is about to argue with her too, until Lavinia starts peeling off the tape that keeps the tube in. She takes a cotton pad and a plaster from her Mary Poppins handbag and applies pressure to the needle puncture to stop it from bleeding, whips the line out and covers the cotton with the plaster and the plaster with her cool hand.

"Your situation," says Lavinia, "is not beyond fixing."

"What about your Frankl quote? What gives light must endure burning?"

"It no longer applies. We need to get you out of here."

"Morris is at Kruger's place," says Raven. "I need a car."

"Don't worry about Morris. I'll get him home safely." She opens Raven's locker and pulls out her clothes.

"Thank you, Lavinia."

"Now," she says in a low voice, "I have a plan."

54 / INVISIBLE PEBBLES

The policemen guarding the door pretend they're not paying attention. They whistle silently and kick invisible pebbles with their department-issue boots.

"I've been thinking," whispers the High Priestess, "and I think that the way to address your… problem —"

Raven smiles despite herself. "Which one?"

"All of them."

All of them that she knows about, anyway. Raven is hoping she doesn't know about the body in the trunk.

"Even," says Lavinia, "the hidden ones."

Raven clears her throat and glances over at the cops. They are definitely listening.

"Because those are often the most dangerous."

Raven sits up. "You have my undivided attention."

"So I was thinking," she says again, "about the space-time continuum."

Raven was expecting more hands-on advice. "You'll have to help me understand. My physics is a bit rusty."

"The space-time continuum is a mathematical model that joins space and time as a single idea."

"Okay," says Raven.

"So space is then three-dimensional and time has the role of the fourth dimension."

"It may be the pethidine, but I have no idea what you're speaking about."

"It's not important."

"It sounds pretty important. It sounds like the universe would fall flat without it."

"Yes, there's that. But for our purposes now, what's important is what you already know. That time is not fixed in the past, just as it's not fixed in the future."

Raven is struggling to see how the theory applies to her very real and present mess.

"I know what you're thinking," whispers Lavinia, "that it's hardly the most practical advice, but I think it's the only thing that'll work."

"What?" says Raven. "What will work?"

"It's the over-arching theme of the multiverse, Raven, dear."

"Karma?"

"Yes. Yes. Karma. Everything that you've done, every choice you've made has led up to this very moment."

"I know. I know that. It doesn't make it easier."

"But it's bigger than you think it is."

"I don't understand."

"It's your karmic baggage. It's throwing a shadow over you."

As she hears the words she knows that it's true. She doesn't understand what Barkridge is getting at but she knows that it is true. "I can feel the shadow," says Raven. "I've always felt the shadow."

"It's the hazard of old souls," says Lavinia. "People — and events — reaching for you from your past."

"The Unquiet Dead," says Raven.

"Exactly."

"But what can be done? What can I do about it if it's in the past, as fluid as the past is."

"You can visit it," says Lavinia. They stare at each other. Raven's brain whirrs.

"You're saying that I need to… time-travel?"

The High Priestess chuckles. "No," she says. "No. Time-travel is extremely difficult. Even for the most proficient witch. The training is extensive and dangerous."

Raven nods. They don't have time. Which is ironic. Which makes her want to laugh, too.

"And, even if it *was* possible — even if you happened to have an extraordinary talent for it — it's too complicated. You can't tell what consequences your actions will have."

"The butterfly effect."

"Exactly. Even a wholly benevolent action could reverberate through the continuum and have severe and unpredictable implications."

"So how do I do it? Visit my past... if I can't travel through time?"

"There are other ways."

"There are other ways to time-travel?"

"In a manner of speaking. It runs a bit deeper than that. I know someone — a witch — who can help you."

"And you recommend I go back, not forward?"

Lavinia's smile disappears.

"Oh, you never go forward."

The High Priestess begins closing the curtain around the hospital bed. One of the policemen, the one with the *boep,* tries to stop her. Lavinia waves a steel bedpan at him.

"Do you mind?"

He steps back, holds a hand up in apology. The wheels spin in the metal rail as she pulls the fabric curtain around the bed. Raven jumps up, strips the cling-wrap off and pulls her clothes on. The dress worries her blisters but she doesn't have time to feel sorry for herself. Lavinia climbs up on her chair and flicks her lighter on, giving Raven a thumbs-up. She looks like some deranged fan at a Rolling Stones concert.

"People always complain about smokers," she says. "But whenever there is a birthday candle that needs lighting, or a smoke detector that needs activating, then all of a sudden they're very happy to have us around."

The wail of the siren makes them both jump. Hospital staff

outside launch into action, yelling instructions at people and shepherding patients towards emergency exits. The cop pulls open the curtain and Lavinia acts pleased to see him. Places a temporarily frail hand on his arm.

"Thank Goddess," she says looking into his eyes, "that we have you here to protect us!"

He clearly suspects them of mischief, runs his fingers over his handcuffs, but then decides against using them. Raven assumes the SAP can't afford any more bad PR this year after the media outcry over their alleged excessive force used in prior months. If anything was to happen in this emergency and it was discovered that he had handcuffed an ill woman and/or her aged companion it would not look good for him, or the station. He looks around to his partner, for assurance, but he's gone. Perhaps, thinks Raven, to help with the evacuation.

"Come on," he beckons at them to follow him. They do as they are told and join the caravan of nurses and gurneys and limping patients in the corridor. "Stay close," he says. It is not a suggestion. Being surrounded by so many people and their jangling nerves makes Raven want to push everyone aside, the sick and wounded alike, and just run for it. They cease to be people in her frantic mind: just obstacles standing in her way of her freedom and her sanity. Her breathing becomes shallow. She needs to get out of here. The cop's grip on her arm tightens. As they get right into the thick of things, Lavinia whispers in her ear and Raven nods.

"Oh dear," says the High Priestess, above the din. "Oh dear."

The policeman furrows his brows at her. It seems that he won't be taking any nonsense from an occult-practising octogenarian.

"I think I'm going to..." she holds a limp hand up to her forehead.

"What's going on?" the man says and then she faints into his arms. Instinctively, he lets go of Raven's elbow to catch Barkridge and Raven immediately ducks under the ocean of people. She has already loped, chimpanzee-style, five or six metres away before she hears the cop shout "Hey!"

In his mind she must have disappeared from right in front of him. A magic trick.

55 / SNOWBROTH

Raven keeps up her monkey stride all the way down the passage and into the elevator which people know to avoid in the event of fire. She presses 'B' for the parking basement, and, once she's in and the doors glide shut she can stand up straight.

"Breathe," she instructs her reflection in the mirror. "Breathe."

Her asthma pump is in her laptop bag. Bloody Kruger. There's no way he could have known but damn him anyway. She considers going back into the hospital, breaking into the pharmacy for an inhaler, but decides against it. She knows she will never make it out again, not as a free woman, anyway. Best to take her chances with her traitorous lungs. Try to stay calm and focused. Try to breathe.

The elevator doors open again and she skips out, then forces herself to slow down. To walk. She scans the rows and rows of multi-coloured cars.

The wasp is in the basement, Lavinia had whispered.

Raven circles the glass-enclosed elevator shaft and sees the row of bikes on the other side. Handsome, polished black motorcycles stand alongside grubby delivery bikes with dented cargo boxes, and then, at the end of the stack, Lavinia's trusty blue Vespa. The helmet and key are inside the stow, exactly as she knows they will be.

Thank fuck! she wants to shout, but instead says, "Blessed be, Barkridge" and her voice seems small in the cavernous underground. She jumps onto the scooter, jams the key in, revs the 150cc engine and pats the helmet onto her head. She kicks the stand up, stutters forward, practices using the brakes, then whizzes away. She has neither a parking-ticket nor money to pay for it, so once she has wound her way up to ground level she just edges past the end of the boom of the exit ramp. Hospitals shouldn't, in her opinion, make people pay for parking, anyway. The parking attendant tries to wave her down but she shows him the back of her middle finger as she zips off.

In hindsight she realises that they probably have cameras at the exits and she has just added further insult to the cops who will be watching her escape. She smiles into her helmet visor.

A dress is not the most practical attire for riding a scooter, but the cool air on her arms and up her legs feels good. Without being conscious of it, her breathing has returned to normal. Beyond the oppressive walls of the hospital she feels like her whole body can breathe, and she relishes the feeling. She takes deep lungfuls of oxygen. Part of her wants to just keep riding away from her falling-down house and bodies under floorboards and bastard lover cops and a possible lifetime sentence. But she knows she won't. Knows she can't. Raven knows that running away always circles back on you and you end up sprinting straight into the shitpile that you were trying to leave behind.

Where are you going? asks the voice.

Well, hello, says Raven. Very nice of you to join us.

Just because I'm not talking doesn't mean I'm not here.

I know, I know.

You'd go mad, you know, if I just kept chattering away to you night and day.

I know.

So?

Yes, yes, I'm grateful that you're not –

No, I mean, so, where are you going?

To see a witch.

Ah. And this will solve your practical problems, how?

I don't know yet.

So you're not sure where you're going or who you're seeing or how it's going to help you.

Yip. As Michael Jackson said, "You've Gotta Have Faith".

I think that was George Michael.

Whatever. It's having faith that's the thing, says Raven.

Hmmm, says the voice.

Faith is... taking the first step even though you can't see the staircase.

Well. There's faith and then there's blind trust. Stupid trust. What if there's no staircase?

That's the thing. You'll never know if you don't take the step.

But if there's no staircase –

Maybe there is no staircase UNTIL you take the first step. By taking the step, you make the staircase appear.

Sounds a bit ethereal to me.

Raven turns off the tarred road leaving the traffic behind and bowls down a sandy lane, whipping up a squall of fine dust behind her. It's apt, she thinks, to have a cyclone nipping at her heels. She passes large plots with simple houses and low fences.

Besides, I do know where I'm going. Lavinia put the address into my Google maps app. Glenferness.

Horse country, says the voice.

Is it?

Horses and hippies. They all stay out there.

That seems to be a bit of a generalisation.

Doesn't make it untrue.

Excellent. Hippie witches are my favourite.

She takes a few turns and the properties get bigger, the land looks flatter. There are indeed horses and stables and bales of yellow straw in the distance.

It even smells horsey, says Raven.

I'm not quite sure I know what a horse smells like.

Oh, come on. Don't be such a city slicker. You know what Apple-jack smells like.

City ponies are different.

Muck and sweet animal sweat. Grass. Leather. Burnt hair.

The app on Raven's phone tells her that she has arrived at her destination. It's a massive, rambling plot covered in trees and creepers and vines. It's not subdivided, as far as Raven can see, but there are four separate letterboxes and doorbells. Raven rings the bell for Bronwynne Snowbroth.

Told you, says the voice. *Hippies. It's some kind of commune.*

Don't say it like that.

Like what?

Like they're weird or dirty or something.

I bet you, says the voice, *that there will be some kind of crystal collection or dreamcatcher in the front entrance. Or —*

The gate shudders open and Raven drives inside. She follows a path through the overgrown gardens to where an attractive woman in a gold-trimmed emerald robe directs her to park. She drives in, switches off and kicks her stand to park. Takes off her helmet and rubs her cheeks.

Snowbroth walks right up to her with open arms. "I'm a hugger," she says.

Of course she is, says the voice.

The women embrace. Snowbroth smells like aromatherapy oils — patchouli and bergamot — and freshly shampooed hair. She takes Raven's clammy hands in her own. "I'm so glad you've come."

Raven feels the dirt on her skin from the ride. She's sure that she stinks of nerves.

"Thank you for seeing me. Especially at such short notice."

She dismisses the favour with a wave of a much-bejewelled hand. "Any friend of Lavinia's…". The gems glint in the sunlight. Snowbroth leads her down a path, past dandelions and creepers and into a quaint thatch house.

"Besides, it's not short notice. I've been expecting you for a while."

In the entrance is a wind-chime and a shelf of Spiritual Bath Salts for sale.

Told you, says the voice.

The front room is cool and dim and smells of straw. The furniture is wicker with 70s-style fabric, bold florals in oranges and browns. A caramel-coloured tea-set is laid out, along with an upside-down pineapple cake. The cake reminds Raven that she hasn't eaten in ages. There is a cheap print on the wall — a sentimental picture of a horse — and a cross-stitch owl. The room is like a time capsule.

"Please," she says, motioning for Raven to take a seat.

Raven sits. She isn't offered the tea or the cake.

"How much do you know about what I do?"

Raven shakes her head. "Nothing at all. Lavinia just said… that you could help me with my karmic baggage."

"That's exactly right. History repeats itself but you don't have to. You can escape the inevitable."

Raven scans the bookshelf next to her. In between *Microwave Meals* and *Grow Your Own Dinners* is a book called *Soul-Mates and How To Avoid Them.*

"She said I need to go back in time but advised against time-travel."

"Absolutely," nods Snowbroth, not pouring tea. "Absolutely sound advice."

"But I'm not sure where that leaves us. You know, I don't understand how —"

Snowbroth cuts her off. "We need to heal your soul."

Oh brother, says the voice.

"It's clear that you are an Old Soul," says Snowbroth, "which means that you have more than one lifetime of karmic wounds to consider."

Heal your soul? says the voice. *Karmic wounds?*

Please keep quiet. I need to concentrate.

You're not telling me that you believe in this hocus pocus, are you?

What do you mean? I'm a witch. My life is based on this 'hocus pocus'. I am MRS HOCUS POCUS.

I wish you could hear yourself, says the voice.

I wish I could *stop* hearing myself, says Raven.

"I can tell that you're fractured," says Snowbroth.

"I'm not fractured."

Snowbroth maintains her eye contact. Beautiful, clear green irises. Fresh ponds.

"Okay. Maybe I'm a little fractured," says Raven. "Isn't everyone?"

Snowbroth laughs. "Indeed," she says. "Some, more than others."

Raven's stomach growls.

"Do you know about the ancient Japanese art of *Kintsukuroi?*"

"No," says Raven. She wonders if it would be rude to help herself to a slice of cake.

"It means to repair with gold. So, a valuable piece of china gets broken, and instead of throwing it away, a craftsman will fuse it together using gold. It's beautiful, and it makes it even more valuable than before."

Raven thinks she understands what the witch is getting at.

"Being fractured — being broken — is not always a bad thing. With some care it can make you a far better person and that is what past life regression therapy can help you with. We can draw on your previous lives, as painful as they may be, in order to enrich your current one."

"I'm willing to try it. I'm willing to try anything."

"Tell me why you're here."

She shifts in her seat. Where does she begin? The murder charge? The body in the trunk? The cop she can't stop thinking about? The house she's about to lose. The sister she's lost. The magic she can't find, the freedom she can't live without. In short, she's here to save her life.

"Your skin," says Snowbroth, motioning towards her blistered arms. "Let's start with your skin. And your blue lips."

Raven tells her about the burning and the way her lungs constantly betray her.

"You're afraid of crowds."

"Yes," says Raven.

"I have a theory. About the skin and breathing issues. But we'll get to that in a moment."

Raven starts to feel restless. All this talking. She wants to *do* something. Get somewhere.

Snowbroth stands. "Are you ready?"

Raven eyes the cake.

"To do what?"

"To go back in time."

PART IV

FIRE

57 / THE GATE OF CLOUDS

Snowbroth instructs Raven to lie down on a quilted bed. From where she lies she can catch a glimpse of the bathroom which includes a sauna and an avocado-coloured bath.

"Past life regression therapy," says Snowbroth, pulling up a chair beside her, "is basically a kind of hypnosis. I'll put you under and then guide you to the Gate of Clouds. First you'll travel back through your current life. A recent moment that holds some kind of charge for you, then a childhood moment. Then you'll find yourself in your mother's womb. From there you can visit whichever previous life you choose."

Raven raises herself up on to her elbows.

"How do I choose?"

"There will be a long white corridor —"

"Like when you die? A bright light at the end of a tunnel?"

"Exactly. But it has doors all along it. All kinds of shapes and sizes and colours. You choose whichever door seems right to you."

"How will I know?"

"You'll know."

"What if I… I don't know… what if I get lost? What if I just… disappear in-between the layers of lives?"

"You won't."

"You're sure?"

"That hardly ever happens."

Whoah! says the voice. *Hardly ever happens? So it's happened before?*

What the –

"And your guides will be with you."

"What does that mean?"

"Your Higher Self knows what needs healing. It'll show you the way. You'll only experience what you need to experience in order to clear your karmic account."

"How will I know what to change in those previous lives?"

"You can't change anything even if you try. You're purely an observer. It's like dreaming."

"But if I can't change anything how will that clear my karma?"

"Observance and knowledge has its own energy, as Schrodinger's cat will attest to."

Raven wonders briefly if cats can visit their past lives. They have so many of them.

"Once you know what you're dealing with you'll be able to work through it. That's why this is called therapy."

Raven lies back down again.

This is ridiculous, says the voice. *Your life is an unmitigated disaster —*

—That's a bit harsh —

It's a mess, Raven. And here you are, lying on some moth-eaten hippie-witch's bed when you should be —

There's something about her that I trust.

Is it the bath salts in the entrance hall? Because you can make those yourself, you know, for a tenth of the price. You just need some epsom salts and food colouring.

I think this might work.

"Focus on your breathing," says Snowbroth. "Close your eyes. Feel your weight on the mattress."

Raven takes a deep breath and relaxes her muscles. She's aware of the length of her body weighing down the bed.

"The earth is supporting you, holding you. You have nothing to fear. Breathe into your scalp, your forehead, your jaw."

They work down her body: relaxing her neck, shoulders, elbows, hands.

"Breathe into each finger."

Legs, knees, ankles, feet, until her whole being is heavy and light at the same time. Snowbroth counts her down from ten to one into a light hypnotic trance. Raven is still aware of the room and the witch, but it's as if her consciousness has split and lifted to a higher plane. She can see the dusty window in the room but she can also see a path in a forest. It's like slipping into a nap-time dream.

"You see a path in the woods," says Snowbroth.

"Yes," says Raven.

"You're not wearing shoes."

Raven looks down and she is indeed barefoot. She can feel the cool soil on her soles. Despite the dark shade of the canopy, the sun is warm on her face.

"These trees are old," says Snowbroth. "As old as time itself."

Raven walks along the path, feels the bark of the giant trunks. She hears a stream and walks towards it.

"You find a stream. It's cold and fresh."

There's a glint of small fish as they dart away from her shadow. Raven follows the stream and finds a waterfall. She wades into the silver water and drinks it from her cupped hands. She wants to stay in the water but Snowbroth says, "You see a cave and you go inside it."

Raven squints, looking for a cave. It's just beyond the gush of the waterfall. She makes her way towards it. The cool air of the cave doesn't chill her. The air is thicker here. Raven feels her breath catch in her throat. There's not enough oxygen in here. She doesn't want to go any further. Snowbroth feels her apprehension; places her hand over Raven's, on the bed.

"Your guides are with you. They'll support you. Make you feel safe."

Raven feels their presence. Feels something. Warmth. Her breathing returns to normal.

"There is an archway," says Snowbroth. "And stairs."

Raven walks through the archway and down the eight white marble steps.

"The steps are taking you back in time."

She counts backwards from eight to one and Raven feels as if she is falling. The white marble disappears and there is nothing.

58 / UGLY BUTTERFLIES

Raven opens her eyes.

The 70s time capsule is gone and in its place is a man lying in his bed. It's Sheldon Bond Senior.

He has Stage 4 pancreatic cancer. He had joked when he called Raven to enlist her services, saying, "There is no stage 5". He needs someone who will be willing to end his life for him when the time comes and is finding that time approaching rapidly. Just a month ago, he had said, he was driving his Porsche Carrera with the top down, meeting friends for lunch, drinking Scotch and following the Premier League. But now he finds his appetite vanished, his balance off. He can't hear properly, doesn't have the energy to drive.

"Can it be true," he had asked her, "that my drive to the café around the corner for the paper was my last? That I'll never drive again?"

It isn't just his beloved car he is mourning, of course, but his independence. His life as he knew it. He's plagued by a constant 'empty' pain in his abdomen that gnaws at his mood. His son will not visit, his wives are all estranged. His doctor says her hands are tied; there are no more treatments available, that she can only make him 'comfortable'. He's not at peace with his impending death but he doesn't want to live like this, not when he knows there will be no improvement.

"I should be grateful, I suppose," he said to Raven, "going downhill so quickly. It's what every terminal patient hopes for... once you reach the top of the hill, that is."

It's difficult to be grateful when you feel your life — a good life — is being snatched away from you. He's not the kind of man who will accept being bedridden or fed chicken broth with a spoon. He's lost 8kg in the past 2 weeks. When he can no longer walk, Raven takes him things to cheer him up. He still likes iced-coffee but refuses berry pinwheel pastries, his former favourite combination.

The curtains billow. The heavens open up and blast the house with a dramatic thunderstorm.

Raven reads the newspaper to him as his consciousness swims in and out of shallow sleep. She tells him the soccer score, who has saved a goal, who has been carded. She has been with him for five days and five nights. Every hour drains her, but she tries not to show it. They do this pretend-dance of patient and nurse until this moment when he takes her wrist in his cool, bony fingers and says he is ready.

The truth is that nothing is being snatched away from him, not permanently. Once his heart stops knocking and his cells power down, his energy will move on to a better place. Not heaven (or hell), not a resting place, but a living place. Raven has counselled him that energy cannot be destroyed, only converted, but his imagination cannot stretch that far. It's not a 'better place' — not necessarily, just different — like a new day. You don't know exactly what it will hold, but it'll surely be kinder to him than this suffering. We are all souls surfing through history. This moving on, this energy conversion, is why Raven has no problem with ending someone's current life if that is what they want. An act of compassion, she knows it's no more sinister than putting a child to sleep.

It's Raven's job to allow the soul to ascend, un-barbed, to its beckoning place. Sometimes gentle help is needed: extra analgesics, if one can get them or a steady pillow over a slumbering face.

'I'm ready,' Sheldon says now, clear-eyed. 'I'm ready to go.'

With a long match, Raven lights the nine black candles in the bedroom and smudges the space with sandalwood and willow. She puts a smooth obsidian stone in his palm; recites the Druidic Death Hex under her breath. The magic electrifies the room. It sounds like a cat purring. She takes out her vial of Poppy and loads up a syringe. Pushes the needle into one of the beetroot-purple veins that snake over his arms. She can see the effects of the morphine cascade over him; his relief is instant. She holds his hand as the spirit leaves his body. There is a pull, a falling away and then it's gone. The room exhales. The wheel turns, the cycle spins. There is no need to check his pulse or put a mirror near his mouth to search for breath. Nothing remains but a skeleton in skin.

Raven blows out the candles and packs her things, including a fat envelope of cash with her name on it. She wipes the house down to obliterate any fingerprints and lets herself out of the house, leaving the polished key under the doormat. The wind has picked up again and dead leaves flutter and swirl across her path like ugly butterflies. The moon is waning and she's feeling older, colder, bashed-about. Burnt out. Ashes to glinting ashes.

“Are you okay?” asks Snowbroth, a God-like voice from the sky.

“Yes,” says Raven. She’s still walking on the pavement outside Bond’s house. The biting wind makes her teeth chatter.

“Are you ready to travel further?”

“Yes,” she says. “I’m ready.”

59 / FOREVER STAINED

There is a pretty, ivory-coloured coffin. Pale masks crowd around a gaping hole in the earth. The soil is darkened by rain. She looks at her hands. They are doll-sized, nails freshly clipped. Her shoes are white, leather buckle sandals. Their newness pinches her feet. She wants to move around but bony fingers on her shoulder keep her still. She looks up at the owner of the bones and sees a very young version of her grandmother, her barely-lined cheeks swollen from being wiped of tears. Brenna sees Raven peeking up at her and winks in response. Her other hand is on the shoulder of Jessica, who looks furious and devastated at the same time. She looks seven or eight, which makes Raven around five years old. Far too young to lose a mother.

The priest is talking about grace under suffering, which Raven's mother experienced a lot of. He's saying how we need to find meaning in Anne's suffering and in our own. How there is a unique kind of beauty that suffering affords us. Raven knows, firsthand, that this is not true, that there is only the rose and the worm and that the insidious beast does nothing but destroy the rose. It adds no grace or beauty. It only takes away.

She is angry with the priest for suggesting otherwise, but what do men of the cloth know of love? Not the airy affection they have for their God, but real, skinless, marbled human love.

Raven doesn't agree with what he's saying but she does recognise the voice. A straight-backed Stephen Bishop speaks earnestly and shoots tender glances at Brenna.

The worm had taken her mother from her bit by bit. First it had taken her energy and her sureness of breath. The sparkle in her eyes. Then it took her breasts and her hair. Took her away for days and then weeks at a time, as if rehearsing for this final departure. Raven had seen firsthand the wrenching pain that had knocked the life out of her mother, had been shocked by the blood streaming out of her nose at inopportune times: family celebrations, an Easter breakfast; a Christmas Eve dinner that had left the good tablecloth forever stained. Raven wonders if Bishop had ever had to hold a bowl under his own mother's mouth as she heaved and heaved into it, wonders if he had ever had to deal with the sour stink of everyday suffering.

Raven's father isn't crying. His face is the colour of the casket he's staring at. Raven wonders if he's already planning his grief getaway, his heartbreak holiday, his escape from the family home left devastated by Anne's ultimate vanishing. A good father, a Real Man, would have stayed with his children, people said. He would have hugged them close and stayed put, instead of packing a bag and getting on a plane. But Raven understands why he left. Why he had to leave. Facing the half-empty bed, the deserted house, the haunted rocking chair every day, looking at her and her sister's bleak faces, so very similar to his late wife's — brutally similar — had been too much for him to bear. He could have stayed but he was sure to have unravelled. It seemed a terribly cowardly thing to do — to run away — but Raven saw the bravery in it too. Sometimes you have to save yourself. She understands that.

"Are you ready to leave?" asks Snowbroth.

Raven feels the edges of the memory blurring. "Yes."

"You're going back to the stairway. One. Two. Three. You're there."

"Yes."

"You're going to go down more steps. Another eight."

Raven walks down the white steps. Again, there is a falling sensation and she finds herself curled up, constricted, surrounded by sticky, warm water. She hears a bounding heartbeat.

"You're in your mother's womb. You chose this life."

It's the safest she has ever felt, the most intimate hug imaginable. She has no need to think. She just lets the sensation of being so close to her mother ensconce her. She wants to stay forever.

"It's time to go," says Snowbroth.

"I don't want to."

"It's time. We have work to do."

Raven is back at the stairway but now there is a big, open tunnel in front of her. It is in another time, another place. Snowbroth counts down from ten to one and Raven is pushed forward towards a bright light. She touches the sides as she walks and the walls are smooth. Doors appear and disappear. Doors, as far as she can see.

"Choose a door," says Snowbroth. "You'll know which one is right."

Raven keeps walking until she sees a slim green door that speaks to her. There is another door right next to it, consisting of old wooden planks that also demands her attention, but she puts her hand on the unpolished copper doorknob of the green door and turns it.

"Where are you?" asks Snowbroth.

"Trees," says Raven. "Another forest. A long time ago. Am I in the right place?"

"You are in the right place."

The air is startlingly fresh. Sweet. Is this what air used to smell like? Humus and rain and pine needles.

"I'm walking away from the darkness."

"To a clearing?"

"To the edge of the forest. There's a village here. It's where I live. Where I've always lived."

She's in a hurry. Out of breath.

"Watch your breathing," says Snowbroth. "Keep calm. What's happening?"

"I have to hurry. I have to get out of the woods."

"Is there something in the woods? Are you in danger?"

"There is danger but not behind me."

"You're running towards the danger?"

"I have to."

The green forest air gives way to manure and woodsmoke.

"What century are you in?"

"I don't know."

"Look at your feet. Are you female?"

Raven looks down. She's wearing unsophisticated boots veined with mud, a faded grey dress of thick wool, hem-spattered. Her hair is heavy: long, and plaited into a bun. Over it, she feels a cotton cap. She's holding a wicker basket heavy with herbs.

"Yes. Dark to Middle Ages, I'd guess. Fifteenth century? Sixteenth."

She starts running.

"Where are you going?"

"I'm going home."

60 / BLACKWATER ESTUARY

Maldon County

Essex, 1579 AD

Poppy runs through the nettles and mud. Her boots threaten to betray her by sticking to the mire. She has, in her basket, the fruits of her morning's foraging: rosemary blossoms, clove stalks and resin of myhrr. She's tempted to abandon the harvest but thinks that the plants might come in handy for what's ahead, so she firms her grasp on the handle and keeps running. Above her, the ravens cry.

Thomas, the bearded dairy man, greets her and she raises a hand in acknowledgement. Her neighbour, Picot, does the same. She smells the ale on him as she passes. She can tell that he wants her to stop, wants a chat, but she doesn't have time. She is needed at her homestead.

The hand-painted wooden sign on her gate says Elderberry Farm, but it's not a farm, not really. It's a modest plot with just enough land to keep her pantry well-stocked and her neighbours sweet with gifts and good bartering. As the village herbalist and honey-keeper, she's known to have the greenest fingers in Maldon county.

Poppy jogs past the town square. The tradespeople are packing up their wares for the day: spun cloth; tallow candles; lavender soap; crusty loaves of rye. She'll bake her own bread in the morning. She prefers a finer grind to what the bakers here sell. You have to be careful of telling people that kind of thing though. You have to buy a loaf of theirs every now and then just to show that you don't think yourself better than them. Poppy doesn't care much about what people think, but she also knows that it's the tallest flowers that get scythed.

At last she reaches her dirt track: the Osgoods, the Middletons, the Giffords and then she bursts through her gate and scrambles into the hall. She can't see her Jacqueline anywhere. Her cat skitters out of her way.

"Poppy!" shouts a man with his hat in his white-knuckled hands. "You're here!"

Lily, his wife, is bent over and groaning.

"Did Jacquie find you? We sent her to find you."

The ravens had sounded the alarm, pulled her from the forest. But that is not for the Glovers to know.

Poppy is perspiring; breathing hard. She moves over to Goodwife Glover and takes her hands.

"Lily. Is it bad?"

"There's something wrong," says the woman, her face as pale as a waning moon. "I can feel it. There's something wrong."

"She's in pain," offers Glover.

"Thank you," says Poppy, "I'll take over now."

The man looks relieved as she leads his lowing wife away. A labour chamber is no place for a man.

There is a welcoming coolness of the stone floors but this won't last long: the fireplace is stocked with wood and kindling, ready to come alive at the flick of a flint. Poppy fills her black kettle with well water and hangs it over the straw, which she lights. She flings off her hat, smoothes her wisps down and scrubs her hands. People scoff at this habit, but she believes that clean hands are an outward symbol of a clean mind and she needs to keep her wits about her if this is going to be a difficult birth.

"When did they start?"

"This morning," says Lily, "but they were easy."

Poppy opens all the lattice windows and drawers, unties all the knots.

"You should have come over."

She gives Lily a Jasper gemstone to hold.

"I didn't want to bother you too soon. I was timing them. But then —" she grinds her teeth, "But then something changed."

"Climb on the birthing stool. Let me take a look."

"Poppy," she says, desperate, grabbing Poppy's wrist. "I don't want the baby to die."

"The baby won't die." Poppy begins rubbing salve on Lily's tightening belly. Perhaps what Lily also meant was, 'I don't want to die'. But that she cannot guarantee.

Three hours later, just as Goodwife Glover's screams threaten to strip the straw from the very roof, just as Poppy is deciding that she will have to cut the baby out, there is a change; a shift. The breeze picks up outside and whistles its news. There is to be a concession for this woman, and, surely enough, the screeching subsides and a waxy grey head appears. One more exhausted push from Lily is enough to deliver him in his entirety, despite his generous size. The baby is limp and blue and isn't taking a breath. Poppy rubs him vigorously with a cloth, trying to wake him up. She smacks his sides, pokes his ribs, speaks to him sternly, telling him it's time to wake up, but the baby does not stir. The women make sad eye contact. Lily is too exhausted to cry.

Poppy lays him on the bed, pinches his nostrils closed and uses her own breath to inflate the boy's lungs. On her third exhalation he starts. He gurgles and coughs. Poppy clears his mouth and breathes into him again and this time he takes the next breath himself and rewards the women with a yell of indignation.

Poppy, lightheaded with relief, cuts his cord at four fingers and wraps him up in swaddling cloth, lays him on Lily's chest, plugs his mouth with his mother's nipple. What happened? What changed the almost certain outcome that this baby would not live? She cleans up while the newborn suckles, then bathes him in salt and honey to dry up his humors and comfort his limbs, all the while sending up a prayer of thanks to the forces that let this be.

When Glover comes to collect his wife and son he is buoyant with gratitude. He bundles them out into the night and into his cart, which he has lined with fresh linen for the occasion. He pays Poppy in cotton shifts and salted meat and she can tell that he wishes he could give her more. Just before he instructs the horse to trot, Lily stops him, and takes a ribbon from around her neck.

"Take this," she says, pressing it into Poppy's palm. "It was my mother's and her mother's before her."

"I can't."

"Take it. You saved my boy's life. I want you to have it."

Poppy opens her hand. A silver amulet knotted onto the ribbon shines in the starlight. The face of a wolf.

"It's Fenrir," Lily whispers, "the Wolf God." But Poppy knows that already.

Jacqueline had arrived home while the birth was in progress and put herself to bed. She is an independent child. She has to be, with her father gone and the hours that Poppy works. She sits on the edge of her seven-year-old's bed, near the purring cat who lifts her sleepy head in greeting. Poppy strokes Jacqueline's cheek, her chin, marvelling at the beautiful creature sleeping before her; marvelling at the terrible love she feels for this being. Still a baby, really, despite her brave appearance and her sword-fighting skills.

Poppy will need her help tomorrow. She's behind on the preserving and pickling of the late harvest and she doesn't like to see one ear of wheat wasted. Jacquie will complain, saying she has a village to conquer — she's going through a Viking phase — but she'll do her chores first. She always does.

There's a knock on the door. The first thing that comes to mind is the Glover baby. Has something happened? Has he fallen asleep and not woken up? She makes her way to the front of the house and pulls open the door.

The fire is fading, so a naked Poppy slides out of her thistledown bed to add more coal. Her braids are undone, her dark hair drifts down her back. Devereaux watches her move in the firelight.

"God, you're something," he growls. "Come back here, you vixen."

"Not a vixen," says Poppy, moving towards him.

He takes her hands. "No?"

She leans towards him, puts his hands on her breasts. Shows him the amulet on her chest. "A wolf."

"Ah," he says, and howls like a homesick hound.

"Shush! Shush!" she says, laughing, covering his mouth. "You'll wake Applejack."

He stops howling, sucks her finger instead.

"You're delicious. Tell me again why you won't come and live with me?"

"Stop it," says Poppy. "You know that's impossible, with your… status."

"Since when do you care what people think?"

"It's not that."

"I could hire you. You could live in the house under the guise of proper employment."

"And what? Become your concubine?"

"My staff are discreet."

She shoots him a look of dubiety. "No thank you."

"It would be a luxurious life, compared to this, anyway."

"I'm very happy here, thank you very much, in this humble hovel."

"I didn't mean that. You wouldn't have to worry about money.

You wouldn't have to work. You could save these lovely fingers of yours."

Poppy laughs. Not work? She shakes her head. It wouldn't be her life.

There is a glint in Devereaux's eye. He's angry.

"It's because of him, isn't it?"

He's always had a quick temper, this pale, high-cheekboned man. He was spoilt as a child is Poppy's guess. Never wanted for anything. As beautiful as a god, but blighted all the same.

"It's because of that bastard."

"Don't call him that. He's my husband."

"Husband?" He laughs without humour. "Richard left you five years ago."

"He's still my husband."

He raises his voice. "You think he'll come back, but he won't."

Poppy knows she should stop the argument, soothe Devereaux with words and caresses, but she's had a long day and is not in the mood for supplication.

"You don't know that."

"You don't even know if he's alive!"

"He's Applejack's father."

"He doesn't give a damn about Applejack."

"Watch your words Devereaux."

"You still love him. You're a fool!" He smashes his pewter goblet on the floor. It clangs against the stone and rolls to a stop.

"I think you should leave."

Devereaux sets his jaw and begins pulling his breeches on.

"And this time… this time, I don't think you should come back."

He puts on his doublet.

"You don't mean that."

"I do. You want to control me and I will not be controlled."

She knows she is playing with fire. He grabs his jerkin off the nearby stool sending the chair cracking to the floor. Shakes it onto his shoulders. He grabs her arm roughly, takes one last hard look at her. She can tell that he wants to strike her. Bruise her. He wants to see her cry.

"You'll be sorry," he says, his irises black with fury. He squeezes her jaw so hard her teeth cut into the inside of her cheek.

She unclamps his grip, returns his solid gaze, although she is shaking inside. The taste of copper is in her mouth. "Goodbye, Devereaux."

Poppy is tending the bees when the Justice of the Peace arrives. The honey yield has been especially good since she's been experimenting with dog roses and wild raspberry. Jacqueline comes to call her. Her lips, hands and apron are spattered with crimson and it makes for a macabre sight.

"Have you finished with the beetroot?" she asks her daughter, patting her head and twirling a loose strand of fringe.

"Yes, Mama."

"Good girl." She looks at the officer, then back at Applejack. "Go wash up and then you can play."

"But I haven't yet —"

"It's all right," she says. "Take a break. We'll carry on this afternoon."

Applejack hesitates, then whirls away.

Poppy shields her eyes from the morning sun. "Good day, Valance," she says, and he tips his hat to her. "Is there something you're needing? More oak tincture for your wife, perhaps? I have some at the ready."

Valance looks uncomfortable. He shifts his weight from foot to foot. "We've had another complaint."

Poppy sighs, crosses her arms. "What is it, this time?"

"Picot. He says that you've hexed his milk cow."

"Will you… will you say that again?"

"His cow. When he retired last night the cow was in perfect health. This morning it won't stand up."

"And how does this have anything to do with me?"

"He says you had an argument last week."

"It was hardly an argument. He owes me money and I reminded him it was overdue."

"He says you cursed the cow for revenge."

"That's ridiculous. Picot is poor and he wants my land. He's always had his eye on it."

"That may be. But, as I said, it's not the first complaint. And your neighbour is not the only one asserting that —"

"Asserting what?"

"Asserting that you've made a deal with the Devil."

Poppy laughs out loud. “The Devil?” she says. “How does one go about doing something like that?”

Valance lifts and lowers his shoulders. His whole body is a shrug. Poppy feels like striking some sense into his barrel chest.

“You spend too much time in the forest,” he says.

“I’m a herbalist.”

“And you know that the forest is where the evil spirits convene.”

“Nonsense.”

“In the woods. The Robbins boy saw you… dancing. Speaking in tongues.”

“That boy is troubled. He is always watching me. He stalks me wherever I go.”

“You were angry. You chased him away.”

“I’m always chasing him away. He’s menacing.”

“When you were angry with him a storm brewed.”

“Did it? I don’t remember.”

“It killed the dog. The Robbins’s dog.”

“What is the charge, exactly? Do you believe I killed a dog?”

“I’m not sure what to believe. But —”

“You know that I am a good woman, Valance.”

“You don’t come to church as often as you used to.”

“I work this land on my own. I treat sick people. I birth babies. I don’t always have time for Pastor Thurlowe’s ramblings.”

“It’s that kind of thing,” says Valance, sucking his teeth. “It’s saying that kind of thing that gets you into trouble. You read too much."

"So I'll be on trial for dancing in the woods and reading too much?"

"We'll begin at four. In the town hall."

"An inquisition?"

"An examination. You have to answer to the allegations. That's the way it is."

"But they're ridiculous."

"That's the way it is."

The town hall is packed by half-three. Poppy has never realised how many people want to see her undone until she walks into the humming, high-roofed room. There is a ripple of quiet as she steps through the threshold. The Justice of the Peace catches a glimpse of her and is relieved. He doesn't want to be forced to arrest her. The timber boards creak under her as she moves towards the front of the room where the pulpit serves as a make-shift witness box. Pastor Thurlowe looks on intently. He has, Poppy is certain, been waiting patiently for this day to come. She looks out into the gathering, seeing men she had saved from the Sweating Sickness, women whose hands she had held through labour, now bouncing on their laps the very children she helped deliver.

"Poppy Gossard, you stand accused," says Valance, "of forming a pact with the Devil. "Of naughty dealings, and, ultimately, of witchcraft."

The crowd murmurs. Poppy's hands are white fists. There is a buzz and a snap in the room as if there is a stormcloud above them.

"Willard Picot. Please come forward and make your case against the accused."

Poppy's neighbour, sober for once, comes up to address Valance. He tells the story of how he oftentimes sees strange happenings at Poppy's home. He smells her potions brewing, hears her cry out at night in pain and ecstasy as she indulges in sexual relations with the devil. Bawdy comments escape the gallery. Pastor Thurlowe's ears turn red and burn at the idea.

"And how do you know, sir, that it's the presence of the devil that you observe?"

"Depraved fornication." Spittle gathers at the sides of his mouth. "If you were to hear it, Justice, you would know it, too."

"No wonder her husband left her!" shouts someone from the gallery.

"She's had her fair share of company since then," says another onlooker.

Picot speaks slowly and deliberately as if he has rehearsed his story. He tells of their argument over his debt, and of how his milk cow is still too ill to stand. "I'll wager right now," he says, "that if I were to pay her the money she's so intent on, my cow would recover forthwith. Otherwise, I don't think she'll make it through the night."

"Do it, then," cries a lout from the gallery. "Pay her and we'll see."

Picot is known for his poverty. The little money he has always seems to find its way to the ale house. When Poppy had sold him the scouring sand he needed she hadn't been expecting a hasty return.

Picot shoots a look at Valance and Valance agrees. "Pay her, Picot and we'll see."

The man pulls out his leather purse and counts out some bronze coins. He counts them twice, then hands them over to Valance, who deposits them into Poppy's clammy palm. Where, she wonders, did he get this money?

"We'll listen to the other witnesses then make our way to Picot's holding."

Other witnesses? Who else will betray her today?

Goodwife Kemp takes the stand. Tells of how her summer crop of rye spoiled before it was harvested. Under questioning, she reveals that she saw Poppy Gossard's striped cat amongst the stalks, rubbing its cheeks on the green of the produce. Six days later the plants were infected with a mould that drooped their crowns and rotted their grains. Bent, crooked, blighted.

"Goodie Kemp," says Valance, "do you contend that the Gossard cat is capable of evil deeds?"

"A cat is a cat," sniffs Kemp. "I afford no special powers to them unless they are bewitched."

"Bewitched?"

"Every person in Maldon County knows that Gossard is a sorceress and that that creature is her familiar."

A low moan emerges from the gallery. Some people toss their heads. Poppy frowns at them, trying to establish the mood of their judgement. Kemp is excused. The crowd waits.

"I request the testimony now of Goodwife Glover," says Valance.

Thank God. A friend.

Lily limps, baby bundled in her arms and sighs in her direction. Poppy can smell the rose oil on the baby's skin. She tells the court of her difficult birth.

"He wasn't breathing," she tells the Justice. "He wasn't moving. His skin was saxe. But Poppy… Poppy brought him back to life." The baby fusses and she rocks him to comfort him.

Pastor Thurlowe cannot sit still any longer. He stands up, bringing the court to attention. He seems genuinely shocked by the testimony. "Brought him back to life? Are we to believe that you gave birth to a dead baby and this woman summoned his spirit to live?"

"I didn't mean —"

"How did she do it?" Thurlowe asks. "Was there a tincture? An incantation?"

"No, no, pastor. All I mean is that I think, with a less experienced midwife, Baby Glover wouldn't be here today."

"How did she do it, woman? Tell us!"

"I was almost delirious with pain. Exhaustion. I may not be a dependable witness."

"Tell us what you saw," says Valance. He is gentle with her.

"She held him up, scolded him, smacked him."

"She struck a newborn infant?" asks Thurlowe, eager to show his astonishment to the gallery.

"It's not an uncommon practice," says Lily. "A man wouldn't know, of course, of the happenings in a labour chamber."

"Go on," says Valance.

"He still wouldn't wake. And by then I was sure that he would not."

"Then what did she do?"

"She… she put her lips to his. She used her own breath to wake him up."

The pastor seems at once horrified and joyous. "Are you saying that this woman, Poppy Gossard, breathed life into your dead infant?"

There is silence in the hall. Lily seems unsure of how to answer. She looks at Poppy, then searches for her husband's face in the gallery.

"Goodie Glover," says Valance, "Is it true?"

"That's not how it was. Or, it's not what you think. It was a miracle. A wondrous gift."

"Blasphemy!" shouts Thurlowe. "Human beings are not capable of miracle-making. Only the Good Lord Himself can do such a thing."

"Perhaps the Good Lord used Poppy as his instrument," says Lily, eyes brimming.

"More like the Devil," says Thurlowe. "The Devil's instrument. The Devil. The Devil. The Devil."

Lily shields her baby from the pastor, as if his words create a sinister splatter about him.

"There was no evil-doing in that room," she urges, looking desperate now to leave the stand, but the pastor won't allow it.

"You said yourself that you are an unreliable witness to the event. You were barely conscious and Gossard took advantage of your vulnerability."

The people buzz with anticipation.

"That's not the truth," says Lily.

Poppy stands. "This is nothing but scandalmongering. I will not be slandered in this way."

Valance steps forward with his hands out. "Good people, please," but the pastor is in full swing. He struts as if on a stage.

"I put it to the good people of Maldon County that Poppy Gossard is a powerful witch, guilty of general *maleficium* and of harmful sorcery against her neighbours."

A roar reverberates from the back of the court. People stand and jeer. Poppy can't tell if they are in her favour or against her. Valance offers his hand to Lily, helps her down off the stand and leads her to her husband, who stands, nonplussed, just outside of the commotion.

"She's a good woman, Valance." He takes Poppy's trembling hand. "You know she is."

"Picot's cow will decide the matter," says the Justice. "We'll be on our way there now."

It's a twenty-minute walk from the town hall to Picot's place and Picot leads the way even though everyone knows exactly where he lives. They walk over a dark patch of hardened sand, stained by the blood of a bear recently baited there and ripped apart by dogs. Picot side-eyes Poppy. Guilt shines from his face. Valance walks beside his charge. Poppy is unsure if he's there to protect her or to keep her from escaping. Where would she go?

They reach the blackjack lane which snakes up to Picot's ramshackle house. The townspeople, their target now in view, hurry past the weeds, tripping on the pink stones. Poppy lifts her woollen shift to avoid the unlucky seeds. Picot, still sober, is surprisingly agile as he strides up to his plot. Before Poppy catches sight of the cow she knows it is dead. Her neighbour wails and curses.

"She killed it!" he shouts, pointing a dirty finger at Poppy. "She killed my cow."

The people gather around the poor animal, belly distended by death fumes, bluebottle flies for eyelashes.

"You said that if the animal recovered it would be proof of my magick," says Poppy. "You can't have it both ways."

"You tricked us," says Picot. "Of course you would not allow the cow to recover if it would be evidence of your evildoing."

"So whether the cow lived or died it would be proof of my witchcraft?"

"You're not called cunning folk for nought."

"I've had enough of this eyewash," says Poppy. "I've honest work to do." She begins walking towards her house, mere metres away, but a strong grip on her arm holds her back.

"I think we need to get back to the inquest," says Valance.

"It was an examination. Now it's an inquest?"

"Now it's a trial."

The Robbins boy comes running up, face afluster. "There's no time for a trial," he says. His breathing is short and sour.

"What do you mean, son?"

"Her magick is too strong. She's already taken revenge all over town."

"Gossard has been in my company all hours today. She's had no time to make mischief."

"Her familiars carry out her demonry for her. I've seen it with my own eyes."

"Your imagination is the thing of demons, lad," says Poppy, "not my work."

The boy ignores her, licks his lips. "It's true. I saw that cat of hers, black and oily as tar slipping into Goodie Kemp's yard and attacking one of her hens. The fowl is dead. As dead as this cow."

A voice from the gathering, "I saw that devil cat go into the house of the Glovers."

The people titter in fright.

Valance turns from Poppy to the boy. "For what? What now?"

"To murder the baby, of course," splutters the boy. "The unbaptised baby. She's taking revenge on all the witnesses who testified today. And when she's finished with them, you will all be next."

Valance seems alarmed.

"That cat," the Robbins boy says, "I'm going to tie that cat in a sack and drown it in the river."

Poppy slaps the boy hard across the face. The onlookers gasp and back away from her.

"Shut your mouth, vermin," hisses Poppy. "Don't you see how dangerous your game is?"

"It's no game," he shouts, rubbing his cheek. "I've seen this witch in the forest, communing with Satan."

"I've also seen her," says Beckett, the cobbler, "coming out of the woods at all hours with her herbs and poisons."

"And me," says Ellis.

"And me," says Landsdowne. "And I've seen her talk to animals."

"She'll kill that Glover baby if we let her."

"Where is Goodwife Glover? Someone must fetch her. Warn her."

"I think we have all the proof we need," comes a voice from the back of the gathering. The people part and Pastor Thurlowe walks towards Poppy and Valance. "Raise your eyes to the treetops. Do you see the ravens gathered?"

The people look up, and indeed, the uppermost branches are host to scores of black birds.

"There is evil in our midst," says Thurlowe. "It is imperative that we exorcise it before more harm is done."

Townspeople prod Poppy in her back forcing her back towards the town square. Thurlowe clutches his Bible and recites verse. She tries to break away from them but Landsdowne brings rough twine to tie her hands behind her back and Ellis threatens to put a sack over her head. Jacqueline comes running, but the villagers keep her away.

"Ma!" she screams, "Ma!"

Poppy thrashes at her captors to get to Jacqueline. She's almost able to touch Jacquie's hand, the soft, hot hands she knows so well, but they pull her back into their marching circle. Poppy's wrists chafe and bleed. She tries to escape again and again and the people become angered by her perseverance. Beckett strikes her to quieten her spirit. Every attempt to get to Jacquie now is met with a hammering to her face or a kick to her stomach. By the time they reach town she can no longer hear well and her face is dripping with blood. Her daughter's screams are dull in the distance. Her dress is torn and she has lost her shoes.

The old gallow-tree is grey in the shade of the triangular tower of the church. Tired sunlight, the colour of orange preserve, washes the top half of the surrounding buildings. Poppy is led up the stairs by Valance, who loses his grip on her for a moment. His hands tremble. The executioner stands alongside pastor Thurlowe, who is crimson-faced and still spouting verse like a madman. The bearded hangman readies the noose for her, but the pastor stops him.

"The mercy of the Lord insists I give you one last chance," he says.

Poppy's eyes search for her daughter in the crowd. Faces, angry and shocked, stare back. People she has shared her modest harvests with, given honey gifts, baked bread for, mixed medicine. Children she has minded, babies she has delivered. She wants to believe this is not really happening, but her mind and heart are so wide awake that she knows this is no terror dream. The noose is real. She can smell the barley breath of the hangman.

"One last chance," says the hell-faced pastor, "to confess your sins and give your life to the Lord."

"I am innocent of the crimes you are so eager to lay upon me," says Poppy. "I have done no wrong."

She sees Devereaux on the steps of the town hall. He won't look in her direction. She wants to call out to him for help. Can't he see what is happening here? Surely with his money and influence he can help her? But then she sees him exchange a few words with Picot and Picot swills from a new cup and then Poppy understands.

"Confess!" the pastor shouts into her face.

"I have nothing to confess."

"Allow the Lord God to show you mercy, child."

"I will not beg for forgiveness for something I have not done."

A blue calm settles over Poppy. A resignation. A knowledge that this is what has to happen.

"Do you think I see not the evil in your body?"

"Any evil you see in my body is in your mind alone."

"Confess!" he shouts again.

"*You* are the wicked one," Poppy says and spits in his face.

Thurlowe lifts a hand as if to strike her, but she does not flinch. His eyes are mean coal-sparks.

"This Satan-worshipper before you," he says to the crowd, wiping his face, "this blackened soul is past redemption."

Cries of assent echo from the crowd. The hangman steps forward again, places the noose around Poppy's neck and tightens it. She battles to breathe. The pastor stops him as before. "Stop," he says and struggles to loosen it.

The crowd is silenced. Valance looks on, clearly hoping for a reprieve. Thurlowe puts his hand on Poppy's shoulder.

"A noose is not enough," he says. "We need to exorcise the very demons that inhabit her being."

The executioner seems unsure what to do. Valance starts to argue but a look from the pastor cuts him down.

"Fire," says Thurlowe, "Only fire will purge the wicked spirit of this woman."

A cry goes up from the onlookers. The Robbins boy is already depositing twigs and other kindling beneath the tumble-down timber platform. Thurlowe helps the hangman lash Poppy to the hanging post.

"Exodus 22 verse 18. Thou shalt not suffer a witch to live," he says to her as he trusses her with a dirty cord. "Thou shalt not suffer a witch to live."

The fire has been lit. Poppy can feel the sneaking warmth on her bruised soles, can smell the smoke. She finally catches sight of Jacqueline who is screaming and flailing below.

"Take her away," shouts Poppy, her voice hoarse. "I beg of you do not let her witness this."

Her legs are starting to burn. She feels warm liquid, like tea, wet her shift. She looks down and sees that her bladder has emptied. Thurlowe is rigid, one arm pointing up to salute his imagined heaven, the fingers of the other hand on his brow, eyes closed, as he mutters his own incantations. A raven swoops down like an arrow and pecks at his eyelid, scratching his cheek. He waves it away and finds blood on his cheekbone.

"Ma! Ma!" cries the girl, still a baby. Still her precious baby. Poppy tries to reach out to her but her arms are firmly bound in place. The fire is gathering momentum. Her dress catches the flame.

"Please," cries Poppy to the crowd. "Please take my Applejack away." She sees the baker's face, the hay-man, the seamstress - all cold and unmoving as winter cliffs. She tries to ask again but she cannot breathe for the smoke. No one heeds her but then Glover breaks through the crowd, calling out and clapping at the people. In his wake, Lily Glover, babe in arms, pushes forward and grabs Jacquie's arm and leads her away.

Poppy can hardly hear or see; the heat is agony. Her skin blisters and pops. Her mind begins drifting to a higher place. She sees the Robbins boy pick-pocketing the gawping onlookers. The pain becomes unendurable. More ravens come, perching on railings and barrels and abandoned market-stalls. Soon the air is black with them.

Glover is bellowing. “Help her, help her,” he is shouting, “she burns too slowly.”

Suddenly people are spurred into action as if woken from a trance and they gather whatever fuel they can and add it to the bonfire beneath her. There is light and darkness and no air to breathe. Poppy sees peach blossoms and lavender and bees and Applejack as a toddler; dimples; clouds; soil. Stars sparkle before her and at last, at last the torment fades, at first into black, then grey, then white.

61 / RUSSIAN NESTING DOLLS

Raven sits up on the bed as if she has been electrocuted. She snatches her hand away from Snowbroth.

"That was difficult for you."

Raven clutches at her body, assuring herself that she is back in her own body, in her own lifetime. Only when she is certain that she has herself back does she relax into weeping. Snowbroth passes her a tissue.

"Difficult is good. It's very good. It means that we're getting somewhere."

Raven keeps sobbing. She cries until her ribs ache. Snowbroth stands to pat her back. "Difficult is good," she says again, and Raven leans into her soft middle until there are no more tears.

"What did you learn about yourself?"

"I don't know. I'm still trying to… process… what happened to me."

"You learned why you don't like crowds."

"Pitchforks."

"And why you have difficulty breathing."

"Yes."

"And your burning skin."

"Yes."

Raven gets up and splashes her face with cold water from the avocado-coloured sink. She pats some of the water on the back of her neck, too.

"It's not over yet," says Snowbroth. "Going back is not enough."

"But you said - you said knowledge changes reality."

"Real Knowledge. Observing is not enough. This is the 'therapy' part of past life regression therapy. We need to *understand* what happened to you."

"I do understand what happened to me. Reckless rumour-mongers put a noose around my neck, women who I helped through the births of their children, whose hands I held when they were at their most vulnerable."

"And your lover betrayed you."

"Yes."

"Do you have trust issues with men?"

"Yes. No. I have trust issues with people. Women cannot be trusted either."

"They all betrayed you."

"Yes."

"Are you able to maintain close relationships of any kind?"

Raven thinks of past lovers, of Jessica and the kids and of Kruger.

“I prefer animals.”

“Animals can’t betray you.”

Raven nods.

“Do you see,” Snowbroth asks, “how things begin to make sense?”

“Yes.”

“Try to think of another example of how your life now is impacted by this particular past life.”

“Applejack,” says Raven, and her eyes begin stinging again. “I lost my daughter. I never want to feel that again.”

“Yes,” says Snowbroth.

“I never want to have children.”

“It’s not that you don’t want to have children.”

“I’m afraid of having children. Life is too easily crumbled.”

“Yes,” says Snowbroth. “Yes.”

Snowbroth gestures for Raven to come back to the bed.

“Now comes the difficult part,” she says.

“NOW comes the difficult part?”

“You have to forgive those people for what they did to you.”

“What’s the point? They’re all three hundred years dead.”

“They’re not. They’re as alive as you are.”

“Why should I forgive them? Why should they be let off the hook for what they’ve done?”

"No one is being let off the hook. You know that everyone has their own karma to deal with."

"Why then? What does my forgiveness have to do with them?"

"You know the saying," says Snowbroth. "about hate being poisonous."

"Hate is like drinking poison and expecting the other person to die."

"Yes. Forgiveness is the antidote. You're not doing it for them. You're doing it for yourself."

"Okay. I understand that."

"But, more importantly, you have to accept what happened because, what was done to you, was done to you for a reason. Those villagers were following their destinies just as you were."

"What reason? Why would it be my destiny to die at the hands of those small-minded sheeple?"

"That's what we need to find out. We have to go deeper for that."

Raven shakes her head. No no no no! She's not going back.

"We'll only know once we find the life that led you there."

"Another previous life?"

"Yes. Usually I wouldn't do more than one session in a day but your case is exceptional. How many other doors did you want to open when you were at the Gate of Clouds?"

"One," says Raven. "One in particular."

"Then that should be enough to solve your current dilemma. To solve the blazing of your skin."

Raven pictures her soul's history as a snug sequence of antique

Russian nesting dolls to be carefully unpacked. How far back will they go? The idea is exhausting.

"I don't think I can go under again. I don't have the psychic energy."

"Once you have completed this journey your energy will return. You will regain your power. You did something that caused that noose around your neck. You need to forgive your executioner, as well as understand what you did previously — before the Middle Ages — to cause that execution."

"I find it hard to believe that I did something so heinous that I deserved to be sent to the gallows by an entire village."

"You'd be surprised," says Snowbroth, "at the things I've seen in this room. Those were bloody times."

Snowbroth counts Raven down and she slips under easily. She makes her way down the white corridor to the door that is calling her: blackened timber planks hammered together with wrought nails. A giant stubborn latch that she has to wrench open.

"Who are you?" asks Snowbroth.

Raven looks down at her hands. Flexes them. They are oversized. Rough. Hairy. She can feel the strength in her arms.

"I'm a man," she says. "Strong."

She looks around. She's sitting at a table in a hall warmed by fire. A feast is laid out before her, roasted meat and sour apples.

"Bone utensils," she says. "Drinking horns. A language I don't understand. It sounds… Nordic."

"You are among friends?"

The hefty men around her bellow with laughter and lick their greasy fingers and rub their oily beards. Someone affectionately wallops her back. "Yes."

"Good," Snowbroth says. "Allow yourself to slide deeper into this life. Listen closely and the words will begin to make sense to you."

Raven hesitates. She has a strong sense of foreboding, as if a part of her remembers this lifetime and doesn't want to re-live it. She feels as though she is hanging onto a ledge. Below her is a swirling abyss. She doesn't want to fall but her hands are losing their grip.

"Let go," says Snowbroth, and she does.

62 / FENRIR

Norway, 835 AD

"Bring us some more wine, boy," says Halstein, emptying his drinking horn as if it's a thimble of dandelion dew. Stig doesn't need to be asked twice. He scampers down the hall. Colborn approves.

"May as well finish our supplies before tomorrow's expedition," Halstein says. His face is full of firelight; his voice is as big as his barrel-chest. He fills his horn again with his clumsy bear hands, neither noticing nor caring how much of the expensive drink he spills. "To the feaste!"

"Aye!" shouts Fiske. "To the feaste! *Skål!*"

Skål! Skål! The cheers rise in the air like arrows.

Colborn joins in the merriment despite the feeling of dread in his bowels. He looks around him, as if for the first time, as if he is a stranger in this longroom which is usually as familiar to him as his own house. He gazes, with a new flicker of tenderness, at Stefnīr. His wife catches his eye and swings her foot, kicking his ankle with a grin. He watches Stig heave another great log onto the red coals. When did the boy shoot up like that? He was just yesterday a babe, mewling and suckling, growing like cottongrass in summer. Now the imp is as tall as a crucible sword.

The Norse men, women and children are all painted warm by the flames in the hearth and in their heads. All manner of food is set before them: pickled duck eggs, cracked and marbled with beet, salted seal-meat, horse fillet from the roasting spit. Stig hurries back to the table balancing two bottles of wine as carefully as if his life depended on it. Halstein takes them from the barefooted boy and rewards him with a back-pat that nearly sends him flying. He stumbles on the woven wattle of the floor, but he is smiling.

"Come here," says Stefnīr. People usually listen to Stefnīr, even those not of her womb, even those older and stronger than she. Before Stig reaches his mother, Colborn lunges for him, drags him, protesting, onto his lap. He musses the straw on his head that passes for hair, his mother's hair. *My eyes though,* thinks Colborn, *and my nose. It's fairer on him than it is on me.*

Halstein leers at Stefnīr. "Give the boy some mead."

"He's too young," says Stefnīr. "He hasn't yet seen five winters."

"Too young?" booms Halstein. "I was fighting Saxons when I was his age."

"Aye, aye," she says, stretching her neck. "I'm sure you were."

The clanspeople laugh.

"I was!" he says. "They used to call me Stalwart Stein. My job was to spear the heads of the monks."

Stig looks up at the man, lips ajar.

"Father would give me a copper coin for every skull I spiked,"

Halstein says. "Before long I was chopping them down me-self. How do you think I got to become a Jarl? My purse of Saint Peters started when I was half the size of Stig."

Colborn catches Stefnīr rolling her eyes; he runs his hand over her back.

"If only yer cock was as swollen as yer battle tales," says Ingvar. There is a sudden stiltedness in the festivities. Halstein frowns at his wife and at the rest of the table. Ingvar stares back at him, sparks in her eyes. The guests busy their gazes elsewhere, wicker-watching. They know better than to show their mirth. But then he tips his great black beard back and roars with laughter. The others take his cue and do the same. Stig doesn't understand the bawdy humour — not yet — but he chuckles with an open maw to join in the fun. Colborn hugs him closer. The boy squirms away and off his father's legs to grab at the honey-smoked hen's leg Stefnīr dangles in front of him.

"We'll sail before sunrise?" Colborn asks his leader. Over the years, as Halstein's girth has grown, so has he appreciated his morning slumber more. The next-to-last expedition saw Colborn having to lever the Norseman off his bench and onto the longboat, his lolling tongue still black with the previous night's wine.

"It's good to leave while the moon is still bright," Colborn says.

"Aye, aye, brother," says Halstein. "And it's a good thing, too, having you keep us on the narrow."

Colborn picks up a sharp henbone from his wooden bowl and uses it to pick errant flesh from his teeth. Under the table, Stefnīr palms the hard muscle of his thigh. This is how they speak, mostly. Through skin-grazing and gesture. It's the best way. The most honest.

Let's get back, then, her hands are saying. *We don't have much time. I want you to myself.*

They fuck once near the entrance of their longhall, Stefnīr pinned up against the daub, and again in bed on the furs. He watches her, astride him, the strength of her body, the softness of her breasts, as she climbs towards her zenith. She makes as much music as she likes. Stig has stayed over at Halstein's feaste. He wanted to hear the minstrels and gleemen play.

Once they are sated, Stefnīr rolls off Colborn and cleans herself. She uses her antler comb on her yellow mane. She comes back to bite his chest, to tickle his ribs and he swats her away. She laughs her lusty laugh, the sound that made him fall in love with her. In moments like this he wonders what he has done to deserve her. He turns to blow out the tallow candle when she stops him.

"You'll be careful tomorrow?"

"Aye," he says. "Always."

"You'll mind yourself?"

"Of course."

"Then I'll give you something to take with you." She bites him again, hard, leaving a leaf-shaped mark on his chest. "There," she says, rubbing the saliva away. "Now you can look at that and think of me."

"You witch," he says, "tormenting your man the night before he sails."

"Tormenting? Is that what we're calling it, now?"

Colborn laughs.

They move closer together so that Stefnīr's head rests in the crook of his arm, and they can look facewards. Colborn's hand lies on his wife's sure hip. She holds his other hand — sex-scented — near her lips.

"Don't go," she says.

"That's what you always say," says Colborn. "And I always come back, don't I, with silver and livestock and… fur blankets."

"We have enough of all that. The farm is in good stead. You'll see, come Harvest time, how much grain we have to store. We'll have more than enough. Besides, I'd rather have you here than all the silver in Essex."

"You're forgetting one thing," says Colborn. "I'm a warrior, not a farmer."

"You could be a farmer.'"

"You know it's not like that. I'm Halstein's second."

"More like you're the leader and it's only fat Halstein who hasn't realised it yet."

"*Och.*"

"It's true. He's not half the man you are. Everybody knows it."

"Aye, well, it's not a sport. He is welcome to his command."

"You won't stay? Even for Stig?"

"I can't stay and you shouldn't be asking me to," he says, taking his hand away.

"Don't be angry. I only ask because I want you. Not like Ingvar, who I'm sure would push Halstein straight out of the door and into the ocean if she could. You're my family; I won't lose my family again."

Stefnīr's mother died birthing her; she had lost her father in a raid.

"I'm not angry," Colborn says. "It's just..."

"Just?"

She steals his hand back. Kisses it.

"It's just that this time I feel it, too."

"What?"

"That I shouldn't get on that boat."

Stefnīr pushes herself up on her elbow, makes wide eyes at him.

"Then for Thor's sake, don't go!"

There is blood in her cheeks.

"You know as well as I do that our death days are already decided by the gods. Getting on a boat won't change that. It's just a feeling. A stupid feeling."

"Maybe you should listen to that stupid feeling."

He falls on his back, examines the rooftree.

"Like I did, when I married you?" he says.

"Aye," she says, "and look how that worked out for you."

She lies back down again, close. She traces the tattoo of the bitemark, then strokes the silver wolf's head on its leather cord on his chest.

"My Fenrir," she says. "My moon-snatcher. My lone wolf."

The charm, a pretty wolf's head, had been a gift to her from her father. It was all she had of his. On their wedding day, after they had exchanged swords and rings, Stefnīr had strung the brooch and given it to Colborn. He had uttered the beginning of a refusal, but she had insisted and had tied it around his neck herself.

"It feels right," she had said. "Do you feel it?" and he had. He still does. He calls it his lucky charm.

Now Stefnīr moves to blow out the flame.

"No," he says, stopping her. "I want to look at you."

The candle burns all night.

At first light the longboat is keen and gleaming in its new clinker skin: the moulded gunwale is polished with beeswax, the woollen square-sail is dry and ready. The air around the North-men is still blue as they grip their oars; the white-breathed thralls push them into the tide. The men are excited and bang their burnished shields. They exchange happy insults as they row. Colborn leans against the bulwark and swallows the last of the elderberry tonic Stefnīr prepared for him hours earlier. It was green with fresh peppermint from their farm, to help settle his stomach, which never enjoyed the roiling of the sea.

"Drinking yer witch's potion again," says Halstein, uncharacteristically bright-eyed for this time of morning. Perhaps last night they had run out of ale.

"Aye,'" says Colborn, throwing the empty swine bladder into the stern-hold.

"Lower the flags!" he shouts, and the seafarers lower the handsome gold-woven Raven banners: the two black birds of blood fold down as if being put to sleep. *Huginn* and *Muninn* — thought and memory — are laid to rest so that the men can approach the Saxons without alerting the sentinel. Although he has seen this many times before, the image stays with Colborn. Something feels different: a premonition that one way or another, this will be his last expedition.

"Now, hear ye, men," shouts Halstein, half an hour away from their landing spot. "It's time to get clear of purpose."

"Aye, aye," say the Vikings. They blow their noses into the sea and rotate their shoulder cuffs. Their feet won't stay still.

"Before ye grab yer breastplates and blades," says Halstein, "I want ye to hear me."

The men keep moving their limbs, keeping supple, but their attention is now on their leader.

"We'll be landing in the Isle of Sheppey where ye know we invaded last Spring."

"Aye," says Fiske. "It was a good haul, Sheppey."

"Aye," say the Norse raiders. "Aye."

"Now we were very kind to them then and didn't spill much blood, but they will be better prepared this time. They'll have weapons and a plan."

The pirates nod and flex their bodies.

"This time you will show no mercy. No hesitation. I won't lose one man, ye hear? Not a one."

"Aye," the men say.

"Ye hear me? Is it clear to ye? No mercy!"

"Aye!" shout the seafarers. "No mercy!"

"I want ye to kill every man you see. Take what they have. And do what ye will with the wenches."

The men whistle, show their tongues and pant like horny dogs. Fiske humps the dragon-fashioned stern and there is high laughter.

"I want ye men to frighten every Saxon ye see. Knock the heads off the men. Terrify the women and children."

"Hold on," says Colborn, tasting the salt in the air. "Hold on. Why will we now hurt the women? The children?"

"Because, Colborn, the more we scare them in this battle, the less resistance we will find in the next." Halstein lifts his bear claw in Colborn's direction. The men quiet down.

"You have a problem with my tactics? Speak now."

"I don't agree with wounding the women unless they pose a danger."

"Ah, lads," Halstein says, fingering his beard. "Get out yer big fat tears. Take yer wails out of yer pockets. It looks like our Colborn here has grown a cunt."

The warship glides onto the tide-flattened beach with a whisper of polished wood greeting sand. The anchor, a rock lashed to a branch and fixed there, is lowered into the shallow brine. The spear-armed men hop off the stern with unexpected grace and fly up the dune like marauding monkeys. Steel glints. Even the seagulls are silent.

Colborn pats his helmet down onto his head and runs along the beach, just ahead of the other marauders. He begins to feel the adrenaline, the vibrating energy, in his limbs. The part of him that is happy husband and loving father separates from his body and flies above him like a calfskin kite. That part cannot do the job of the warrior. That part cannot endure the shock of war. He feels the hot blood beginning to beat in his ears. He sniffs. He gnashes his teeth. He is animal. He is Fenrir.

The first of their victims are fishermen taking stock of their day's haul. Five men smelling of cod and seagrass fall to the earth at the same time, hands wrapping around the strange new arrow-shafts planted in their chests as the tangs shock their hearts. More fishermen and more well-placed arrows until they reach the settlement of huts and halls with turf for roofs.

A woman stirring the steaming contents of an iron cauldron atop a kindling fire looks up and sees the army. She drops the spoon and screams, until an arrow finds its way into her chest. Now their shroud of silence falls to the ground. The raiders shout and bite their shields. Spears wing through the air. Cries, both shrill and deep, pierce the land along with swords and spikes and long-handled axes. Creamy throats are slit open, bodies fall into mud.

Colborn cuts down his twelfth Christian: a padded man who was swinging some kind of stick at him. Colborn feels no fatigue in his sword-arm or in his fighting spirit. Here is another Saxon who doesn't stand a chance. Colborn impales the man without hesitation or pity. All around him there is shouting and moaning and the clashing of steel on steel and steel on bone. Red ribbons of blood spurt skywards like a gory Maypole dance. Meaty maroon mixes with mud. Colborn kills another man, and another. He has a dark power rushing through him. He is a giant. He is a conquerer. He is in the prime of his life. He stabs a curly-haired leather-tanner, and a blacksmith in a scorched tunic. The darkness is like a swarm of black bees in his veins, in his head, pushing him to keep killing, keep plundering. It's like a pair of giant bat wings driving him forward. He slashes and steals and stabs until he is ankle-deep in greasy clay and treasure and still-warm bodies.

And then there is a woman's face in his, her cheek smeared with soil and crimson. She won't let him enter her hut. He pushes her aside but she is stubborn and flings herself back into his path. He smacks her head, hard, and she cries out and falls at his feet. Even so assaulted, she hangs onto his legs to hinder him. Colborn is overcome with fury. The black bees pour into his head, blotting out all reason and rationality. He bends at the knees and roars.

"Terrify the women!" he hears Halstein yell. It's a requisite; a battle tactic. It will cause future fights to be less cruel. It will mean less blood leaking into the ground. It's his duty to show this wench her place. The fury makes him kick the woman up, off his shins and he grabs her arms and jettisons her against a giant standing rock.

"No!" she screams into his face. Her ear is bleeding from his blow.

Colborn squeezes her against the stone: a warning to stay back now while he raids her hut. He loosens his grip and turns towards her home.

"No!" she screams again, falling after him and Colborn loses his temper.

"Terrify them!" a phantom Halstein roars in his ear. The bees in his head and veins buzz wildly and take over his body. He slams her against the rock again and tears off her shift, revealing full, white, milky breasts. Before he knows it, his cock is in his hand and he is forcing it under her dress and into her flesh. She cries out in horror and in pain. She scrabbles at his neck, tries to dig her nails into his throat. He grips her hands and pins them back against the stone while he finishes attacking her. There is no pleasure in his orgasm. It feels obligatory, like a spurt of warm blood once an artery has been ruptured. Colborn pulls away and tucks himself back into his trousers. His anger is gone; he feels disorientated. Did this just happen? The woman's mask of horror assures him that it did. He will plunder this home now. He will get what he has fought for.

She tackles him; grabs hold of his ankle. There is no anger left in him. He hauls her up and head-butts her with his iron helmet. She melts away into the mud.

"Brenna!" comes the call. "Burn! Burn! Burn!"

It's time to go and to leave the village afire. The homes all around him become lamps. Suddenly, whatever wealth this particular hut hides, no longer appeals to him. He wants nothing of it; no reminder of today's battle. He feels the need to flee, to get back to the longboat and the seawater and just row, row, row, until they are at home and at peace and he can hold his wife and son again.

His neck is bleeding: his fingers come away incarnadine. The skin on his throat is a knot-work pattern of fingernail cuts. How will he explain it to Stefnīr?

Fiske marches past, handing him a flaming brick of hay. Colborn holds the firelighter to the thatch of the hut, lights it in three places. Let it all burn, he thinks. Reduce it to ashes. I never want to think of this day again.

The roof begins to crackle and steam. There is a searing surge of furious flame. The fire gains momentum quickly like a body rolling down a hill. Pieces of fire drop down into the interior and eat up what is inside. Colborn feels the wall of heat against his chainmail, his helmet. He steps back to ease the burn and, as he does so, he hears something; a strange sound. He shakes his head and hears it again. Is it a lamb protesting at being dragged onto the boat? No, it's coming from this bonfire in front of him. A choking sound. Screaming. Was there an animal inside? He steps forward again to look through the tiny opening in the wall. His armour takes on the heat of the fire and bites into his skin, blistering his torso and forehead. That's when he sees the wooden crib on fire. Sees the crying baby in it.

His instinct is to barrel into the furnace, scoop the burning baby up, but he knows it's too late.

Too late for the baby, who dies right then before him as the house turns into a ball of fire.

Too late for the baby's mother whom he has all but destroyed.

Too late for himself, because all his loving and valorous moments fall away like old scales as this horror becomes his defining moment and he cannot live with that. Cannot bear a future of looking backwards, of seeing this window-framed picture of cruel burning cot, cradle set on fire by his very hands. He won't be able to bear touching Stefnīr or Stig with these self-same hands. And what is a life if he can't do that?

He grabs at his injured throat for the silver wolf's head. He needs to touch it to remind himself of who he is. But it is gone. Torn off in the assault. He has lost it because he doesn't deserve it any more. He falls to his knees and pushes his hands into the mire. He trails his fingers through the blood and sand hoping to rake up the leather thong. Fire falls all around him, as if from the sky, from the gods. The smoke makes his eyes water and tears stream down his battle-smeared face. As he sinks further down his hot armour is cooled by the mud. His soul keens. Fenrir is lost.

That is how Halstein finds Colborn, weeping in the dirt.

"Well," Halstein says, leaning against the great standing stone and taking in the unconscious woman and the defeated warrior, admiring the bruising on both. "Isn't this a pretty picture?"

Colborn has offered Halstein a hand up on so many occasions when Halstein has found himself sprawled on the wattle, post-feaste, wine-drunk. Halstein does not return the favour.

"Everyone is on the warship," he says, "spoils included. All there but one."

"Go," says Colborn. "Go without me."

Halstein spits on the ground. "No," he says, "I won't. It won't end like this."

"Just go," says Colborn, on his knees.

"I didn't come to find you to take you back on the boat."

Colborn looks up at him. Halstein is iolite in the dusk. White moonshine smoke trails up behind him. His sword is drawn. He looks like nothing less than a god: Odin.

He has something in his fist; something he has taken off the rock: a silver charm. Fenrir.

"Now Fenrir bit off the right hand of his god," says Halstein. "Then Víðarr laid waste to the wolf. That's the way the story ends."

"Aye," says Colborn, "that's the way it ends."

"You would have been better off," says Halstein, "if you hadn't challenged me in front of the men. If you hadn't bitten off my right hand."

"Aye. And, more to the point, I would have been better off if I hadn't married Stefnīr."

"Aye. That was your first and most fatal mistake."

"My second mistake was trusting a friend," says Colborn.

Halstein laughs.

"I don't see any friends here."

Colborn braces himself. He thinks of his farm under a clear sky and his impish, barefooted Stig. He sees Stefnīr's sweet, warm skin as if she is right in front of him. He hears her laugh and feels her biting his chest as Halstein runs his crucible sword through his ribs. The ravens shriek.

There is no pain, just the emptying out of the black bees and an exhalation as the evil leaves him. Colborn has already departed the realm when his body topples over next to the woman's. It will be her sole comfort when she wakes.

63 / THE WASP TAKES WING

When Raven wakes, her amulet is burning her neck. She scrabbles to take it off but Snowbroth stops her.

"I don't want it anymore," she says.

"Your amulet is a powerful magical tool."

"I don't want it. Evil thing!"

"It cannot be blamed for what happened."

"Every time I see it I'll be reminded of —"

"And you will forgive yourself, just as you have forgiven others. And soon your acceptance will be complete and your power will be restored."

"How do you forgive yourself for something so terrible?"

"You've already lived your punishment. You've dragged your burden through entire lifetimes. You have suffered enough. It's time to let it go."

As Raven calms down, the amulet cools. Her skin feels different now — immune to fire — and she can breathe freely.

"You are well on your way to your recovery. Do you feel it? The karmic shift?"

"Yes." There is a force building inside her. It propels her off the bed.

"Fenrir will protect you. He is your inner warrior. You will need his strength in the coming hours."

"Yes," says Raven, yet still she hesitates. She feels she's stronger but there is still fear.

"You know that quote," says Snowbroth. "About the warrior and the storm?"

It sounds familiar. What is it?

Snowbroth takes her hands. "Fate whispers to the warrior: You cannot withstand the storm. The warrior whispers back —"

Raven says: "I am the storm."

She makes her way towards the door and hooks the Vespa keys off the coffee table. Hugs Snowbroth, thanks her. She puts on Lavinia's helmet and hops on the bike. Kicks the stand up.

"Blessed be."

Snowbroth holds up her hand in farewell as the wasp takes wing.

Raven sorts through the violent images in her mind as she zips along the roads away from the flat land and the smell of horses. The vibration of the Vespa travels into her hands and up her arms. A tingle of energy. A hint of what's to come. She's been a murderer and a midwife, a taker and a healer. What will she be in this life?

She knows where she has to go; what she has to do. It's waiting for her — a crucible — a final forging. She reaches the tarred road and accelerates into it. The air has never felt clearer.

64 / THE CRUCIBLE

Raven reaches her house and circles the block to gauge the Pitchfork situation. The crowd has doubled, tripled and is pulsing with chaos but Raven is no longer afraid of them. She pauses. This shouldn't render her foolish, though. She still uses the hidden door at the back of her house to enter the property. The Grimm Brothers bound up to her and almost knock her over in their delight. She sees a lupine quality in them now that she has not noticed before. She gets down on her knees and buries her face in their fur. She thanks their spirits for their unwavering devotion. They whine and pant and slobber.

"Raven."

Raven shoots up off the floor. Lavinia is standing in her lounge. The crowd jeers from outside.

"The session went well," says Raven. The Grimm Brothers stop whining. Their ears prick up. They dash outside, most probably to terrorise the protestors.

"I know," says Lavinia. Of course she does. Clairvoyancy? Scrying? Telepathy?

"Snowbroth called me. She said you didn't even hang around for cake."

Raven casts around for her other animals. Are they safe? She hasn't seen a feather of Eli since the Danielle incident.

"But besides that, I can see the change. Your face is clear. Your eyes, they're different."

"I feel different." Older. Wiser. More powerful.

They exchange keys: Wasp for Morris.

"Thank you so much for letting me have your bike. And for taking care of Morris."

"I enjoyed the company," says the High Priestess, "of your passenger."

Raven wonders how a scattering of pigeons ever worried her. "Thank you. For everything."

Raven throws on her witch's cloak and pockets her wand.

"What will we do," asks Lavinia, "about the gathering outside?"

Raven spies through her curtain. The fence is teetering from the force of the crowd. An angry-looking man in a navy golf shirt slings his banner to the tarmac and kicks one of the fence-planks loose and then another. She sees his face: it's that scheming journalist, Devereaux.

"They'll be here soon." She checks the lock on the front door which is as good as useless with the middle panels of glass missing. She fetches her nail gun and some orphaned boards left at the foot of the stairs and gets to work bolting the ragged aperture closed. She does the same to the broken window in the lounge. The nails bite into the timber with satisfying bangs.

Lavinia closes all the windows — no small job — while Raven

padlocks the kitchen and back doors. The large sliding doors onto the verandah are more difficult to secure. It will be easy enough for the Pitchforks to smash the huge panes of glass. She knows the angry crowd will get in if they want to. She's just buying time.

She fetches Danielle's gun from the freezer and hands it to the High Priestess who doesn't seem surprised to see the cold metal in her palm. She takes it, spins the barrel, checks the safety catch and tucks it into her waistband. "You should call your cop."

"I have."

Outside, a man with a toolbox makes a beeline for the navy-shirted man breaking the fence. He pulls the intruder backwards and climbs through himself. When the journalist tries to get through again, the new man shakes a yellow hammer at him and he backs away. When Devereaux tries to gain access a third time, the carpenter uses his powerful right swing. One perfectly-aimed punch to the nose is enough to fell the trespasser.

In a curious echo of what Raven has just done inside her house, the man with the toolbox, with a practised hand, picks up the planks off the grass and begins nailing them back into place. He repairs the large gap, then, with nails between his lips, moves on to the smaller ones. Raven would recognise that glow-in-the-dark toolbox anywhere. Thank the goddesses for Benjamin.

Someone knocks loudly on the front door making them both jump. Someone has — somehow— sloped through. Raven draws her *athamé,* Lavinia the Beretta.

"Who is it?" She's had enough enemies pass through this particular portal.

"Kruger," comes the reply, but she will not fall for fake identities this time. The door remains locked.

"Prove it."

"You have a tattoo of a pentagram on the back of your neck."

It's definitely Kruger. She'd know that voice anywhere.

"Anyone with an internet connection could know that."

"A leaf-shaped birthmark on your chest."

Raven hears the happy barking of the Grimm Brothers as they accost him on the other side of the door. One of them whines and scratches the wood, telling his mistress it's okay to open up. She hears a loud sneeze from outside and then another.

They put away their weapons and she opens for him. Kruger has brought gifts: her laptop bag and a glowing Stephen Bishop, by the scruff of his neck.

"This man says he knows you," says Kruger. "I found him creeping onto your property."

Raven feels a tenderness towards the old man and his long-ago sorrow. The perennial irritation she has always felt for him has vanished. She thinks of the lace-edged vintage shoebox in her office, next to Max's favourite spot on the bookshelf. Moth-eaten heartache. She knows now that she can trust him.

"You can let him go. He's my neighbour."

Bishop adjusts the back of his collar.

"I was coming to see you," says the priest, opening his jacket. "I have Eli."

The African Grey hops onto Bishop's proffered bony finger and is transferred to his perch.

"Thank you."

"He's been with me for the last couple of days. He seemed nervous to come back. I thought I would show him that it's safe. Although, now —" he gestures towards the crowd, "I'm not certain that it is."

Kruger hands over her laptop bag. "I was right. I didn't find anything."

Raven pockets her asthma pump and slides the laptop under the couch. She sneaks another look outside. People have overcome the carpenter and are again breaking down the fence. There are ten of them and only one of him and he can't keep up.

"In fact," he says. "I have good news. I submitted my report and the charges have been dropped. All the charges."

"That won't stop the kangaroo court on the pavement," says Lavinia.

"No," says Kruger. "We'll have to do that."

65 / PITCHFORKS

Fred is screaming and screaming. The Grimm Brothers are still outside, running circles around the house, stopping to bark and growl at anyone who sticks an unlucky foot through the splintered wooden planks. Applejack, confused, is frozen to the spot. Despite the efforts of Benjamin and the dogs, people begin slipping through the cracks and onto Raven's property. They carry their banners as stakes. The rest of the crowd is emboldened by the intruders and fight to get in too. They multiply inside the perimeter, like Raven's rabbits.

"I'll call for back-up," says Kruger.

"What do they want from you?" asks Bishop. He'll only know what he's seen in the newspaper. Raven can't imagine him reading social media.

"A day of reckoning," she says. "They've decided it's judgement day and have appointed themselves as judges. That's what Pitchforks do." She unlocks the verandah doors and folds them open. They glide on their rails and clatter together.

"What are you doing?" asks Kruger.

"Giving them what they want."

Raven refuses to be a Marie Antoinette in her ivory tower. She knows that if she doesn't go to the crowd — doesn't present herself for their rickety trial — they will storm the house and she cannot have that. Not Brenna's house. She won't have them sully it with their messy prejudice. She won't have them destroy what she has fought so hard to keep. She steps out onto the verandah, walks up to the railing. She's flanked by Lavinia and Bishop: a High Priestess and a priest. Kruger, his gun drawn, but hidden, takes a post a few feet away and watches the mob with electric eyes. The press is there with their microphones and cameras. People hold out their phones in front of them, taking pictures and videos. Children have joined their parents for the show.

The proliferation continues before their eyes: the people and their banners swell and split like multiplying cells, like the intimate genesis of a foetus, or a tumour. Thirty, sixty, a hundred and twenty people stand and bay at her. They call her a murderer, a devil-worshipper. It's nothing she hasn't heard before.

The sun is beginning to set and it lends an artistic effect to the colouring of the scene. She thinks of other horrific *milieus* made to look beautiful by an artist's brush.

How funny, Raven thinks, as she watches the peoples' mouths move in slow motion as they squawk their profanities, that such ugly behaviour can still be beheld as beguiling. Beautiful, even.

But then something happens to smack Raven out of her reverie. Her disconnection to the danger before her is snapped open; adrenaline punches her heart. The scarecrowess has been abducted from her car and is being carried to the middle of the mob. It bobs head-and-shoulders above the crowd until it reaches its spot where it is hoisted and impaled on a spike. There is more movement as the horde throngs to and from the doll, laying parcels at its feet. Raven can't see what they're depositing there, but guesses, before she glimpses the hunks of firewood. No no no no no, she thinks, not so close to the house.

"Please," she says. "Don't do it."

The mob shouts at her, calls her names. Some of them laugh. They're happy now. They have the power. They have the witch under their collective thumbs. She can no longer ignore them. Now she has to listen to them. Devereaux has found his way in along with his camera crew. He keeps mopping at the blood from his broken nose.

More firewood is ferried to the feet of the scarecrowess. Children bring kindling that they've collected from under the apricot and fig trees. Raven looks on as the doll's dress — her red dress — flutters in the warm evening breeze. A breeze that could easily carry a flame from a bonfire to the tinder-box beside it.

"I'm here to listen to you," says Raven. "I want to hear what you have to say."

"Satanist!"

"Witch!"

"Killer!"

"Tell me what you want from me."

"An eye for an eye," says a voice in the crowd. She recognises it before he steps forward. Sheldon Bond.

The people like this sentiment. The words reverberate from a hundred different lips. An eye for an eye. An eye for an eye. An eye for an eye. A Biblical dagger hangs in the air. Raven guesses that the turning-the-other-cheek passage is temporarily — and conveniently — forgotten, as is the rest of the text.

"People," says Bishop, holding up his hand. "Please."

He's wearing his perennial dog-collar. This has a momentary sedating effect on the crowd. They must be confused. Why is a Man of God consorting with a witch? Maybe he's trying to save her? Maybe he's on their side? Maybe he'll wait till she is standing close to the railing and then push her over into their gaping maw?

"It is not our place to judge," he says.

Raven is surprised by the depth and resonance of his voice. He seems to have a certain power of his own. "Only the Almighty can do that."

"She's a sorceress," shouts someone from the middle of the mob. "She killed my brother with her dark magic."

"And my wife," shouts someone else. "She cast a spell over her and stole her life. She cursed our whole family. Blighted our whole neighbourhood."

"And my father!" yells Sheldon, now wearing a mask of frantic insanity, moving towards the scarecrowess. "Raven Kane is nothing but evil." He takes out a lighter. "And she must face the consequences."

Raven thinks of the drop of blood that spilled onto the doll as she was making it. If it goes up in flames, will she burn, too?

"If you knew God," says Bishop, "you'd know that mortals — mere humans — are not capable of the kind of enchantment you are talking about. Only God can perform plagues and miracles."

There is a murmur from the mob. They're too angry to listen to either sense or sermon.

"It is neither a witch, nor devil, but a glorious God that maketh the thunder."

Raven recognises the quote by Reginald Scot, one of the few Christian leaders in the 16th century who railed against the idea of empowered women being maleficent.

"Man has no say over how snow shall fall. It says in the scriptures that only our one true God maketh the blustering tempests and whirlwinds."

If his elegant speech has had an effect on anyone, it doesn't matter, because at that moment Sheldon holds a flame to the pyre.

66 / NAKED

"Stop that man!" shouts Lavinia, pointing her arm at Bond. Raven half expects lightning-bolts to shoot from her hand and long-distance taser him. Kruger is right by Raven's side. She wonders why he isn't out there, trying to control the mob, but then realises that she is his first priority.

No one moves to stop Sheldon. No one wants to. They're here for the spectacle. They've paid their dues: hours of languishing on her pavement, painting placards, tweeting their opinions, making sweaty cheese sandwiches and weak tea in styrofoam cups at the refreshment station. Why would they stop him? The show is just getting started. This is what they came to see. Lights, camera, action.

The kindling takes and, within seconds, there is the rushing sound of flame, the rushing of retribution, of destiny. The sound the air makes as you fly past it after being pushed off a cliff.

The crowd cheers.

Raven runs inside to get the fire extinguisher. A silly little thing when you look at it now, compared to the huge, seething bonfire the Pitchforks have made. A bright red toy in her trembling hands. She moves to go down the steps, to enter the crowd, but Lavinia stops her, pushes her back. She takes the extinguisher and strides down into the garden, into the shrieking horde. They swallow her up. Raven moves to help her, but Bishop holds her back.

"I have to help her," says Raven.

"She has a chance of surviving the mob. But for you, it's certain death." Raven knows he's right. She knows they will tear her limb from limb like hungry jackals. Kruger leaves her side to follow Lavinia, perhaps to protect her, or to round up some of the more violent members of the crush. She feels exposed. The flames climb the straw woman's legs and catch the dress, which burns with quick drama, leaving the victim naked. The people cheer again. Girl Fawkes. The doll now has a skin of flame. The breeze feeds the fire and the fire eats her up. Raven checks her skin: it remains unblistered. The smell of woodsmoke, which before was fragrant, now sweeps towards them. The grey cloud makes their eyes water. When the smoke moves again, dispatched further by the breeze, Raven catches sight of the front row of the Pitchforks. They are doing something. They bend and straighten again, collecting something off the ground. Up and down, then they look directly at her. Dresses and shirts held like apron cradles, bulging. The people go up and down, hands full of — what? What is happening? And then she's razed by a realisation. They're collecting her adder stones.

Before she has time to act, a white stone whizzes straight by her head. She tries to glimpse where it came from, but all she sees is a sea of masks. Another flies by her and another hits her hard, on the chest. It shocks her. Adder stones are sacred, inherently charmed: meant to protect their owner from venom in all forms. Raven knows she needs to run now, to take cover, but she sees a face among the masks that she recognises. It's an ivory-coloured child with long dark hair and mesmerised eyes. It's Becks. And she's holding her own stone.

67 / HOT POISON LEAKING INTO BLOOD

The bonfire is now in full force. Raven can feel the heat on her skin. The people are forced to back away from the sacrifice. It pushes them further into the garden and closer to Raven. They seem to permeate everything. They are hot poison leaking into blood. Some carry makeshift torches from the pyre to set other things alight: the hen house, the dogs' kennels, the tomato trellises, the peach saplings, until the whole back garden is steaming and crackling with jumping yellow fire.

The others pop up and down, filling their palms and their pockets. Their faces are blurred. The only faces in focus now are her niece and her sister — Jessica is striding angrily towards Rebecca with fury on her brow. More stones fly at Raven, but she is paralysed. An adder stone hits Bishop on the arm and he cries out, turns away. Jess reaches Becks and shakes her so hard that it seems her head may roll off her shoulders. She wrenches the girl's fist open, takes the adder stone from her and drops it on the ground. She takes her daughter's cheeks roughly in her hands, her own face red with shouting. Rebecca blinks, as if waking up from a trance and her mother pulls her by the arm, away from the mob. Raven calls out to them but both their heads are turned and there is too much jeering and hissing and baying for them to hear her. She takes another hit, this time on her leg, then another on her stomach. She has to go inside now to find shelter. As she takes a step backwards she sees a missile from the corner of her eye: a smooth white stone like a pigeon's egg sails through the grey-perfumed air. It cracks her with force on her left temple. The jolt of pain is immediate and electric; it short-circuits her brain. Then the hurt fades, along with everything else.

68 / HUNTER'S TROPHY

When Raven regains consciousness, Kruger is again by her side. Rabbits hop and shiver all around them. There is bright light behind him and he is topless. She wonders briefly if she is, in fact, dead, and this is some kind of fantasy limbo she gets to indulge in before moving on to her next life, but the stabbing pain in her head brings her back to reality. Also, there is Jake Grimm licking her palm and Bishop sweating behind him. Someone — her guess is Kruger —has dragged her inside. Stones are clapping and popping on the folding doors beside them, leaving small spider-webs in the glass panels. Lavinia is there, too, thank the Goddesses, but her clothes are torn and there's bright blood on her singed silver-blue hair.

"I did what I could," she pants, "slowed it down. Bought some time. But the fire is still raging."

Raven reaches up to feel her injury but there's a sodden bandage in the way - a piece of Kruger's shirt. Eli is flying around inside, in a panic, smashing into things. Bishop manages to catch him and hold him under his jacket to calm him down.

It's near dark outside. There is the sound of a windowpane breaking in another room of the house. Then another and another. Bathroom, bedroom, office. Then more glass smashes as unseen things are thrown through the openings and break on the wooden floor. Kruger, weapon drawn, goes to investigate. Lavinia, pistol shaking, follows him. There is more of that rushing sound, that storm of fire. Raven smells petrol.

"They've set it alight," shouts Kruger, running back. "They've fire-bombed every room."

Raven pictures the Molotov cocktails, ready to explode. She has to get them out. She'll throw them back out of the windows. Lavinia holds her back.

"We need to get out of here."

"I can't," says Raven, eyes throbbing. "I can't leave this house."

"We have to."

"My animals!"

As they hesitate the fire in each room creeps to join that in the others. Cabinets, paintings, curtains catch fire right there, before them: the family photos, Brenna's antique prints, the Pacific Island Devil Masks. Lavinia goes to unbolt the front door but can hear the horde on the other side. The kitchen door is the same. "They're everywhere," she says. "They're keeping us in. They want to watch us burn."

Raven stands up, unsteady on her feet. Bishop offers her his arm and she takes it. She looks through the hot, cracked glass past the pyromaniac zombies, past the bits of flame falling onto the verandah like burning snow. She sees the giant oak tree, which is, miraculously, not yet aflame. It stands tall within the hungry fire like a cool green beacon, its huge trunk seemingly immune to the lapping flames at its roots. It is the opposite of the Biblical burning bush in the desert. There's a white animal in the branches: Lightfoot, the cat. Almost invisible beside her is Cocoa. Yin and Yang. They are calm despite the madness below.

"We need to get to the tree. The oak tree."

They can get the animals up there too. Most of them.

"That tree will blaze just like this house," says Kruger.

"No," says Raven. "I can protect it."

Kruger is dubious.

"Trust me."

"I do," he says.

"How will we get there?" Bishop points at the mob on the verandah who are kicking the doors beside them. They'll be inside within the minute. "We're trapped."

An axe comes through the wall right next to where Raven is standing. She screams and jumps away. Kruger and Lavinia point their guns at the axe. It's shaken loose, then it comes through again, making a bigger hole. Kruger moves towards the maimed wall. "Stop, or I'll shoot."

The axe keeps coming. Kruger steadies himself and aims. Finger on the trigger.

"Don't shoot," shouts Raven. The axe is neon. Kruger doesn't lower his revolver.

Benjamin sticks his head through the hole in the wall - a hunter's trophy. He kicks and chops until there's a hole big enough for them to squeeze through. He thrusts his hand towards Raven. She takes it and he pulls her out to the other side. She's surprised to see Luella, who doesn't smile at her.

"We need to get —" says Raven, but Luella isn't listening. Instead she throws a black bag over Raven's head and when Raven protests she grabs her arms and forces her forward, towards the chanting crowd in the blazing garden.

69 / BARK

Raven is led, sightless, down the verandah steps and towards the mob. She doesn't understand what's happening. She struggles, but Luella pinches her arms together from behind and it forces her to keep moving.

"Luella," she says, "Luella," but if the witch hears her she doesn't react. Raven stumbles blindly, falling over other people's feet, but someone walks beside her, stops her from falling and guides her with a firm hand. A minute of this drunken walk and then she is stopped. Luella takes her hand and puts it on the thing in front of her and Raven reads the bark as if it is braille and she understands. She feels for the familiar foothold, reaches up for the first knot and hoists herself up. She finds her other natural rungs and climbs the oak tree easily, despite not being able to see. Once she's safely inside the canopy she pulls the suffocating bag off her head and wipes the perspiration from her face. Lavinia appears next, shaking from exertion or nerves, or both, and Kruger is behind her, helping her climb. Before she can say anything he disappears back down the trunk. Raven grabs Lavinia and they sit high in the tree and shiver together despite the heat.

The eleven Twisted Sisters have formed a circle around the base of the tree: a human shield against the people trying to climb up. They are armed with swords and crossbows and wear their black, hooded robes. The mob seems suitably fearful of them. The women break their chain only to allow Kruger back through, and Bishop, as the men bring Raven's animals to the oak. They work quickly, passing up downy rabbits and startled chickens and a slightly charred albino peacock. Eli is already on his favourite branch. He and Fred are uncharacteristically quiet. The Grimm Brothers bound up themselves. Afterwards Bishop stands back. His hand is on his heart and Raven worries that the strain tonight will kill him. But he stands upright again, straightens his back and climbs up the tree to join them.

With Kruger, Bishop and Lavinia in the dark green leaf awning, Raven does a quick headcount of the animals. Is everyone here? She can't focus enough to be sure. She looks out and watches her fruit trees burn: the fig, the pomegranate, the apricots. She catches sight of Applejack, still paralysed with fear. Despite the creeping flames surrounding him, the fiery grass, he cannot move or be moved.

"Applejack," she shouts, but she knows there is nothing to be done. Toby the tortoise is also gone. He was the first to go with his millimetre-per-minute pace. He never stood a chance against this reckless fire. She closes her eyes against the cruelty. There is no time to cry. The blaze is getting nearer. The Wicked Witches below have to rein in their circle to avoid the heat. It'll burn this tree down just like the others if she doesn't do something about it. Lavinia is the most powerful witch she knows. Lavinia can save them.

"Lavinia," she says. "We need to protect this tree. What's the best way?" But the High Priestess is finished. Blood and soot and livery skin: she seems centuries old. She looks like a papered-over skeleton.

"I'm sorry. I can't do it. You'll have to do it on your own."

Far below, the Wicked Witches have to abandon their post. They throw off their burning robes and walk naked away from the fire, which is now beginning to lick the base of the oak tree.

Raven looks around at the expectant faces in the tree, panics. Too many lives depend on her. Too much madness against her.

Suddenly she feels something pulling at her foot, at her feet. A person. She looks down and sees a dirty hand grabbing her ankle. She tries to kick the hand, but its grip is too strong. She sees Sheldon's face, flickering. He has climbed up the trunk.

"Get off me!" she shouts into the noise of the panic and the fire.

He pulls her ankle, hard, and she falls, smacking her elbow on the timber planks. Pain shoots through her arm, joins the pain in her head, making her dizzy. She tries to kick him off, tries to kick his face, but he dodges her heel and grabs on with his other hand, too. He pulls her down, so that half of her body is now outside the safety of the branches. The flames are all around them. She remembers, with terror, the strength in his arms. He won't be satisfied until he sees her burn. It happens so quickly that no one sees Raven being pulled down into the fire. She tries to catch someone's eye, but they have their backs to her, entranced by the fizzing earth below. No one sees her.

The mob, finally realising the danger, grab each other, run over others and sprint away from the house.

She whistles for the dogs and immediately they turn around and see that she's in trouble. They leap down at her to investigate, almost knocking her out of the tree altogether. They notice

Sheldon and growl — a violent, malefic growl that Raven has never heard before — and jump down on top of him. He cries out as Jake sinks his teeth into his forearm, forcing him to let Raven go. Bill bites his leg so that he loses his grip on the oak and falls to the ground below, into the flames. The Grimm Brothers fall too and they all catch fire. Sheldon screams as he watches his shirt turn from cotton to flame. The Rottweilers whine in fright. They dash away, fiery pelts circling the tree, and make their way back up the trunk. Bishop and Kruger are shocked to see them and help them roll on the platform to kill the pungent glow.

Sheldon's whole body is on fire now. He screams and swats at himself making the flames hungrier. Raven looks around — is there no one below who can help him? — But it seems the heedless stragglers are doing what they can to save themselves. The heat is building and her wolf's head amulet burns her chest. She has the unreasonable urge to jump down into the fire; to use her witch's cloak to douse the flames that are eating him alive. She feels the need to rescue her attacker, to stop his screaming torment. But she knows that, if she does that, she will die and everyone in the tree will die. She needs to save herself. She turns her back on his flailing and begins designing a spell to protect the oak.

70 / WAITS FOR THE STAIRWAY TO APPEAR

A spell comes to her. But will it be powerful enough? She can't cast a circle here, or light the requisite green candles. She doesn't have the milk, the sugar or the saffron the spell asks for. If she could just combine forces with Lavinia that would help. She reaches for the High Priestess's hand but Lavinia gently takes it away. She leans back against her branch and falls asleep.

Raven breathes to clear her head. She lets go of her immediate fear and relaxes into the spell. She builds her sorcery up in layers in her consciousness. She sees the light and the colours. Feels the charge.

"I have been with you," she starts, "I have been with you from the beginning." She feels the magic in her fingers, in her chest. It's there, it's undeniable, but she knows it's not intense enough to protect them all. She doesn't despair. She has faith. She waits for the stairway to appear.

In her mind she sees a gossamer glimmer of Brenna, silent, smiling. She catches another glimpse of her. Raven stands up and pours all her concentration into calling up her image. There she is: resplendent, in her perennial white. Then she visualises two other women, one dressed in red, the other in black. The three women move towards Raven in her mind's eye and merge into one figure who places her hands over Raven's.

Raven begins the spell again, holding on to her amulet. This time it's stronger. She feels it building.

"I have been with you from the beginning."

The heat is searing, forcing the crowd to disperse to the cool streets.

Raven is on a precipice. She can feel that the spell is almost complete but she's taking strain. Bishop steps up to her and takes her hands in his. His eyes are closed and he's muttering something under his breath. A prayer? They join voices, even though their words are different, and then there is a cool stream of power in them, through them and around them. The tree begins to vibrate and a circle of light spins and revolves around it, as fresh as water vapour. They stand like that, hands clasped, until the force-field stops trembling. Once it's established, Raven and Bishop break away and fall apart. There is light everywhere. They are safe. Raven binds the spell and releases the circle.

So he IS some kind of wizard.

She expects the voice to reply. She expects him to say something like, *In his own way, perhaps.* But there is no longer a voice.

The rabbits are all gathered around Lavinia's unconscious body. They snuggle on her lap, in the crooks of her arms, in her matted hair. Raven knows that she is forgetting something. It nags at her throbbing head. She does the headcount again and again, and then she realises that there are only two cats with them.

"Max," says Raven, bereft. "We don't have Max." She looks out at the crackling house, points at her office window. "He'll be in the study, on the bookshelf. That's where he always goes when he's afraid."

Kruger moves towards her to comfort her. She closes her eyes and leans into his chest. She's exhausted.

"You saved everyone," he says.

"Not everyone." When she opens her eyes again, Bishop has disappeared. "Where's Stephen?" They peer out just in time to see the priest going into the inferno of the house.

"He's mad," says Kruger.

"He's gone to get Max."

They wait, hardly a breath between them. Raven pictures Max sitting there between the smouldering encyclopaedias and the flaming world atlas - a purring book-end. He always purrs when he's nervous. They see a flash of Bishop appear in the window. His smock is off, he's using it to shield his mouth from the billowing smoke. He vanishes, then appears again, cradling the ginger cat in his arms.

"He's got him," says Raven. "Now get out, Bishop, get out!"

But the priest hesitates. Something has caught his eye.

"What are you doing, man?" shouts Kruger. "Get the fuck out of the house!"

Raven realises what he has seen. "Oh no," she says, "oh no!"

Bishop uses a heavy book to smash the office window further, creating an exit. Raven thinks he will escape, but instead, he throws Max out into a safe patch of bushes and hunches down again, out of sight.

"Oh no!" She knows that he has found the shoebox. His photos and letters to Brenna.

"Damn it, Bishop, move!" shouts Kruger, but the end of his sentence is lost in the fiery blast as the house explodes and sends glittering pieces of debris hurtling all around them.

PART V

SPIRIT

EPILOGUE

REALM OF SMOKE & ASHES

Raven wakes up to black. Witching Hour. The night sky, starless, is a clean dark slate. Her body is supported by soft soil. She lifts her hands to inspect them: black on black, her skin powder-coated by the soot of the blast. The hand she holds in hers is Kruger's. She can feel his warmth. He is alive. How long have they been knocked out for?

The treehouse is gone, the animals scattered by the explosion, but one by one they return to where she lies. Does she still have all her body parts? It's difficult to tell. There is a numbness, also dark in colour. The Grimm Brothers are sniffing silhouettes; she can see the silver shine of their pelts. Their midnight noses are cold on her cheeks. Her fingers search her neck for Fenrir but the amulet is gone. The dogs whine and pant.

Slowly, she rises from the cool ground. She has her legs, her feet, her toes. No bone seems broken. Surely this is its own magic? She casts her eyes around at the ashes that remain and her animals beside her. Not unscathed, not quite, but close enough.

She's lost her house, her laptop, her life's work. The voice is also gone. She misses it, misses the intimacy, the immediacy, but she knows that it's not truly vanished. Instead, it's travelled deep inside her, so that when he talks, she now hears it in her own voice, instead of his. The voice has become part of hers, perhaps the way it should always have been.

Raven's strength gathers like thudding stormclouds. Not only is she unhurt, but her lungs have never felt this strong. Her skin has been transformed from delicate membrane to ebony armour.

"Kruger," she says. The night is warm ink soup: still and thick around them. He doesn't move. "Kruger." She puts a hand on his chest. It rises and falls surely under her palm just like she knew it would. She gives him a shake and sees the whites of his eyes as his lids spring open. He grabs her wrists, fierce in his shock.

"Are you okay?" he demands. "Raven!"

The Grimm Brothers, excited by his outburst, clamber all over him.

"Heel!" she says and they obey. She finds the garden tap and lets it run while the dogs drink from it.

Kruger seems to be in one piece, too, as he stands up. Shaken, but all accounted for. Together, they call for Lavinia. She doesn't answer. Raven is certain the High Priestess will emerge from the smouldering rubble: also painted black; also stronger. They call and call, but all they hear is the scurrying of the searching dogs.

The rabbits draw their attention to her body, mangled by its fall from the oak. The baby bunnies cover her in a rippling blanket of live fur. Raven kneels beside the High Priestess and places a palm on her cold cheek.

"Wake up, Lavinia. Wake up." But she knows as she says this that it will not happen. She knows that the High Priestess has used the last of her life force. She can see that the shrunken form before her is no longer Lavinia, but an abandoned husk. Raven's not supposed to feel grief for the loss of her friend. She knows that the spirit of Lavinia is alive and well — and most probably on an amazing, joyous journey of rushing colour and light as her energy seeks its next incarnation — but she can't help feeling an intense loss, as if her heart has been hollowed out. At the same time she knows that this is the way it has to be. Kruger offers his hand and she takes it. She uses his strength to lever herself up. He doesn't say anything, but hugs her body close to his as an offer of condolence.

KRUGER STAYS WITH LAVINIA. He'll make the necessary arrangements, he gestures, while Raven explores the extent of her loss. Who else is gone? Applejack, of course and Toby the tortoise. She finds his giant blackened shell and now, when she kneels down to embrace it, her tears flow freely, falling onto his hot hard-baked hull, washing the soot away. She starts when she feels movement. She waits for more and, when nothing happens, she thinks she must have imagined it. But there's motion again and Raven squints into the dark to see Toby's ancient head emerging from his fuming pod. His legs appear, too, and, completely ignoring her wonder, he begins his unhurried creep towards what used to be the vegetable garden.

There are voices, now. People enter this dream realm of smoke and ashes. The Grimm Brothers hurry up to them, barking, signalling to Raven that they are friends. The faceless people approach slowly, surveying the damage, combing through the debris for lost treasure. Luella is there, as well as some of the other Twysted Sisters. She has her doctor's kit with her and has been treating people with superficial burns. Raven walks towards them, finding Max in her path, purring on a scrap of Bishop's smock, recognisable only by the singed white collar.

She hears a familiar voice, a sweet ribbon in the bitter air. A small girl bolts away from the rest and runs into Raven's arms. She is talking and crying and Raven can't make out a word. She smells like melted sneakers.

"Becks," whispers Raven, squeezing her. "Becks." Still the girl sobs and babbles. Jessica is next, leading Applejack.

"Applejack!" Raven drags her attached niece to where the pony stands and throws her arms around the animal's neck. "How did you —?"

"Rebecca saved him," says Jessica. "He wouldn't move an inch when we tried to lead him away. There were three of us trying to drag him, but he wouldn't move. He was too scared. The heat was... but then Rebecca managed to coax him away from the fire."

The girl tries to control her weeping. She smudges her eyes and wipes her nose on her arm. "I wasn't going to throw the stone at you," she shouts. "I wasn't going to!"

"Okay," says Raven. "Okay."

Rebecca cries some more. "It was the one from you. The stone I was holding was the one you gave me. It was to protect you."

Raven's chest burns with a sudden and fierce affection for the child.

"Thank you, Becks."

"But then I couldn't save you. The magic didn't work. So I saved Applejack instead."

"How do you know the magic didn't work?" asks Raven. "I'm alive, aren't I?"

Rebecca's small face is a mess of soot and snot. Her shoulders jerk with sad hiccups.

Raven slips down onto her haunches so that she can look directly into Rebecca's eyes. She takes her niece by the shoulders and whispers into her ear: "You are a magnificent witch."

LUELLA, having just realised Lavinia's fate, comes forward to embrace Raven. Someone has flung a jacket around her but she is still cold. They hold each other for a moment.

"High Priestess," she says. It takes Raven a moment to realise that Luella is addressing her. She kisses Raven on both cheeks. When she moves away, Raven feels something warm on her neck. Fenrir. The amulet has been returned.

"Thank you," she says to the shivering witch.

"They thought they could burn us," says Luella. "They didn't know we were kindling."

LIGHTFOOT, the cat, picks her way carefully through the wreckage. She is slinking towards them with something in her mouth. Her clean, white form is in perfect contrast to the darkness that surrounds them.

"Cleaning up, again, Lightfoot?" says Jess. "You've got a big job ahead of you."

Lightfoot ignores her and drops the gift at Raven's feet. She's rewarded with a firm stroking. Raven picks up the piece of paper expecting it to be litter, but it's one of Bishop's 'Seven Loaves' flyers, miraculously un-scorched. Her disdain is replaced by an overwhelming gratitude to him. For once, she doesn't crumple the advert. Seven Loaves, it says, is a community greening and gardening initiative. It's dedicated to teaching hungry people to grow their own food.

As soon as the banks open, she'll transfer what is left in her account to the project. It feels right to be rid of the inheritance: the obese, smelly monkey on her back. Almost eight million rand. It never truly belonged to her anyway.

Her phone rings. It's the Unknown caller on the line. For once, she wants to take the call.

"Hello?" she says to the Unknown.

"Hello?" says the American woman on the other side, who sounds surprised to find herself on the line despite being the one who has dialled the number. "Raven Kane?"

"Yes?" Raven walks away from the gathering. In the distance she can hear the sirens of the police cars, the ambulance, the errant fire engine.

"Sorry, I wasn't expecting you to answer."

"Why not?"

"The time difference. I'm in Texas. It's probably really late there?"

"Yet… you still called?"

Raven looks up to the sky. Some cheeky stars have surfaced from the gloom.

"I emailed you earlier. I didn't get a response."

Not surprising, thinks Raven, given the state of her laptop cinders.

"And I didn't want to wait till morning. Is it a… good time to talk?"

Raven nudges a black rock with her shoe. It's still warm. She strolls over what is left of burnt grass, like charcoal urchins underfoot. "I suppose it is."

"I'm Rochelle Strauss."

The name sounds familiar. The hard accent makes it feel like a dream.

"From Finch Press."

"You're… calling about the book?"

"Of course I'm calling about the book!"

When Raven doesn't reply, Strauss barrels ahead. "I've just finished reading the proposal you sent us. I love it. I think it's smart and funny and important. I think it will resonate with every woman — every human — who reads it. And you'd be a dream to market. I mean, who wouldn't love a… a what? A hip, hexing-and-texting witch?"

"I'm afraid to answer that question."

"We'd like to offer you a contract —"

"It's too late," says Raven.

"You've already sold it? Have you signed anything yet? I think when you hear how generous the advance is that we can offer you —"

"No, it's not that."

"Whatever it is," she twangs, "I'm willing to work around it. I really do love what you sent us —"

"It's not something that can be… worked around, unfortunately."

Kruger walks up to Raven.

"I lost it," says Raven. "I lost the manuscript. I lost everything."

"But…"

"It's gone."

Kruger frowns at her. "What?" he mouths.

"My book," she whispers. "It's okay. I don't need it anymore."

She knows now that she has what she needs. She always has.

"It's not gone," he says.

"Just give me a second," Raven says into the phone, then covers the microphone. "Of course it's gone. My laptop was in the house."

"I backed it up," he says. "It's procedure. I copied your hard-drive at the station. It's under lock and key."

Raven looks at Kruger. There is blue light in his eyes.

She pulls him closer. The disembodied voice of Rochelle Strauss from Finch Press says "Hello? Are you still there?" Raven chucks the phone on the ground and looks up at Kruger.

"I don't need rescuing, you know."

"Believe me," says Kruger, "I know."

They stand together in the night, connected by skin and by cosmos. They watch as Raven's friends rake silently through the darkness. Fred, the singed albino Peacock, screams. The Grimm Brothers lope towards them. Kruger strokes them, tells them they are Good Dogs. They smile at him as if to say that he isn't too bad, either, then steal Raven's phone for a game of Fetch. Eli swoops down from the inky swill of sky and lands on Raven's shoulder. His head swivels, surveying the scene, and for once, he is lost for words.

Raven kisses Kruger. He doesn't sneeze.

* * *

The End

ALSO BY JT LAWRENCE

* * *

FICTION

WHEN TOMORROW CALLS

• SERIES •

The Stepford Florist: A Novelette (Oct 2017)

The Sigma Surrogate (2018)

1. Why You Were Taken (2015)
2. How We Found You (May 2017)
3. What Have We Done (October 2017)

* * *

STANDALONE NOVELS

The Memory of Water (2011)

Grey Magic (2016)

* * *

SHORT STORY COLLECTIONS

Sticky Fingers (2016)

Sticky Fingers 2 (2018)

Sticky Fingers 3 (2018)

* * *

NON-FICTION

The Underachieving Ovary (2016)

* * *

Grey Magic is a work of fiction.
Names, characters, places and incidents are the product of the author's imagination or are used fictitiously. Any resemblance to actual persons, living or dead, events, or locales is entirely coincidental.

Published in South Africa by Fire Finch Press.

www.firefinchpress.com

Book cover design by Christian Bentulan

ISBN: 978-0-9947234-7-5

Created with Vellum

Printed in Great Britain
by Amazon

62793804R00281